WHEELER-DEALER

The Ghost & the Camper Kooky Mystery Series

Book 1

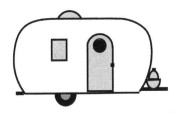

RITA MOREAU

DEDICATION

This book is dedicated to George,
the author's husband, and my best friend.

Savannah, GA

My name is Mabel Gold, and over the last couple of years, my life took an unexpected detour. What was to be the golden years, you know—playing with grand-children and lots of baking—turned into the *Are You Kidding Me* years when my husband Jack lost his mind and traded me in for Tiffanie.

She's about the same age as my youngest daughter, Bianca, but with bigger boobs—store bought. I've been trying to get my life back, driving a pickup and towing a vintage camper around this beautiful country. My five kids think I've lost it and maybe I have because I have company. A specter, a ghost, a spirit—whatever you want to call her.

Her name is Irma, and I can see her as plain as day. Neither of us knows why. We're still trying to figure that out. She's as stubborn and hard-nosed as me. It's a wonder we can even talk to each other since we both never learned to bite our tongues.

Irma is stuck in purgatory. You know, where you go to make up for past deeds when you were among the living. She checks in with Saint Peter from time to time at the Pearly Gates. She says it reminds her of checking in with her parole officer. So far, he has sent her pack-ing each time. Back down the Rainbow Bridge she goes until she serves her time, and Saint Peter hands her the get out of jail card—but I digress. This is how it all be-gan. Buckle up—you're going for a ride, and I hope you like camping.

WHEELER-DEALER

"I told you I would get you the money. You know I always come through."

"He's tired of waiting. Get this done and consider your slate wiped clean."

"Poof—all gone."

"I need more time."

"No more time. One week."

"One week? What if I can't get this done?"

"Then, if I were you, my friend, I would get my affairs in order."

A week later, he was dead.

His affairs were a mess.

CHAPTER 1

Boca Vista, FL

"Mother, you have trouble driving at night, let alone driving a trailer," Meg said. "I think you need to see your doctor and make sure this is something you are allowed to do."

Meg is daughter number one and a real worrywart. But of my two daughters, I'm closest to her. The other one is younger—a millennial—if you know what I mean.

"Meg, it's a camper. Not a trailer. Not that there's anything wrong with that. You don't drive a camper, you tow it. This one is light and small enough to be towed with an SUV but I'm towing it with an F-150."

It was time for a diversion.

"How about a drink?"

"It's one o'clock."

"It's Florida," I said with a wink and a sigh.

Meg had flown in from Long Island, with my only grandson, Sid. I was so thrilled to see him. We had a special bond. Grandchildren are a blessing. They make up for some of your grown-up kids, who think they know what's best for you. Like this daughter.

The recent purchase of the Ford F-150 and a vintage camper, with its recognizable shiny aluminum curved body, prompted this visit. "What's an F-150? It sounds like some kind of gun. You don't still have that gun Dad got you? I hope you sold it like I asked the last time we talked."

"Oh, I did, Meg. I did. I sold it."

Yeah, I sold it and replaced it with a bigger one and a concealed weapons permit tucked in my wallet right behind pictures of the grandkids. No point in opening up that can of worms. I had my hands full with what was parked out in front of my house.

"Mom, an F-150 is a pickup truck with a lot of horsepower. I think it's very cool. Gram is rad."

Sid gave me a wink, and I gave him a wink back. We were on the same wavelength when it came to his mother.

"I'm not so sure that it's safe."

Meg looked at her son for support. Sid gave her a blank stare and shrugged his shoulders. I could read his mind by the look on his face. *"The ball is now in your court. Good luck with that."* I just smiled, but I was biting my tongue, literally.

Sid was working on my laptop. Like all teenagers, he was very good with computers and cell phones, tablets, your basic devices. It seems it's important to back them up—in case they crash and burn. Way over my pay grade.

"Gram, why do you have duct tape wrapped around the top of your laptop?"

Whoops. I gave my grandson the same look I used to give my five kids—*because I'm your mother–that's why*—it didn't work. His mother's paranoia came to my rescue.

"She's taped the camera so no one can watch her. You haven't noticed the duct tape on my laptop and tablet?"

Sid gave us the OMG look, but being a smart kid, he changed the subject.

"Gram, can I drive your truck?"

Sid had recently started driving. His mother had not quite come to terms with that milestone. Her husband, Seymour, had prevailed and just bought more insurance. He's grounded in reality (thank goodness).

"Sid, why don't you take your grandmother's laptop and work on it out on the lanai?"

"Sure."

He got up with my laptop and gave me a conspiratorial wink on the way out. This family is big on winks.

"Don't be looking at any of those porn sites."

This prompted a ha-ha from Sid and a look of '*really*' on his mother's face. I just winked at him.

"Oh, lighten up, Meg. Now for that drink. It's Florida, where five o'clock comes early."

"It's noon."

I rolled my eyes as I watched the calculating mind of my daughter give in to an early cocktail.

"I'm driving."

"Your condo is five minutes away. Let Sid do the driving."

"Okay, but make it a really small glass of wine and then, Mother, you have to start from the beginning and tell me how this all happened."

"All of what happened?"

I got up and walked over to a small but well-stocked bar and slowly fixed our drinks, knowing full well what she meant. Sometimes I play the old card with my kids. It doesn't always work with Meg. She was a lawyer. The sort of lawyer you need if you murdered someone.

Meg got up and walked to the large bay window and pointed at what was parked in my circular drive as if she were in a courtroom. She was trim. She looked like an athlete. Not an ounce of fat on her frame. She watched every little calorie. Her shoulder length hair, cut and highlighted to perfection, kept her beautician, sorry hair stylist, happier than a clam.

"All that happened."

I poured her a teeny bit more than a small glass of wine. I handed it to her as she sat back down. She eyed it, but decided not to argue. She probably needed it for the cross examination she was about to conduct. I took a sip of my Cosmo. A double shot of vodka was just what I needed.

Meg is the smartest of my five kids, book smart, that is. She graduated top of her class in college and then law school. First, she became a prosecutor. Then, after seeing the shenanigans pulled to convict someone in order to score a win, she went to the dark side. In a courtroom, she was a different person.

When she married Seymour and finally got pregnant, she made the decision to stay at home and raise children. Like I did. Only I never went much past high school. I grew up in a walk-up flat in Brooklyn, a city that still defines me. I like to think of myself as a graduate of the Brooklyn School of Hard Knocks.

Her husband is in business with my oldest son, Jack Jr. They are money doctors, financial planners. Jack Jr.

watches over my nest egg I was granted when his father divorced me and married Tiffanie. Legally it's Tiffany, but she spells it 'Tiffanie,' according to Bianca, my millennial daughter, who remained a neutral party during the divorce.

It's not an ostrich egg, but it's a little more thanks to my CPA Mary Catherine, who used to work for the IRS. She found some offshore bank accounts Jack totally forgot about. The IRS wasn't happy about that either, but Mary Catherine convinced them I was an Innocent Spouse. That's a tax law rule that allows one spouse to avoid taxes owed to the IRS from errors made by the other spouse on a joint return. Errors they weren't aware of when they signed that return and then got divorced. Like leaving off income and stashing it in an offshore bank account. Jack got stuck with that tax bill.

Jack and Tiffanie recently had twins. And the new stepmother actually asked Bianca and my youngest son, Henry, another millennial, to be their godparents. The christening is coming up. This I know because Tiffanie sent me an invitation.

Bianca thinks I should attend. I haven't quite figured out how to communicate with this daughter. Sometimes I even wonder if there was a mix-up at the hospital when she was born. But then she has my eyes and quick tongue.

Tiffanie was a waitress at a bar Jack inherited from a rich uncle on the Jersey shore. The only time I stepped foot in that bar was when I found out Jack was spending a lot of downtime with Tiffanie. That's when the fighting began. He should have known better than to pick a fight with a gal from Brooklyn.

I kicked him out. The fight escalated, and before we knew it, there was no turning back. We got divorced, and he turned around and married Tiffanie when she told him she was pregnant. I got enough money to tread water and move to Florida, the Land of Oz—for old people.

Jack is a plastic surgeon. The kind you need if you're going into witness protection. We had been high school sweethearts. He was a few grades ahead of me and we got married right after I graduated. We moved in with his parents until he finished medical school. That's what we did in those days.

While Jack was in school, I worked in my father's restaurant. I was good with numbers, so I kept the books and helped out behind the bar. That's why I can still make a great Cosmo.

Jack had brains, and his family had more money than mine. His father was a bookie and his mother, Big Stella, had family closely connected to the mob. Really close. My parents were thrilled. I married a doctor. His mother, not so much. Big Stella wasn't shy about letting me know she wasn't happy with her son's choice. I wasn't Italian. I wasn't Catholic. Worse, I was Jewish. As far as Big Stella was concerned, her beloved son had married an alien. Looking back, now that we are divorced, I'm convinced Jack married me just to spite his mother.

Once Jack graduated, we looked around for the best place to start his practice. I suggested Long Island. After all, when you are a plastic surgeon you go where you're needed. And there were a lot of rich women there who always needed something to perk them up, if you get my drift. He had a steady stream of work. Plus,

I was happy to put some distance between me and Big Stella.

In the beginning, I worked in Jack's office, managing his appointments and the books until our five kids came along. The practice paid the bills, and we bought a nice home. Life was good, but it wasn't until Big Tony, a made man, walked in one day that Jack started making real money.

It started off innocently enough. Jack gave their mistresses boob jobs and facelifts and tummy tucks. But then it picked up from there. His patients needed new faces to go along with new identities. For those who needed to run. I knew Big Stella had a hand in this. I didn't like it, but we had five kids to feed.

One of Jack's patients turned out to be someone connected to the CIA. Next thing we knew, Jack was working for them. They can be tougher than the mob. When they offered him a safe and secure government job working exclusively for them and the FBI and some other deep alphabets, he couldn't say no. Not if he wanted to stay out of prison.

The alphabets had a lot of work for Jack, bringing in spies from the cold, sending people into witness protection and stuff even the president didn't want to know about. His handler, Cliff, kept Jack insulated and safe in the background.

As for Jack's mob connections, most of them are dead or living new lives. That is, except for one. I like to think of him as Jack's skeleton in the closet. One he doesn't want to get out. Unfortunately for Jack, I have the only key to that closet. It gives Jack a lot of heartburn.

Meg was pacing back and forth. I get a lot of inside information from Meg, even more if we have cocktails.

She was daddy's little girl and still hasn't forgiven him for hooking up with Tiffanie. She had finished her wine as quickly as I knew she would. I got back up to pour her another *small* glass and freshen my Cosmo.

"Not too much for me."

With my back to her, I rolled my eyes. She thinks I'm old and deaf, so she repeats a lot. Sometimes it's a good thing. I'm not deaf, but I do tend to forget easily.

Meg and Seymour have a condo here in Florida. I used to come down in the winter to visit. After the divorce, I thought what the hell I might as well get as far away from Jack and his trophy wife and live in sunny Boca Vista.

I discovered lots of older women like me live in Boca Vista. Too many perhaps, but we make the best of it. We even have a book club. The members of the club haven't gotten around to giving it a name, so it's just called the Book Club. Mostly divorcees and widows.

We meet to talk about books and drink. There's no requirement that you read a book. Sometimes we don't even pick out a book. We just talk about books and drink. We network. You know, share notes. Divorced women our age have to stick together.

The widows like the club a lot. They laugh and forget their grief for a few hours, and like the divorcees, try to move forward, many alone for the first time in their lives.

I dragged my friend, Lili, to a couple of the meetings. She actually reads books. I really admire Lili and am lucky that the feeling is mutual. She managed some of the biggest estates on Long Island. The Downton Abbey wannabees. She was prized because she kept their secrets and never betrayed a confidence.

The girls in the book club immediately took to Lili. In no time at all, they insisted she become the president. She accepted. No one would call her a wallflower. Lili is black. I'm sorry, African American, as my two millennials have corrected me. So, what can you expect from a Brooklyn gal who grew up back in the day?

Anyway, I once asked Lili if she is offended if I used the term black. She looked me straight in the eye and said, "Mabel, you are the most color-blind person I know, and that's a good thing."

I was happy when, a few months after I moved down, Lili decided to join me in Florida. She could afford it. A few years back, one of her wealthy Long Island clients left her a tidy sum. It was enough for her to retire. Lili is frugal, and like I said, smart. She's probably better off financially than I am.

She is my only true friend. I think both of us liked the idea of having each other's back. Life can be scary when you become a divorcee or a widow, like in her case. She is the one who suggested the camper.

"Mabel, get with the program. Jack has moved on—you should too."

Lili was never one to sugar-coat. She did have a point. It had been a few years since the divorce. I had reached a plateau—like you do when you go on a diet, and the weight loss comes to a standstill. That was where my life was, so I gave it some thought and decided to make a leap of faith. As long as my kids don't get in the way, I'm heading in that direction.

That's why Meg flew down. She claimed it was for some work on their condo, but I know the real reason was she was here to check on me. I dipped into my nest egg to make my recent purchases. No doubt Jack Jr.

spilled the beans before the ink was dry. The two of them were probably worried that I had a boy-toy and was spending money on him. You know, the rebound from a humiliating divorce. Lose a lot of weight and find a younger boyfriend. A lot of divorced women in this town take that route.

"Cougars," Lili calls them. And a good number of them belong to the book club.

Just because Jack was stupid enough to fall for a gold digger, didn't mean I was going to get back at him by dating someone the same age as our youngest son. I'm still working on losing that weight.

"You need to move on, Mabel," Lili told me when she arrived in Florida. "Shake those hips your mama gave you." Looking me straight in the eye, she added, "With someone new."

Like I said, Lili doesn't hold back. That's one of the great things about her. I could always count on an honest answer.

"I forget how to do it, Lili."

She walked up to me and looked at me with her dark eyes and whispered in my ear, "It will come back, Mabel. Like riding a bike."

Lili had moved on. When she came to Florida, Bob, a long-time friend of her late husband Carl, more or less followed her. Carl was an NYC firefighter and Bob, a retired homicide detective from LA, was divorced. She had known him for years but connected after Carl passed. Eventually they married.

"Tough to stay married as a cop," he told me when we first met. He was white.

"Always liked white men," Lili joked with a sheepish grin on her dimpled cheeks when she introduced me to Bob.

Since his retirement, Bob has been traveling with a group of RV owners. That's how all this started. Lili and Bob invited me to travel with them this summer. They were heading out West. Stopping along the way at national parks and points of interest parks, but I didn't want to be a third wheel. I had enough of that after Jack and I divorced and he dropped me for someone who looked like she was just out of high school.

"You poor thing," our friends would say with a condescending tone in their voice. I could read their minds, *"Glad it's you and not me, sister."*

I was tired of hearing that, and before long, my friends dropped me socially. I understood. It was awkward since their husbands were Jack's friends and moved in the same social circles. The connection we shared was broken.

"It's time to find someone else."

Lili was right, but not with a boy-toy. My choice of toys was a pickup truck I named Thor and a vintage camper. When I made the decision, Bob helped me pick out my rig. I returned with a second glass of wine for Meg and a second Cosmo for me.

While Meg delicately took a sip of her wine, I sat down and waited for the lecture. I needed my two oldest kids to stop worrying about me. Mainly Meg. I decided it was time to present my case, and so I began.

"Lili and Bob have a camper like mine, but bigger. During the summer months, they travel with a group of like-minded RV owners. Most of the campers are vintage, usually Airstreams or Bluebirds—canned hams."

"Canned hams?"

I took another swig of my Cosmo. I had this all thought out and had rehearsed my story, but this was before Meg, the lawyer you need if you buried a bunch of bodies, showed up.

"They are retro and look like a ham in a can."

"Oh yeah, yeah."

I could see from the look on her face the light bulb came on. She keeps busy on Pinterest.

"Lili and Bob took a short trip to the Keys and invited me along. We stayed at a state park in Marathon. I loved it, Meg. It was a beautiful park, and their campsite was near the water. I felt free and not stuck in that dark place where I have been since your father lost his mind."

I paused here and gave Meg a chance to take a sip of her wine. She half-finished it. She was relaxing, and I knew she'd let Sid drive them back to their condo.

"She's going to take him for everything he's got. Jack Jr. is worried."

I gave her the Jewish mother *oy vey* look and a shrug. Although we went through a World War III divorce, I decided not to trash talk Jack with our kids. I didn't need them feeling like they had to pick a side. I left the trash talk for the book club. Lots of venting went on during our meetings. Even the widows joined in. I continued my story.

"After that trip, Lili suggested I join them this summer when they head out west, but I'm tired of being the third wheel and so I decided to buy my own rig. Bob helped me pick out the camper. It was a deal. I got it out of an estate. Vintage but refurbished, top to bottom, like new."

I quickly downed more of my Cosmo.

Meg was in full lawyer mode and was listening for a flaw in my story. Like I said, she turned into a different person as a lawyer. I sometimes wondered if that was the real Meg.

"I know, mother, but I thought you were planning to join us in the Catskills."

I had done that every year since the divorce. Although I enjoyed visiting with my grandchildren, I felt like a leftover meal. I spent my days with the other old farts and could only take so much bingo and card playing and bus trips, not to mention putting up with the old codgers hitting on me. They came equipped with plenty of their blue pills.

Even after all those years of marriage, Jack and I still had a fireplace in the bedroom. Okay, it wasn't a roaring fire, but it was still fire. Women my age were brought up in an era where you were told you had to be good in the sack to hold on to a man and that if you couldn't hold on to him it was your fault. At least my millennial daughter doesn't think that way. I have to give her that. She also is not married to the idea of becoming a mother. She's happy with or without children.

"If they come along fine, if not, that's fine. Not so sure I want to bring kids into this world," Bianca told me one day. "You know, with all the global warming."

"What about a husband?"

"What about it?"

Bianca is a very independent woman, more so than Meg. I don't have to bribe her with booze. In fact, she buys drinks and dinner. As typical, she was supportive when I mentioned the camper and going out on the road.

"I think that's awesome."

This daughter is a woman of few words but speaks her mind. Underneath that exterior she has a soft heart, but she doesn't wear it on her sleeve. She's an idealist and feels it's important to give back. Interesting how there is a difference in generations between my two daughters.

No, I needed a change. Some fresh air, so I could figure out where I was going for the rest of my years, instead of my kids doing that for me.

"Meg, let's go outside and take a look at the camper, and then we'll go to lunch."

I could see I wasn't going to convince Meg anytime soon to hop on board with my camping trip. I got up and said loud enough for my grandson to hear me.

"Sid, do you want to drive my new truck and take your mom and me to lunch?"

I turned back to Meg, who I knew was obsessed with her diet.

"There's a new Greek restaurant I've been meaning to try. You can order a Greek salad."

"Mother!"

Meg went to high alert like a Category 5 hurricane was approaching.

"We're not finished talking here."

"We'll talk over lunch."

Sid moved quicker than a New York minute. "Let's go, Gram," he said as he placed my computer down.

Before Meg could protest, I got up, grabbed my purse, and started toward the door after Sid.

I took one last swig of my Cosmo. I never waste good vodka.

"We'll talk at lunch and you can have more wine. Sid's our designated driver. He can keep the truck until you come back for your car."

"She's wound as tight as a rubber band," Lili always says whenever I mention Meg.

Before Meg heads back to Long Island, we have plans to take her to a book club meeting and introduce her to some of the cougars.

"It'll do her good," Lili said as she wiggled her hips. "Loosen her up."

CHAPTER 2

Meg would not step foot inside the camper. Her way of protesting the idea. Sid was eager to get a peek inside.

"Gram, this is so rad."

I nodded my head. I've picked up a lot of new words from my grandson. Sid is an only child. Meg and Seymour wanted more, but it never came to pass. Finally, after several miscarriages Sid came along. It was no surprise that she was overly protective. It's more about her than Sid. At some point, she will have to let him fly. That's the way it was with my kids.

One flew off to Broadway, and the two millennials are still learning to fly. They have a cupcake business. Bianca is a chef, and her brother Henry helps her in the cupcake shop, for now.

He went to law school but didn't like practicing law. Henry found out to make money as a lawyer you had to stretch the truth or lie. He just didn't have the personality for it. The two of them are closet socialists, but then again, they're young.

Jack Jr., on the other hand, is a lot like his father, conservative politics, and street smart with a silver tongue, which in his business comes in handy. His wife

Carmela and I never got along, but I play nice, so I can visit my two granddaughters.

She reminds me of a younger version of Big Stella, my mother-in-law, may the woman rest in peace. Meg and Carmela don't get along either, which is problematic since their husbands are business partners.

I turned back to see my daughter standing there like a deer in headlights. She definitely needs to drink more.

Sid and I stepped inside the camper. On one side was the galley or kitchen. It was updated with a new refrigerator and Corian countertop. A new range, which I would have to learn to use if I intended to do much cooking. The camper had a small microwave and enough amps to operate it, which Bob said I would come to appreciate.

Across from the range was a dinette. At the front of the camper was a sleeper sofa with plenty of storage underneath. At the far end of the camper there was a shower and a small bathroom or head as Bob called it, a nautical term.

"Is this the original brochure?" Sid picked up the brochure from the dinette.

"Yes. Bob downloaded it from the camper's website. The previous owner did a top-to-bottom restoration. I have all the papers. These campers have quite a history despite being older, like your grandmother." Sid gave me a loving smile which melted my heart.

"How cool."

We stood in the small interior as he looked from front to back.

"Leather?" Sid pointed at the white sofa at the front of the camper.

"Yes. The interior is fully updated. It was built in 1968, but these campers are so well built a good number are still on the road. In fact, in 1969 when the astronauts returned from the moon, they were quarantined in one of these campers because they are built so airtight."

"Really?" Sid had an interest in aeronautical engineering and wanted to work for NASA.

"They wanted to make sure they didn't bring any moon bugs back."

"Oh, like bedbugs."

He had a quick wit. He got that from my side of the family, not Jack's.

"Bob told me the company is coming out with a retro that looks just like this one since it's one of the most popular and recognizable of their line of campers. Vintage ones hold their value in case I do have to sell it down the road. Or pass it on to the next generation. Yep, this baby might be yours, down the road."

"Way down the road, Grams." There was the look that melted my heart.

"The exterior is aluminum. That's why they are nicknamed Silver Bullets."

"Wow. Can I come out and visit? I'd love to see the Grand Canyon."

"Yes, but we'll blow up that bridge when we get to it."

I nodded my head toward the open door. Meg was standing out there with her hands on her hips.

"Copy that." He continued to look around. "You don't think it's too small, Gram? Will you have enough room? How long is it?"

"It's 17 feet, and that's all I need. I don't want to tow a large camper. It weighs less than 5,000 pounds."

I pointed toward the dinette. "This has room for four and converts easily to a bed. I like this little vintage camper. It's a classic, like me."

Sid gave me a hug and then I nodded my head toward the side window. "We better get going, your mother looks hungry."

I didn't want to add, *"And angry."*

"She's always hungry because she's always on a diet."

Meg did not have a weight problem, but she lived on Long Island, where she had a lot of peer pressure from her social circle. Lili calls them 'The Wives of Long Island,' like that reality show on cable.

"They're all bone. Some men like their women boney. Lucky for me Bob likes a woman with a booty." She slapped her curvy hips.

To stay bone-thin, Meg and her country club friends don't eat and take a lot of tennis lessons with young and sexy tennis pros or work out with young and sexy trainers. Meg knew all about the latest diets. Lately, she's a vegan. Sid and Seymour live with her cooking and hate it.

As Sid stepped out of the camper, the corner of my eye caught something. For a second, I thought it was Meg, but she was still outside tapping her toes.

I looked around one more time, and that was when I saw Irma for the first time. She was standing there at the back of my camper with her hands on her hips, and she looked just like my favorite Aunt Sadie, all Jewish and bossy.

I blinked my eyes once, and she was still standing there. I blinked them again, and she was gone.

"Gram, are you okay?"

Sid was waiting for me to come out of the camper. He reached up and helped me as I stepped into the bright Florida sun. I froze in place. In a minute, the two of them were all over me.

"I think I just saw a ghost. It looked like my Aunt Sadie."

I immediately regretted saying it when I saw Meg in a panic.

"Mother! Maybe we should go to the ER? You might be having a stroke? Stick out your tongue."

I obediently stuck out my tongue.

"Now follow my finger."

Meg stuck her pointer in front of my nose and moved it from right to left. I tried to follow it with my tongue. I took a deep breath and put my tongue back where it belonged.

"I'm fine. I'm fine. No stroke. Maybe I'll skip lunch and take a nap. I'll call you later. We can meet for dinner. You're only five minutes away. I probably had one too many Cosmos." To make sure she didn't drag me to the ER, I added. "I was just kidding about Aunt Sadie."

She eyed me like a cat about to trounce on a mouse. I quickly gave them a hug, and before Meg could protest, I headed back into my house.

"Got to get out of this heat."

I felt better once in the A/C. I watched from the window while they stood there looking at each other.

"Dang."

I saw Meg heading right back toward my house. Sid said something, and she stopped and turned around and shook her head. I stepped right back outside so she could see I wasn't having a stroke. I didn't need her calling 911.

"I'm fine. I just got overheated in the camper. Much better now that I'm in the A/C."

I watched her assess the situation, looking at me and then Sid and then back at me.

"I'm fine. Go have lunch."

"Okay Mother, I'll call you later."

Sid blew me a kiss as I waved goodbye. I got back in my house and watched from the window as they got into their SUV and drove off. I was happy to see that Sid was driving. Progress.

As I stood there, staring at my camper's reflection, like a mirror in the bright Florida sun, I started to have dark thoughts. Meg didn't come right out and say it, but I could read her mind. Maybe the camper and the pickup were an overreaction to my husband of many years, dumping me for a barfly.

Yes, it's time to move on, but at my age, what are my choices? Join the other old farts in town for early bird specials and plan the move down the road into the retirement home. WTD–'waiting to die' is what Lili calls it. Nope. I don't think so.

I walked over to my bar, fixed another Cosmo, and returned to staring out the window. I found myself doing that a lot lately, meditating like they do in yoga. I learned that from my millennial son, Henry, who has taken yoga for years and now, along with helping his sister in the cupcake factory, teaches yoga instead of practicing law.

"Maybe he's gay." I remember Jack saying to me back when we found out Henry didn't like being a lawyer and decided to teach yoga and bake cupcakes.

"What if he is, Jack?"

"Well, there's nothing wrong with that. Just trying to figure out where he's going in life."

"He's teaching yoga. Law wasn't right for him. Probably tried to compete with his big sister."

Actually, Henry is gay. I knew that early on. Everyone did but Jack, although he probably suspected as much. After we divorced, Henry decided to tell his father. I remember when Henry called me that day,

"I told him."

I could hear the emotion crack in his voice. I held my breath.

"What happened?"

Saying a quick prayer in my head and making the sign of the cross like Big Stella used to even though I was Jewish.

"He gave me a big hug, and then he looked in my eyes and said, 'I was wondering when you were going to get around to telling me.'"

Jack and I may have split, but we share a secret. I keep it safely tucked away in a safe deposit box. Both our lives depend on it, but mostly Jack's. I have the only key. We agreed to talk on the first Friday of each month about the safe deposit box. The conversation is short.

"You have the box."

"Yes, Jack. I have the box."

Then I hang up before Jack has a chance to say anything more. We'd been divorced awhile when I began to hear rumors from my kids that the honeymoon was definitely over.

"Can we talk, please, Mabel?"

"No, Jack."

As of late, I could detect a plea in his voice.

"Please, Mabel."

"Nope."

I knew Jack, and I figured he wanted to talk about restructuring my alimony payments. According to Meg, Tiffanie has expensive tastes and spent money faster than water pouring out of a broken pipe.

When we first opened the safe deposit box, Jack decided the box should be in my name only. A decision he came to regret. I knew he had lost his key, and unfortunately, he never got around to getting a replacement. During the divorce, the bank would call me weekly to report that Jack dropped by the bank trying to get another key. Nope, was always my answer.

Although we went through a contentious divorce, we have five kids, three grandkids, and a secret that could get us both killed. When one of the grandkids landed in the hospital, he was the first to call and tell me. It was then, when I saw him at the ER that I agreed to a truce.

"Please, Mabel. We need to talk from time to time. I think you know why. You have that key. You know, the only key. We need to talk about that. Our lives depend on it, and maybe even our kids."

Jack had a point.

"Okay, Jack."

That's when I agreed to talk to him once a month. As far as I was concerned, Jack could take a long walk off a short pier. I had no doubt before long Tiffanie would push him off that pier and clean him out. Good thing he had that safe government job.

Jack had called last Friday to check in. I was about to hang up. "Mabel, wait. I need to tell you something. It's for your protection."

I decided this time to hear him out. "I'm listening."

"Have you been watching the news? It looks like Vito is throwing his hat in the ring."

"It's all over the news. He is the governor of Florida."

Vito is our code name for the skeleton in the closet. He was one of Jack's mob patients and came out of the closet some years ago. He got into politics. Not much of a change going from the mob to politics. Same rules apply.

In his prior life, Vito was an accountant. Like Jack, he started to acquire mob clients. He soon had an exclusive job with the mob. He was their money man.

In the safe deposit box were before and after pictures of Vito. Jack always took before and after pictures of his patients. He just made copies and saved for future use. I had a feeling that Big Stella suggested it as some kind of insurance.

The governor is still a patient. After all, he has to look young for his constituents and he wouldn't dare go to a new plastic surgeon. If the pictures got out, it would be front-page news, and the rumor that he was the mob's numbers guy would be all over cable news.

"Pictures don't lie. The before pictures of Vito tie him to certain mob bosses," Jack told me.

Vito no longer keeps their books, but he is tied at the hip to the mob. They helped him get where he is today. It takes a lot of money to run for political office. Plus, his politics lean toward the religious right. They would forgive him, but they certainly wouldn't vote for him. Not if he had his sights on becoming a senator from Florida and moving to Washington, home of the real crooks. He doesn't know about the before and after pictures sitting in my safe deposit box, or Jack would be swimming with the fishes, and I might be joining him.

But that's not what really worries Jack; he crossed that bridge a long time ago when he became the top doc for the mob. No, what worries him is that his friends at the alphabet agencies would put him and Tiffanie in witness protection. Tiffanie likes her present life. She would not be happy. She'd be gone quicker than a New York Tick-Tock and so would Jack's money. Meg told me they were having problems. The honeymoon was over.

"Tiffanie has a boyfriend, one a little closer in age. Seymour thinks she's had this boyfriend all along. Probably set Dad up. She's also hired a nanny—she didn't take to motherhood."

Jack would be broke, and in witness protection hell for the rest of his days. Not to mention my alimony would dry up. So, whether I like it or not, from time to time, Jack and I have to talk and work together.

I was staring at my camper and sipping my drink. That was when I saw her again. The door of the camper swung open, and she stood in the doorway. She raised her pointer finger, just like my Aunt Sadie, and curled it, motioning me to come out. Then she was gone, but the door was still wide open.

Maybe I was having a stroke. I almost called Lili, but then I decided to pull up my big girl panties and check it out. You know, face your fears. I heard that recently on a TED Talk.

I walked over and almost poured another shot of vodka, but decided I needed to be able to walk. I took a deep yoga breath instead, in through the nose and out through the nose, and headed out my front door. I had my cell just in case I needed to call 911.

CHAPTER 3

The sun had dropped behind a cloud, and I felt a nice breeze from the Atlantic. I had the smallest house on the block, but it was oceanfront. My lawyer, Limo Louie, found it for me. It had been tied up in an estate for a long time. The kids who had inherited the house were squabbling. They finally made peace because they needed the money. They listed it at a price for a quick sale. It was a good deal.

At the time I met Louie; he worked out of his 1975 Cadillac and used it for Uber when he was tight for money. When I moved to Boca Vista, I needed a lawyer for the sale of some real estate I got in the divorce. Met him one day when I was having a drink at a bar on the Intercostal waterway called Hotel Florida. The state of Florida was like that; you can check in but never check out.

The bartender Ernie and I struck up a conversation, and I told him my sad story. Funny how you'll spill your guts to a bartender you never met after just a few drinks. "Cheaper than therapy," according to some book club gals.

After a couple drinks, Ernie made a call, and that was when he introduced me to Louis Fox, Esquire.

Louie was kind enough to drive me home in his limo. I was living in Meg's condo, and I told Louie I was looking for a house which is why I was selling the real estate. Turns out, the limo had a nice little bar in the back where we had a few more drinks and chatted about selling the property.

"This is my law office. I don't need the overhead, but I may need to find an office before long. I'm getting too old to cart legal files and boxes up to my place when I get home at night."

We talked for a long time that night. Seems like Louie and Jack had mutual friends in the mob, and interestingly enough, he told me Ernie, the bartender, probably had mutual friends with Jack's pals at the alphabet agencies. He shared with me that Ernie was a spook and probably knew Cliff, Jack's handler.

Louie had left all that behind him when he sold his law practice in Miami and moved up the east coast of Florida, to Fish Camp, which is next door to Boca Vista. Fish Camp is a smaller version of Nashville, and Boca Vista does its best to be a smaller version of Palm Beach.

Recently, he'd opened an office in Boca Vista, right down the street from my CPA, Mary Catherine Mahoney, but everyone calls her MC.

A friend of Louie and Ernie, MC was someone who knew her way around the IRS. She helped me out of an IRS audit of the last joint return I filed with Jack. Got me a waiver of all the tax and penalties the IRS had set up. It's called the Innocent Spouse Rule.

MC also found a hidden offshore bank account Jack had conveniently forgotten to tell my lawyers about during the divorce. It was where he had stashed the money he was skimming from the bar. MC called it a cash hoard.

That was when I moved the box that held the pictures of Jack's patients to a different bank. I had closed the one on Long Island when I moved to Florida and placed it in a safe deposit box where I do my banking.

MC suggested moving it to another bank, different from where I do my banking. She had a safe deposit box at the bank she suggested. It seems it was a Greek family tradition to keep money in a safe deposit box once they decided not to keep it under mattresses any longer. MC definitely knew her way around the IRS since she used to work for them in a special group buried deep in the IRS.

I also heard from Louie that she was psychic. Didn't hurt, I guess, if it helped her find offshore bank accounts. It sure helped my finances and helped me hang onto this house.

I introduced Louie to all the women in my book club, and business was picking up as well as our friendship.

Like Lili said, "Time to move on."

I stepped out of my front door. I told myself there was nothing to be scared of. Still it did occur to me that I could go back for the revolver I keep in my nightstand. Growing up in a tough neighborhood, I was not new to guns, and back when Jack was doing remodeling work for the mob, he thought it was a good idea. I kept one for protection.

Some of the ladies in the book club were taking a self-defense course at a martial arts studio because the instructor was hot. I joined them and was surprised to find out I was stronger than I imagined, and I liked martial arts.

The instructor thought I was a natural, so I kept up the lessons, plus he was easy on the eyes. I was thinking about my self-defense training and kept walking, going slowly, and that's when I saw her again. She appeared in the doorway of the camper. It was also the first time I heard Irma's voice.

"Hurry up. What are you waiting for, Hanukah?"

I stopped dead in my tracks. She sounded just like my Aunt Sadie.

"Aunt Sadie, is that you?"

I couldn't believe I was asking that question. Maybe Meg was right. The stress of the divorce was taking its toll on me. Plus, I just started a new medication, and I looked it up online, and it said a side effect was hallucinations and/or death. I hate to take medication. I was already re-thinking the latest prescription.

"No, I'm not your Aunt Sadie. The name is Irma. We need to talk."

I blinked my eyes again. She looked like she was about my age, maybe younger. She was very curvaceous. She had red hair and piercing green eyes. One look at her and I knew that when she was younger, she had been drop-dead, movie star gorgeous.

"Who the hell are you, and what are you doing in my camper?"

I took the self-defense stance, right foot forward, chin up, hands ready at my side.

"Your camper? Ha! Listen, honey, this is my home, and I've been living here long before you. Unfortunately, for both of us, I'm not going anywhere soon. How about we get out of this heat so we can talk? I thought you were having a heat stroke earlier. I'll meet you inside your house at that—what do you call it—the lanai."

No sooner had she said that when she whooshed past me and was gone. Like something out of Ghostbusters. I turned around and had a decision to make—call Meg and go to the ER or fix another drink. I was at a fork in the road. Meg and the ER led to the old folk's home and no road trip. I made my decision right then and there. I was taking blood pressure, cholesterol, and thyroid medication, all with side effects that were worse than the reason you were taking the pills. What did I have to lose?

I closed the camper door and made my way back into the house, fixed myself a stiff drink, and headed out to the lanai. I'd taken that fork in the road.

CHAPTER 4

The lanai was my favorite place in the house. It looked out over the ocean.

"If you're lucky enough to live by the ocean, then you're lucky enough," Lili told me when she first saw the house.

I walked out on the lanai, and when I first looked around, I saw no one. I closed my eyes and shook my head and was about to sit down, but when I opened my eyes—there she was—sitting in my favorite chair. I would have sat right on top of her.

"Have a seat, honey. We need to talk. We need to figure something out."

She raised her arms in the air, just like Aunt Sadie. I stood there, staring at her. I closed my eyes, took a deep breath, and downed my drink. When I opened my eyes, she was still there, staring at me with the Aunt Sadie look I got many times as a kid, still sitting in my favorite chair.

"You made the right call, Mabel. No need to call your daughter. You're fine. We just have a situation we need to discuss. Go freshen your drink," Irma said and pointed to a little bar in the corner.

She looked human, but I knew instinctively she wasn't, she was a ghost. I had seen them as a kid, usually long-gone relatives. They became my imaginary friends. It was my Aunt Sadie who told me that some of us could see them and not to be afraid.

"They're called specters, and they are still tied to the earth and need to work that out." Once I was grown, the ability to see them seemed to disappear—until today.

"Can I fix you one?" I said to Irma out of habit and maybe in shell shock. I pinched myself. Okay, I wasn't dead.

"I wish. I'd love a gin and tonic Mabel, but you see, I'm dead, and one of the downfalls of being dead is that you can't drink or eat. But where I'm stuck, you still remember what it was like. As if you had cravings. How about you fix me one and just place it here next to me."

I watched as she pointed at the wicker table next to where she was sitting. Her hand slipped right through the large conch shell sitting on top and back up again.

"It will be like I'm having a drink with you, and you can finish it after we talk. You're going to need it."

"I don't drink gin," I said to Irma, mentally thinking I've probably reached my limit, and I was going to pay for it tomorrow.

She had her arms folded in front of her. I couldn't believe I was talking to her, but she did sound like my Aunt Sadie, who I adored as a kid.

"Well, get used to it. I like gin, and where I come from, we never wasted booze. You're not dead. So, deal with it."

I decided to go along and fixed a gin and tonic for Irma and vodka with plenty of water and ice for me. I placed her drink next to the conch shell and sat down across from her.

"Okay. Start talking. My daughter Meg might be back at any minute."

"I never had a daughter. Just a son and I had to give him up at birth for adoption."

"Oh. I'm sorry."

"No need. It was for the best. I was too young when I got pregnant, and well, it didn't exactly fit into my work schedule."

Irma looked out at the Atlantic. "You see those clouds. Those are cumulous. Might be a storm heading in this way."

Irma reached for the drink, and her hand passed right through the glass. I watched her as she looked at me, and then I could see her shrug her shoulders. I sat there, mesmerized.

"Relax, Mabel. You're fine."

I could sense she was as confused as I was.

"If I'm fine, why the hell can I see and hear you?"

"I don't know, but I'm sure we will find out. This isn't a coincidence. I've been dead a long time, and you are the first person who has been able to see me and talk to me. There has to be a reason."

I thought about this, "When I was a kid, I could see dead people, but when I got older, that went away."

"Sometimes, small children do have that ability, Mabel. I stay away from them. Don't want to scare them or worse, become their imaginary friends. Too much work. I'm not a nanny."

"So, what are you?"

"You mean who was I? The name's Irma and I was a hooker in Las Vegas. First, I was a showgirl and then got into hooking, as we girls called it back then. You sort of fell into it by happenstance, and then you were hooked, hence the name *hooker*."

She looked at me with emerald green eyes that looked all the way back to a prior life.

"Anyway, I was real young when I got pregnant. I discovered it when I was in jail on trumped-up charges. I called my sister, Betsy, and we agreed that it'd be best if she took the baby. So, she and her husband adopted him. They already had a houseful of kids. One more was no big deal. I was able to watch him grow up from afar. We never met. After all, I was a hooker, and eventually, I became a madame of my own cat house. Well, mine and the mob's. They don't let you alone. I did business with them just like your ex."

"You know about Jack?"

"I know everything about the owners of my camper. You buy the camper and along comes your baggage."

I watched as Irma got up and slid across the terrazzo floor. She stood there, staring at the ocean. I was getting pretty close to calling Meg and was just about to dial her when Irma turned around and floated right in front of me with her hands on her hips.

"I wouldn't do that, Mabel. They'll put you in the old farts' home. Trust me on that." She stuck her pointer finger really close to my nose.

"Please tell me you cannot read my mind or worse, you can see the future?"

Looking at the ghostly finger right under my nose, it looked as real as mine. The more she talked, the more human she looked, but I knew she was a ghost because she was dressed like I used to in the 1980s and with that really big hair.

"No, I can't see the future or read your mind, thank the big guy up there."

She pointed upwards as she sat back down in my chair. I took another sip of my drink, and I leaned closer to her.

"Look, Irma, why don't you cut to the chase before I fall asleep in this chair. What are you doing here? What is this, *Beetlejuice*?"

"You do love movies, don't you?"

"Yeah, sort of."

"Well, I'm stuck in purgatory. My last deed on earth got me into purgatory. It could have been worse. You see, I took a bullet for my son."

Irma placed her hand gingerly on the front of her large chest, near her heart.

"Geez, that sucker did hurt."

"You did? What did you do, step in front of him?"

"Yeah, something like that. My son's name is Walt. He became a detective. One of my girls overheard some made men planning a hit on him. I had put out the word that if they ever heard anything about Walt, they were to come to me. They didn't know he was my kid. For that matter, Walt didn't even know. I kept an eye out for him."

"So, you never got to see him growing up."

"I watched him from afar. I told my sister it would be for the best. So, in a way I did see him grow up and like I said I kept an eye out for him. I grabbed my white mink and stuffed my Glock into my pocket and rushed over to the campground where Walt was living."

"I waited outside and when the guy showed up—his name was Luca—I watched as he broke in. I snuck up to the window. I could see him holding a gun on Walt. I knew he was going to kill him. I held my gun up to the window, and that was when Walt saw me. He was standing at the back of the camper, and Luca was standing by the dinette and had him blocked. Walt didn't flinch, but Luca must have caught something in his eyes because he turned around and saw me standing at the window with my gun pointed right at him. I got off a shot. Unfortunately, so did he."

"Next thing I know I'm on the ground. Then Walt was kneeling down and holding me in his arms. Only when I saw him look at his hand did I realize I was bleeding. I grabbed on to his finger and held tight. I remembered the night he was born. They let me hold him for a just minute. He grabbed my finger. It was so tiny but strong. He wiped away a tear rolling down my cheek. Of course, he didn't know who I was. But for a moment he was looking at me like he recognized something."

"Did he say anything?"

"He kept saying, 'Ma'am, I called for back-up. You hold on now. You saved my life and I want to thank you properly. You hear me, ma'am. Hold on."

"I did hold on very tight to his finger. Then when I felt the last ounce of life leaving me, I said, 'Mom. Call me Mom."

I got up to get a cocktail napkin to blow my nose and wipe away a tear.

"It sure made me mad that I ruined that mink. It was so pretty. But it was worth it."

"What happened to Luca?"

"Arrested and sent to prison, where, not much later, he got what was coming to him. Someone cut his throat. He knew too much. He went straight to hell."

I watched Irma take an imaginary sip from her gin and tonic. The drink came up off the table and close to Irma's lips and then back down on the patio table.

"You can move things?"

"Yup, I can. Since you're a movie buff, you remember the movie Poltergeist? Well, that's me. I'm a poltergeist, a ghost with some physical powers. I try not to do too much, but it's mostly out of boredom. Saint Peter is not always happy with my antics and threatens to add on to my jail time."

"So, to make a long story short, I haunt this camper. Walt moved out the day after I died and the day he found out I was his mother. Betsy sat down with him and told him. He came to my funeral with the first of my future daughters-in-law."

She brushed what looked like a tear rolling down her cheek.

"You know what he said when he came up to my coffin? 'Mom, I wish I'd had a chance to get to know you.' It touched my heart."

Reflecting on her life, I saw the ghostly tear evaporate. I guess we had bonded as mothers who have held a tiny finger do.

"So, Mabel, pay attention, it works like this. I'm not going to repeat this more than once. Until I can leave purgatory I am attached to this camper where I died. It's been sold a half dozen times over the years. If I don't like the new owners, I cause such a ruckus that they sell the camper. On the other hand, if I like my owners, I leave them alone. Sometimes, I've even helped them out of jams. I found out it helps with Saint Peter, and he credits my good deeds against the time I've got to spend in purgatory. They always give their guardian angels all the credit or that Saint Anthony. Guardian angels, my ass." Irma said, tossing back her red hair without lifting a hand. "We *ghosts* who are working off our time in purgatory are the ones watching out for you."

"Anyways, to make a real long story real short, the last time the camper was sold, the owner moved it to Florida and I was thrilled. Winters spent in storage up north were boring. I usually went into hibernation mode."

"The owner before you was a real nice guy. Sadly, he never got a chance to use the camper. Had it restored like new. Then his wife died in her sleep, and he got sick and died not long after her. I see that happen a lot with the one left behind. He went straight to heaven, and she met him at the front gate where Saint Peter let him pass."

"Not me. I meet with Saint Peter from time to time. He reminds me of my parole officer. So far, he has sent me right back to purgatory every time, and so I look for ways to do good deeds to whittle away at my sentence. Anything that will shorten my time. I asked him about early release, but he told me I'd have to chalk up some good deeds. He'll take them into consideration at my next parole hearings."

"Stepping in front of bullets wasn't enough?"

"Let's just say I have a colorful past he has to take into consideration."

"I get it. How has doing good deeds worked out for you?"

"Not so good. I take two steps forward and then two steps back. Since you can see and hear me, for some reason, maybe you can help me with that, Mabel. Perhaps we can work as a team and find ways to do good deeds. The sooner I'm out of purgatory, the sooner I'm out of your hair."

She had a big grin on her face. I could see she had huge dimples. Looked like little balloons.

"So, Irma, what you're really saying is that as long as I own this camper, I have no choice but to help you. Or I will spend the rest of my living years with you tagging along."

"Well, look at the bright side. It'll certainly reduce your time in purgatory because I highly doubt you are going straight to heaven."

When you're my age you start to think about what looms ahead. She was right. I was no saint. From the look on her face, I figured Irma knew that already.

"Mabel, I'm so ready to finally get to heaven. Not that I know too many folks there, but I was awful good at making friends in my lifetime."

I felt a headache coming on.

"I'm willing to do whatever it takes to get you out of purgatory, so sign me up. The sooner, the better, so I can have my camper back."

This prompted a big smile on Irma's face. Her dimples looked like balloons about to bust.

"So, Irma, either I'm crazy and you are a ghost, or I'm the one who is dead."

"No, not yet." Irma looked at me with those deep green eyes.

"What does that mean? I thought you said you couldn't see into the future. What! Can you see my death like the ghost of Christmas past?"

"Oh, heavens, no. I mean, you're no spring chicken. That's all. By the way, Betsy is what I call your camper. After my sister. She went straight to heaven. I'm looking forward to seeing her. She will be the one waiting for me at the front gates. Like she did when I was alive, and she came to bail me out of jail."

"What happened to your son?"

"Walt got married and he has two daughters. Beautiful girls. They've got my eyes. Grown up now and doing well. Unfortunately, marriage never worked out for him. Sort of like what your friend, Lili, told you about Bob and his luck when it came to marriage. A cop's life is tough. But Walt is doing okay. When he retired as a detective he retired to a small town out west. He's the sheriff now and one of his girls is a lawyer. Like your Meg."

I now had a full-blown headache.

"So, what's the plan? You're tagging along with me in the camper? And I'm supposed to help you do good deeds along the way? If I do, then you'll get out of my hair?"

"Pretty much, Mabel, and remember—I live in your camper. Well, living might not be exactly the right word, but pay attention. As long as you own Betsy, I'll be around. Of course, when I get that get-out-of-jail card, I'm out here and Betsy is all yours."

This prompted another smile with those big dimples. I reached over and had a sip of the gin and tonic, made a face, and put it back down.

"Yuck. Maybe you can try vodka next time. Any idea how long this purgatory thing will last?"

I was hoping she'd didn't have much longer but she just shook her head.

"Can I say a prayer to Saint Peter at your next parole hearing? You know, move things along? Like a character witness?"

"The last time I met with Saint Peter, he must have been in a good mood because he told me he was putting me on the fast track program. I will be called on to handle some challenging work and that should speed things up. I think he's looking forward to the day I get into heaven. I probably drive him batty. Maybe that's why I can see you, and you can see me. I have a feeling that you are going to be a real challenge for me, Mabel. I should rack up a lot of extra credit just dealing with you."

"Ditto," I replied.

I watched as the specter rose and walked all the way down to the beach, and in a flash, she was back sitting next to me. It made me a little dizzy.

"Yeah, I think you are my ticket out, Mabel. I'm ready to do whatever it takes to get out of this joint. You should meet some dead people stuck here. They're a bunch of whiners. You got to work to get out of here. No free passes. Maybe there is something in your lifetime that you have to work out so that when the time comes, you'll be able to skip purgatory all together."

"Like what?" I asked. "Almost shooting my ex for dumping me for a tart the same age as our youngest daughter? I had a gun with me when I walked into that bar we owned in Jersey when I found out about her. I pulled it out of my purse. I came pretty close to shooting him. I know how to shoot a gun. He called our oldest son, who drove me home and unloaded the gun."

"Mabel, I don't know. For some reason—who the heck knows—you can see me. Maybe your ability to see the dead never left and it's come back. You know, like arthritis setting in from an old injury. It might have nothing to do with the two of us. I have noticed that's how the big guy works." Irma pointed to the sky. "It happens, Mabel. Sometimes it happens for no good reason. At some point, you have to move on, or you'll find yourself stuck in a purgatory, right here on earth."

I stared at Irma, and I knew then that I was hearing the voice of my Aunt Sadie, a message from beyond the grave.

"I think you're taking a step in the right direction by hitting the road with Betsy and me, if that is any solace."

I heard my Aunt Sadie now as clear as the day she left this earth.

"You sound like my Aunt Sadie."

"Sometimes they speak through me. She was sending you a message."

"Thank you."

"Yes, well, I allow it because I get extra credit with Saint Peter."

The movie star smile appeared on her face.

"In the meantime, I'm on this fast track to getting the hell out of purgatory. Dang. We're going to have to clean up our language. Saint Peter doesn't like a potty mouth. What I do know is that I am going to be called on to do some challenging work, as St. Peter puts it. Good deeds and helping people out of jams, stuff like that," Irma said, looking at me. "Maybe you're the one who needs help. We'll find out sooner or later."

"By the way, Mabel, when Saint Peter went over the program he told me it would involve the same thing that I took a bullet for."

"What did he mean by that? A murder? That's what you took a bullet for, you know."

"It's not an Alfred Hitchcock movie, Mabel. I don't know. Never question the bosses. One more thing, Mabel, I'm not on the same time zone as you, so get used to that."

And with that, Irma evaporated, and I passed out on my lanai.

CHAPTER 5

I woke up the next morning with a nasty hangover. At my age you can't drink like you used to, but that doesn't mean I'm giving up my cocktails. I had managed to send a text to Meg and begged off dinner last night. I went straight to bed, even though it was early. I could see I already had a text from her, so I texted her back that I was just getting up and having coffee. I left off the part about the hangover and Irma my new friend. Hopefully, that would be enough to keep her from running over and checking up on me. Over my morning coffee, I decided it was best not to mention Irma to a soul, especially Meg, who would think I was gaga.

If Irma showed up again, I was thinking of calling MC who got me out of that jam with the IRS. Besides knowing how to handle the IRS she had psychic abilities and her two Greek aunts were fortune tellers. Those three could hold a séance and have a chat with Irma, maybe an intervention. Ask her politely to leave. Or if that didn't work MC could call on her two nun friends. If anyone could get Irma out of my camper it would be those two scary nuns.

A few days went by, and no Irma. I began to talk myself into believing that my ability to see the dead had not returned, and my mind must have been playing tricks on me. It was probably a dream, or I shouldn't have mixed that new medication with booze. That had to be it.

I just wanted to get out on the road with Lili and Bob and my camper, Betsy. I liked that name. I called my F-150 Thor. I love those movies. I had a Groot bobble-head sitting on the dashboard of my pickup.

A couple more days passed, and I forgot all about Irma. I knew Meg was heading back north soon. She got busy with some unexpected repairs on their condo. Sid had flown back to Long Island, and I missed my favorite grandson.

"Stay out of trouble, Gram."

"Yeah, you too and eat your vegetables," I said loud enough for Meg to hear when we dropped him off at the airport in Palm Beach. In his ear I whispered, "Have a big hamburger with those veggies." He gave me a big hug.

"Of course, Dad and I will be having veggies tonight with our burgers. Potatoes, or as we know them, French fries." And off he went.

On the drive back from the airport, I had mentioned the book club meeting and asked Meg if she still would like to attend. To my surprise, Meg said she would.

The next day I called Meg. It went to voice mail. "The book club meets tonight. Do you still want to attend with Lili and me?"

A little while later, I got a text from her, "Sure. What time?"

I texted back the time. Lili and I would pick her up. I gave Lili a call and told her Meg was coming along.

"Great. I'll drive and be our designated driver. That will put her at ease, and maybe she'll relax."

"Oh, she'll relax all right. I'll make sure of it."

It was a big meeting at the club. Several of the cougars were heading back north, so tonight was a going-away party. Meg didn't know that. She thought we were discussing a book, like a regular book club.

Since Sid had gone back, Meg had been busy with work on the condo getting it ready for the winter rental season. It kept her out of my hair, but I knew before she left, she would re-visit my decision to head west in a camper.

Lili picked me up, and we went up to Meg's condo to see the renovations.

"What do you think?"

Lili had overseen many renovations on the large homes of her clients and was serving as a sounding board since none of Meg's friends were nearby. Lili was impressed, and while Meg showed her around, I decided to fix myself a drink. I was never good at decorating. I went over to the bar to fix myself a cocktail and was surprised to hear Meg's request for a drink.

"Mom, fix me one if you don't mind."

"All right," I said. "Small glass of wine?"

"No, fix me a Cosmo."

I caught a look from Lili.

Well, this was going to be an interesting book club meeting. Meg had decided to loosen up tonight. Wait till she met the cougars. It was going to be an earful. We finished the tour and our drinks and headed out. Lili drove along A1A, and in a few minutes, we parked in front of a mansion.

"Wow," Meg said looking at a house as big as a hotel.

"Wow is right," Lili said. "Wait till you see the inside."

The mansion by the sea belonged to Babbs LaFleur, the self-crowned queen of Boca Vista. She was a divorcee, but not a cougar. Her last husband was a partner with MC, my CPA. His name was Charlie LaFleur, and I had met Charlie while MC was working on my IRS case.

"He's a bad boy," Babbs told me when she heard I met Charlie.

Although divorced, they remained good friends but not as good as Bruce, her chauffeur, confidante, and food tester. Bruce was gay and a member of the book club. The women loved him, and he fit right in. He had especially connected with Lili. They were best buds. He answered the door with a martini.

"Girlfriends come on in, and this must be your beautiful daughter Meg." Bruce took her arm and whisked Meg to the bar.

"What are you drinking, sweetheart? How about a martini?"

"Sure," I heard Meg say. Well, surprise, surprise. Meg was going to become a member of the book club tonight.

Bruce finished fixing our drinks and whispered in my ear, "Don't worry; I made her a light one."

Lili apparently had told Bruce all about my daughter. Bruce gave Meg a tour of the house and introduced her to all the book club members and fixed more drinks.

Meg did not turn down another martini. I gave Bruce the thumbs up and mouthed the words, "Lili is driving."

By the time Meg joined Lili and me, I could see she was tipsy.

"Are you okay, Meg? I don't think I've seen you drink this much," I whispered to her while Lili stood by for moral support.

"It's Florida, Mom." Out came the words with a slight slur. "Introduce me to your friends. I'm dying to meet all of them."

I looked over at Lili, who said, "I see Queen Babbs, and she's heading this way."

Well, Meg was a grown woman, and I wanted her to relax, and it looked like she was relaxing–big time.

"Hello, Mabel, Lili, and who do we have here?"

The queen had arrived and was gracing us with her attention. Babbs LaFleur was one of the richest women in Florida. She owned a large grocery chain. Her father started the business. It began as a front for the mob and was used initially to launder money. It's all legit now. Once Babbs took over the reins, she saw to that. Her parents died tragically. Her mother died suddenly. Shortly after that, her father checked out. He was sitting in his favorite Italian restaurant and was served fettuccini, along with about a dozen bullets. Her Uncle Sal raised her, and ran the business until he passed, and Babbs took over after a struggle with her nephew, Dominic, who met his maker in Davy Jones' locker.

She recently sold it to a conglomerate. She liked being a social butterfly. She wouldn't know one aisle of a grocery store from another. Bruce took care of all that for her. He ran her household a lot like Lili ran the households of the rich and famous on Long Island. Currently, Babbs was the reigning queen of Boca Vista. She was in her element.

Bruce came by and swooped Lili away to catch up.

"Babbs, this is my daughter Meg," I said, and before I could finish the introductions, Babbs spoke.

"Charmed."

She extended her hand in a queenly gesture. Meg politely shook her hand.

"I'm very happy to meet you. You have a beautiful home."

"Let me introduce you to some of our book club members," Babbs said and took Meg's elbow. "I understand you are a criminal lawyer and a very good one."

As Meg was led away, she gave me a look and tried to hand me her martini. "I think I've had enough."

"No, I think you need to hang on to it. Trust me. You're going to need it."

Lili returned to my side. "Well?"

"Very strange goings-on here tonight. I've never seen my daughter drink this much, and what is up with the queen?"

We watched the Queen making the rounds and introducing Meg to the members as if she were a royal guest.

"She's usually very cool."

"Not sure," Lili said, "but that woman is calculating. She has something in mind, and she obviously thinks Meg is the one for the job."

"She said something about Meg being a criminal lawyer. How did she find that out?"

"The woman has connections."

"Oh no, we better go rescue her," I said as we watched Babbs introduce Meg to the cougars, and she was now surrounded by those women.

"She's fine. Freshen up your drink."

I looked down and saw that my Cosmo was dry. I started to head over to the bar but stopped because two cougars and Meg were heading our way.

"Let me go get you another drink," Lili said with a smile.

Roxie was now standing in front of me with her partner in crime Thelma. They were probably my age, but you would never know it. They had several plastic surgeons on retainer who were devoted to keeping these women happy and wrinkle-free from top to bottom and everything in between. These two women had boyfriends the same age as my youngest son. Actually, they both had several boyfriends, but their boyfriends didn't know they were not exclusive.

"Why not?" Roxie said when I first met her. "We are in control now," and she gave me the universal hand sign that meant I've got the money, so I call the shots.

Roxie owns a sports fishing boat and a big one. She was very good at sports fishing and entered contests all around the Caribbean and Florida. She kept her boat in Key West and had a pilot on call to fly her down there. Her oceanfront home is right down the street from Babbs. Thelma's money was inherited from trust funds. She had also been married a couple of times.

"Just never worked out, they were always after my money."

Thelma also had a home nearby and a collection of vintage cars she enjoyed exhibiting at shows and auctions. Roxie's taste in men ran to pirates, while Thelma favored race car drivers.

They were now chatting away with Meg, who was mesmerized by these two women who were different from her country club set on Long Island. Surprisingly, Meg seemed right at home with these two. Lili and I watched as they chatted about diets and exercise. It was quite a transformation. Meg was a hit and was inducted as an honorary member of the book club. They all agreed to keep in touch via social media. It seems a lot of them were on Pinterest.

Lili drove home after the book club meeting, and she dropped Meg and me off at my house. Meg was going to spend the night. Meg and I sat out on the lanai for a nightcap.

"Mom, I loved your book club."

"You seemed right at home."

"I've been thinking of going back to work. Sid is old enough and practicing law again will be good for me. Actually, Babbs convinced me. And even Roxie and Thelma agreed."

"What brought that on?"

"It's time. I need something to do."

"Other than worry about me?"

"There is that. Although I still don't like the idea, I am proud of you. You're living your life. Good for you."

She gave me a hug as she headed to bed.

"Night, Meg."

It had been quite an evening. Glad Meg came to the book club. It did her good. When I drove Meg to the airport a couple days later, I asked about her plans.

"I'm giving it some serious thought."

Then she gave me a laundry list of what I needed to do while on the trip west, including calling or texting her daily. I saw what was happening. I was becoming her child. Daughter number one had returned. So much for the book club transformation.

"Meg," I said as she grabbed her carry-on luggage. I got out saying goodbye under the watchful eye of the airport meter maids. *"Move along, nothing to see here."*

"I will be okay. You need to stop worrying about me. I think returning to the law is a good thing for you or maybe another baby?" I said half-jokingly. I knew that, over the years, Meg and Sid had tried and even considered adopting.

"Mother! A baby would be more work than returning to law, but I'll give it some thought."

I waved goodbye and watched until she disappeared.

CHAPTER 6

Bob helped me pick out the camper. He also told me that I needed to learn how to tow my seventeen-foot vintage camper.

"This one is a beauty. It's updated from top to bottom, but Mabel, it will not drive itself."

Bob agreed to teach me how. He was very patient with my lessons, which took place in an empty Walmart parking lot located in Fish Camp. No way would the movers and shakers of Boca Vista allow a Walmart in their little Palm Beach town. A new super Walmart had been built, so for now, there was plenty of room in the empty parking lot to maneuver. We practiced backing it into a simulated campground site. It wasn't easy, but he told me not to worry—he could always back it in if it came to that. But I needed to learn how to do it. Bob told me we would always try to book a pull-through site at the campgrounds we would be stopping at along the way.

"It makes it real easy. No backing up. Just pull in and stop. When you leave, you just drive straight out. No hassle. No accidents," Bob explained.

"Oh yeah, I always try to do that when I'm shopping."

During my last lesson, Bob had me drive out of the parking lot, drive around the neighborhood and then drive back home. I passed, but today was my final exam. I was heading out on the highway.

"I'm a little nervous, Bob."

"Nerves are not a bad thing, Mabel. Mine saved my life more than a couple of times."

I had no problem with driving Thor. My new pickup was a step up from the mini-vans I drove to the ground while schlepping five kids around to school and after school and everything in-between. Not to mention a zillion birthday parties. Unlike Meg, I was never so happy when they were old enough to drive.

But driving and towing a camper is new territory. Luckily, it's small and light. When I first bought it, I thought I'd use my SUV. But it had a lot of mileage and Bob suggested I needed a reliable transport. You don't want to break down when you are towing a camper. I invested in a pickup and appreciate the extra horsepower, although even a VW Beetle could tow it. There's a photo of one doing it back in the '60s.

We took a couple of laps around the parking lot for a warm-up, and then we headed out of the safety of the Walmart parking lot. We were leaving soon, and the plan for the final exam was to drive on the highway that will take us north out of Florida, I-95. It runs north and south along the east coast. It ends right below Miami, and then the road to the Keys begins.

Bob was sitting next to me in the passenger seat, and just as we were heading to the on-ramp to I-95 during rush hour traffic, Irma decided to make her appearance and pop back into my life. I'd been nervous enough as it was, but when I looked in the rear-view mirror and saw Irma sitting there, I just about had a heart attack.

She just smiled, dimples popping out on her cheeks, and gave me thumbs up. She was wearing a bright orange neon dress matched with black stiletto heels and black nylons and a garter. She looked like she was going to a Halloween party. She looked so real, but I knew she was a ghost. I had almost forgotten about her. I had been telling myself that she was a figment of my imagination. Or the new drug I was on. My ability to see spirits had returned in full bloom, along with Irma. What lousy timing. I just hoped she hadn't brought any company.

I looked over at Bob. He had his head cranked around, looking out the rear window. He was checking traffic as I slowly ventured onto the highway. He was looking straight through Irma.

"What the hell are you doing here?" I mouthed to the ghost in my rear-view mirror. "You look like a street-walker."

Bob turned back around and was now looking at the passenger mirror.

"I was a showgirl, remember? By the way, I never walked the streets," Irma said angrily. "I thought I told you to clean up that potty mouth. That's one thing I expected from my girls, manners and civility. What do you think I'm doing? I'm here to help. Keep your eyeballs on the road, Mabel. I want to make sure you don't wreck this rig. I'd be stuck in a junkyard for the rest of my sentence. I drove an 18-wheeler for a short time. I was trying to change occupations. It didn't work. Some truckers recognized me from the cat house I ran as the Madame."

"Mabel, keep your eyes on the road." Bob gave me a puzzled look. "You're doing fine. Nice and easy does it." Obviously, he could not see or hear Irma, but she was back like a bad dream.

"Sorry, sometimes I talk to myself."

I smiled at Bob, hoping he didn't think I was losing it. I wanted to pass this test so we could hit the road. I quickly looked up at the rear-view mirror. Backseat driver Irma was gone. "Thank you, Saint Peter," I said and made the sign of the cross.

Bob looked at me funny. "Don't worry you're a natural."

I now found myself in bumper to bumper I-95 traffic. For once, I welcomed the slow traffic. Bob told me to stay in the far-right lane except to pass.

"Slow and easy. Who were you talking to?"

"My Aunt Sadie."

"That's fine, but I'm sure Aunt Sadie wants you to keep your eyes on the road, hands at 10 and 2. Got it?"

"Yes, officer."

"I want you to pull out and pass this slowpoke in front of you."

"Okay."

I could feel the sweat on my hands, gripping the steering wheel with white knuckles at 10 and 2. I was about to attempt my first pass on the highway. I was happy to see that the surrounding drivers gave me a wide berth as I moved into the middle lane to pass the car in front of me, who decided to speed up and pull in front of me.

"Damn."

"Relax, just remember you are driving the truck and towing your camper. Pull back over into the slow lane now. Just drive the truck, not the camper."

I got back in the safe lane and took a big breath. I looked up in the rear-view mirror and still no Irma. After that, I calmed down and actually was enjoying driving and towing Betsy until some hotshots zipped past me and honked and gave me the finger. That's when Irma popped back and stuck her head through the closed rear window, and I heard her holler at them. She gave them a whistle any New Yorker would be proud of and then stuck her head back through the window.

"Assholes."

She gave them two ghostly middle fingers and then disappeared. Bob saw me staring in the rear-view mirror again.

"Eyes on the road, Mabel. Straight ahead, not behind."

"Roger that," I said with one last look to make sure Irma was gone. Saint Peter's not going to like that, I thought.

"Are you okay? What are you mumbling about?"

"Sorry. Just a little nervous. I want to pass this final exam so we can get out on the road. Those hot shots threw me for a loop."

"You will get used to that. Everyone is in a hurry nowadays. I'll take care of that. I'll install a horn that you can use when you run into jerks like that. It's a trucker's delight and it's loud. You pass, Mabel. Let's head on back and have a drink to celebrate. I'll call Lili, and why don't you call your friend Louie."

"Okay." I was happier than a kid to get off the highway and head home.

Louie, my lawyer, and I were good friends. We were both happy to keep it at that, for now anyway, although the cougars at the book club had other ideas.

"One day at a time, girls. One day at a time." I told them.

"That's what we don't have, Mabel," Lili said. "Time."

Just the same, I wasn't ready for a serious relationship. Frankly, it surprised me, but I was beginning to like being single and independent, just like Bianca. Although at times it was lonely, so having Louie as a friend was nice. He and I were on the same wavelength, for now, anyway.

I parked Betsy with no problem in front of my house and managed to unhook my camper from the pickup. It took a little muscle, but I did it. Knowing Bob was there to help was reassuring, but I needed to learn how to handle things myself.

"You pass, Mabel. I think we are ready to hit the road and it's time to celebrate."

For the first time in a long time, I felt good about myself. I knew now that my ability to see the dead was back, and that first meeting with Irma was real. As weird as it was, I was happy that I was going to have some company on the road, even if it was a ghost and someone who drove an 18-wheeler.

I let Bob in the house, and he said he would fix up a batch of margaritas. I told him I'd be right in after checking out the camper. I climbed up the step and poked my head in.

"Irma. Are you there?"

"I'm here."

I took a step in and looked around. She was sitting on the sofa "So, you are really real?"

"Well, as real as a dead person can be. I am real, and I am dead, and everything we talked about that night on the lanai was real."

I thought back and tried to remember that conversation.

"I had another talk with the big guy about this fast track program while you were learning to tow Betsy."

"What did Saint Peter have to say? Have you tried asking him to let you pass through the gates and ask God for asylum?"

"I tried that, and it won't work. He said I had to face the challenges. Whatever they are and somehow they are related to the night I died."

"How? Why? Do you have to go back? Live it all over again. Some sort of Groundhog Day?"

"Yep. Groundhog Day? Another movie?" Irma was now standing in front of me.

"What about me?"

"Well, Mabel. You bought this camper, and now you are along for the ride. You got your sight back. You know, 'I can see dead people' so you can see and hear me. So, my best guess is that you will get to assist me. Remember, I was a Madame. You appear to be train-able… but we'll see. The sooner we get going, the better, and then I will be out of your hair."

"If I didn't already drink, you'd drive me to it!" I said and closed my eyes. When I opened them, she was gone, but now, I knew she was not a figment of my imagination. She would be back. Like the Terminator, "I'll be back."

Well, my choice was to not go on the trip and sell the camper or head out and see where the road will take me. I decided on the road.

"Okay Irma, you win," I said to the empty camper.

"Roger that Mabel" Irma popped in front of me with a big grin and a wink, and then she was gone.

"Roger that, Irma, Roger that."

Chapter 7

The weeks were flying by as we made plans for the trip west. Ultimately, we would make our way to the Rocky Mountains and then take a new route back home to Florida in the fall. "When the pumpkins return," Lili said. I felt like we were settlers heading out in our wagon trains to settle a new land.

Bob mapped out the trip. We were leaving Boca Vista, and the first stop would be Daytona Beach. Over lunch at a spot on the water in Boca Vista, Bob discussed our trip with Lili and me. Irma had been quiet, but I knew she would return. Like she told me that first night, "I'm not in your time zone."

"Our first stop is Daytona Beach. Get your feet wet," Bob said. "We'll spend a day or two there and then head out. Then, we will meet up with two RV'ers at a park in Savannah, Georgia. We will spend some time in Savannah, and while we are there, see Savannah and Tybee Island. Get to know everyone and make sure we all get along."

"If we don't?" I asked.

"Oh, we will. Don't worry about that," Bob said with a twinkle in his eye.

"You know, Savannah is known as the most haunted city in the country," Lili said.

She was from New Orleans and knew a bit about the dead. I was coming pretty close to telling her about Irma. I had to talk to someone about Irma, and I had decided Lili was the one. I was waiting until we were on the road. No turning back then or calling my kids.

"The other members of the RV'ers group elected Bob as the leader," Lily said. "Think of it as a lot like our book club. Instead of a group of divorcees and widows banding together, it's a group who want to travel in their RVs."

"Bob is both retired military and cop. He is a natural leader, and likes calling the shots," Lili said, giving Bob a wink. "The RV'ers who make up our club were more than happy to let him take over as the leader of the group."

Will we stop at Ashville? I asked.

"Ashville, North Carolina, we will save for the trip back. Much cooler then and the leaves will be turning," Bob said. "We will spend a couple days in Ashville and visit the Biltmore Estate, which is America's largest home, built by George Vanderbilt. It's a grand estate in the Blue Ridge Mountains."

"I think a number of movies have been filmed at the Biltmore Estate," I said. "I remember one, *Being There* with Peter Sellers. Remember him from the Pink Panther?"

"I do and the movie *Forrest Gump*, my favorite, which was filmed in Savannah," Lili said.

"Next, we will land in Nashville and spend some time in Music City," Bob continued. "We should make it there right after the CMA Music Awards."

"Wow, Lili, we might see some of our favorite country stars. I can't wait."

"Wait, there's more," Bob said with a chuckle. "We will travel to Mount Rushmore and then the highlight of our trip, the Grand Canyon. In between as many national parks as we can visit before winter. So, in all, there will be four of us in the caravan. Our campers are known for traveling in a group. We will be a sight to see traveling on the road."

"So, who are the other members of our group?" I asked.

"I haven't met them in person, just online. Josh and Peggy Crawford are retired school teachers. Oscar Johnson, retired military, and his wife Eleanor."

"So, do you check them out before you agree they can join the group?"

I was thinking about what Irma told me and her fast track challenge that was going to take place on this trip. Bob's prior life as a cop might come handy.

"I'm retired and no longer have access to run background checks."

I knew he had connections because Lili had told me as much.

"But I do what I can. Basically, I talk to them. You can tell a lot about a person from a conversation. Remember, I was a homicide detective before I retired."

"So, what did you find out?"

"Josh and Peggy are both schoolteachers. From our conversations, Peggy is the boss."

"The other couple?"

"I spoke to Oscar. He's a hard read. Retired military. Dabbles in investments was all he shared."

I looked at Lili, who was silent and busy eating her lunch. Lili was not shy about speaking up, but she picked her moments.

"But there is a lot you can find out on the internet," Bob said. "They live in Fort Lauderdale, on Galt Ocean Mile, in a condominium. Nice one."

"Well then, they have money. Coming from Long Island, I'm familiar with that area. It takes money to live on that beach. Anything else?"

"No."

But I knew his radar was up and he would continue looking into this couple.

"So, you don't have a real good feeling about this couple?" I said.

"We'll find out more once they join the group," Lili said. "They'll show their cards."

Lili was a mean poker player.

After many years of dealing with powerful families and running their households, Lili could read people. She did all the hiring and firing of staff. Keeping the secrets of powerful people was paramount. She would send you packing if you dared to gossip. I don't think it was an acquired trait. She just knew instinctively.

"Well, I'm looking forward to visiting Music City," I said, and Lili smiled.

Both she and Bob loved country music. Fish Camp had a row of honky-tonks, and a bar that resembled a famous honky-tonk in Nashville. I was looking forward to learning how to line dance. I couldn't wait to hit those honky-tonks with my dancing shoes. Or I should say boots. Lili is going to take me shopping for a pair.

We finished our lunch. No doggy bags for us but we did leave room for a little dessert. After lunch, they dropped me off.

"We're going shopping for some last-minute items," Lili said. "We are heading over to the Harley store in Fish Camp."

Bob had a Harley he planned to bring on the road. I had watched with amazement the first time I saw him drive it up the ramp to the extended bed in his pickup.

"I've had a bike all my life. I rode a Harley as a cop."

Lili shared that Bob would like nothing better than to settle out west.

"He would love to live in Colorado or Wyoming."

"How about you?"

This was before they were married.

"I'm okay with it as long as I don't have to spend the winters. My bones won't take it."

"You got the spare bedroom in my house. It has your name, so don't worry about that."

"Then I will have the best of both worlds."

I felt comforted by that fact. Plus, Lili liked to cook and me not so much.

CHAPTER 8

The next morning, I was sitting on my lanai with my tablet and coffee. That's when Irma popped back in with her two cents. I was getting used to her appearances and disappearances. She looked as human as I did, but I knew she was a spirit. She had died a long time ago, and a lot of technology had come about since her death, and sometimes it showed, like right about now.

"You need a TripTik, Mabel, from Triple A. I don't trust those—what did you call it— Geepers."

Today, she was wearing another bright neon outfit, looked like something from the eighties. Her hair was teased as big as the hair was back in those days. The dress was short, and I could see she had long legs.

"It's a GPS, Irma," I said, looking up at her standing in front of me. She was definitely tall, probably six feet something. "How tall are you?"

"I don't remember, Mabel. It was a long time ago. Let's just say I was showgirl tall." She took that as a cue to strut around my lanai.

"So, in purgatory, you can wear different outfits?" I pointed to her outfit. "I suspect the one you are wearing will need to be returned to the eighties. Yep, I think they are calling."

"Funny Mabel, everyone wants to be a comedian. To answer your question, I can pop into my closet anytime and any year. I was a hooker, not a preacher. Although we had our share of those as clients. Wink-wink."

"Well, how about something from the movie Grease?"

She was gone and back in a split second. She was wearing the poodle skirt and the jacket I recognized from Grease.

"Holy smoke. Good grief. You have quite the closet."

"It sure came in handy, if you know what I mean."

She vanished and left me alone to drink my coffee. I loved coffee and usually brewed a pot in the morning and afternoon. Coffee didn't bother me like most folks.

I gave Irma's suggestion some more thought and conceded that Irma did have a point. I'd been a member of the well-known auto club since the kids were little. It was like insurance to have their roadside assistance. Everyone my age at one point or another had ordered a TripTik for an upcoming road trip. All that paper! Something about going into the office and watching the agent print out the pages of your trip and handing it to you in a nice spiral booklet. Plus, you got a personalized map and tour books for all the states you would be visiting. Today your cell phone and GPS are all you need. But technology breaks down. There's nothing like a good map. But then a GPS will make sure you don't get lost.

So, I decided to drop into the local office over in Fish Camp to order a TripTik, even though I didn't know the entire route. I had a doctor's appointment in the morning to make sure I had all my prescriptions lined up for the road. I hate taking pills, but when you get to be my age, they start multiplying, like fleas on a dog. After my doctor's appointment, I parked and went inside the AAA office. The young woman, whose name tag read Natalie, was so excited when I told her about the trip and itinerary. She couldn't believe I was heading out in a pickup and towing a vintage camper.

"They're well built. My grandmother and grandfather had one. They sold their home and traveled all over the country for years. My grandmother sent me postcards at each stop along the way. I still have those post cards."

Turns out she was named after her grandmother who was quite the adventurer.

It was close to the middle of May and Bob said we would start back when the Aspen trees turn a shade of gold in Colorado, probably September. I couldn't wait to see that.

"It happens almost overnight," Bob told me. "The Aspen is Colorado's only widespread native tree and can be found from 6,500 to 11,500 feet in elevation. The leaves and their vibrant fall color are often displayed as their state symbol."

It didn't take long for Natalie to prepare the TripTik, and when she finished, she gave me her business card with her number.

"I'm so excited for you. How cool. I wish I could come along!"

Natalie was more excited than any of my kids. "My grandmother did a lot of cool things when she was my age. She served in Vietnam. I'm so proud I was named after her, but I'm not doing anything with my life."

"You will, Natalie, give it time."

I smiled, thinking how the roles between my kids and me had changed. They were now the parent or at least my two oldest thought that way. I was careful now when I talked to them. They were likely to view motherly advice as interfering in their lives. They knew it all, or so they thought. The only one who was still close to me was Henry, my gay son. After Lili, he was my confidante. I could talk to him. He texted every couple of days, and he kept me up to date on his sister Bianca, who was too busy to call or text. I had to make an appointment to talk to her.

"Mrs. Gold, call or email me along the way, and I'll update your TripTik if you take a different route."

"Call me Mabel. How will you get it to me?"

"I can email it."

"Oh, yeah, I am bringing my laptop. But I won't have a printer." It was more difficult traversing the road of technology than it was driving my rig.

"Mabel, do you have a smartphone?"

"Oh yeah. It's smarter than me."

Meg had just updated my phone not too long ago when she first found out about my plans to take the road trip.

"You can't go out west with that flip phone. How will you call anyone? I need to be able to get a hold of you."

After that she and Sid went through my needs on the road and she got me whatever Sid suggested, including the new smart phone, a tablet and a top-of-the-line GPS unit. I pulled out my phone and handed it to her.

"Sweet, an android. Do you mind if I put my personal number in your cell?"

"No, no, go ahead."

I watched as Natalie put her number in. "I can always send it to any Triple A office along the way and you can pick it up. How's that?"

"Perfect. Thank you, Natalie," I gave her a big hug. "I wish my kids were as excited about my trip as you."

"To be honest, if it was my grandmother, I'd be a little worried."

Well, she had a point and was forgiven for the age reference, but who was I kidding, I was old enough to be her grandmother. I waved as I went out the door with my TripTik and bagful of tour books for Florida, Georgia, North Carolina and Tennessee. Plus maps, old school. On my way home, Irma popped into the shotgun seat.

"I'm so excited."

After spending years in a storage facility, I could see how it would be a nice change. She could take an active role in the trip.

"I'm so excited." Irma sang to the song that was playing on the radio. "I remember that song."

"Do you know you have a pretty good voice?"

"Well, I did tell you I started out as a showgirl and had hoped to make it big in show business," she said with a look on her face I would come to recognize as regret.

"Don't wait until you're dead, Mabel, to do things you should have done while you were living. It doesn't work out well that way. You only get one life."

"Well, in a way, you are getting a second life. Coming along on my second life."

"Not really, Mabel. Don't forget I'm stuck in purgatory with a bunch of whiners. I'm ready to walk through those gates and meet my maker. It's time. Let me have that," she said, pointing to the Triple A bag sitting between us.

We had stopped for a red light. I pulled out the Trip-Tik and started to hand it to her, but then realized I had no idea how to hand it to her.

"Just place it on the passenger seat."

As I did, it appeared on her lap. The light turned green, and I drove home watching Irma out of the corner of my eye flipping through spiral pages. It was suspended in midair, being held by her ghostly hands.

"You can do that?" I said as I parked.

"Oh, you'd be surprised what I can do Mabel. You'd be surprised."

CHAPTER 9

One beautiful morning in May, we left Boca Vista. We were taking the scenic route–A1A and then cutting over to I-95 and heading north. Limo Louie got to the house at dawn to send us off and get the keys.

"I don't do dawns, Mabel. Only for you," he chuckled as I handed him the keys.

He was going to house sit. Check on it and use it as an excuse to keep in touch with me. He handed me a bag from Dunkin Donuts.

"They do dawns."

"Louie, make sure the pipes don't burst."

"This isn't Jersey, Mabel. You don't have to worry about a freeze."

"Well, you just keep a sharp eye out. Enjoy but no wild parties!"

"At least you don't have cats. I'm allergic to those critters."

We were standing next to Thor and Betsy while he was giving me last-minute directions for the 100th time.

"Okay, you have my number. Please call or text, anytime. In fact, why don't you text as soon as you get to Daytona. So, I know you're safe."

Today we were going to make our way to Daytona Beach, our first stop. A little over a two-hour drive. Bob and Lili arrived ten minutes ago and were waiting for me to say goodbye to Louie, or maybe it was the other way around.

"Don't worry, Louie! Relax. I'm not heading out alone." I pointed at Bob and Lili, who waved. "It's not like we're heading out to sea and going around the world."

"Don't forget, I can drive this rig," he said, pointing toward my camper.

I had no doubt that Limo Louie could drive my rig. We took it over to the empty Walmart parking lot to help me practice, and he did exactly that. That was when I agreed that he would be my backup plan—in case of an emergency.

"You might get out there, Mabel, and decide the camping life isn't for you."

"I'll be fine! But it is reassuring to know that you have my back."

"Just the same, I can fly out and drive you home. They don't call me Limo Louie for nothing, you know."

"I know and thank you, Louie."

I did feel a sense of relief knowing that Louie could bail me out, instead of my kids. It gave me the confidence to leave the security of my home. We talked about him flying out for the trip home. That was all we did, though, talk.

"I'll miss you, Mabel."

Louie reached over and gave me a hug, and at that moment, we were real close to a first kiss.

"I'll be fine, Louie. Hold down the fort."

I was looking into his eyes while we both considered a goodbye kiss. I guess we decided it was no time to start down that road as I was leaving and would be gone for the summer. That would involve more than a Trip-Tik.

Plus, down deep, I knew if I kissed him, I might be ready to come home at the first-time things got uncomfortable. I'd be safe again like I was all those years I was married. Not that it was a bad thing. It was a wonderful thing to know someone was there for you. I looked forward to finding that again, but not just yet. It was time to learn to stand on my own two feet and with no safety net.

"Hold that thought, Mabel," he whispered in my ear as he released me into my new life.

"I will. See you in September."

"I'll be waiting."

I got in my pickup and waved goodbye. I kept looking in the rear-view mirror until I couldn't see Louie anymore. It was time to say goodbye to my old life and move on, finally.

"I'm not in Kansas anymore, Dorothy. Or should I say, Irma?" I said out loud.

I had half expected Irma to answer me, but luckily, she had stayed away. I didn't need her to see the tears I wiped away.

CHAPTER 10

Of course, she couldn't stay away too long. At the out-
skirts of Boca Vista as soon as we got on the A1A, Irma
appeared in the shotgun seat. Up ahead, I could see
Bob's Airstream. He had hooked up walkie-talkies so
we could keep in contact hands-free when we needed.

I heard his voice. "Doing okay?"

"Doing great, Bob."

"We'll stay on A1A for a bit and then cut over to I-
95, probably close to Stuart. I'll let you know."

"Roger that." I heard him chuckle. "Eyes on the
road, soldier. Don't be talking to your Aunt Sadie."

No, I wouldn't be talking to my Aunt Sadie, but by
the looks of things, I would be talking to Irma.

"You should have kissed him goodbye, Mabel."

I looked over at Irma. Today she was dressed like
she had the lead in *Grease*. She was wearing her Olivia
Newton-John outfit. I looked down, and I saw she
added a pair of boots that were made for walking—
white, knee-high, go-go boots.

"I don't think those boots were in *Grease*. More like
Nancy Sinatra?"

Irma chose to ignore my fashion tips. Probably
smart. I took a deep breath.

"I know. I almost did, Irma, I almost did. But I decided I could only make so many changes in one day, and today, it was this one."

I pointed ahead at Bob's Airstream. Even though Daytona Beach was a little over two hours from Boca Vista, Bob told me it would take longer towing campers. My GPS would tell me how long and from the looks of it, so would Irma.

Out of the corner of my eye, I saw the TripTik suspended above her ghostly lap. A few minutes later I heard it fall on the passenger seat.

When she popped back, she was dressed like she was heading out on a safari.

"In my profession, we did a lot of dress-up."

I glanced at her. She had a whip in her hand and I almost ran off the road when I heard it snap. I watched it zing right through the passenger window and then it disappeared into thin air.

"Good grief, Irma. Please. I have to drive, and I don't need a side-show. Why did you change? I love Grease. How about some West Side Story? What the hell are you dressed for now? You look like you're heading out to do some big game hunting."

"I've lined up a lot of costumes for the road. This is going to be so much fun." Her hands weaved in and out as she ghostly clapped them together.

"Great. I can't wait to see them." NOT!

In the center of the dashboard, the GPS sat right below Groot. Irma was mesmerized by it because it could talk.

"This is all new to me. I'm sure the previous owners of Betsy had one of these Geeper things, but I stayed in the camper. Never rode shotgun." She brought her nose close to the GPS and sniffed it like a dog.

"What the hell are you doing?"

"I told you to clean up your language. You sound like a sailor and trust me; you're giving them a bad name."

"Okay, okay." She was right. "I'll bite my tongue. Remember, I grew up in Brooklyn."

We rode along in silence for a bit. I could tell she was thinking about something. Her eyes were somewhere I could not go.

"What are you thinking about?"

"I'm thinking about a good friend who took me under his wing when I first arrived in purgatory. He's an Indian chief, a Cherokee."

I rolled my eyes. I could hear Bianca. "Native American."

"Chief Little Bear lived in North Carolina, a couple hundred years ago. He's been hanging around in purgatory for a long time."

"What did he do to get such a long sentence?"

"Well, Mabel, my guess is that he angered a few folks. But he had good reason; they were trying to steal his homeland. The Cherokee Indians were one of the largest tribes that settled in the Southeast. When gold was discovered on their land they were forced out. By the way, Cherokee women were immensely powerful. They owned all the houses and fields, and they could marry and divorce as they pleased."

"Really? I like the idea of women in power. They were way ahead of their times."

"He got his name because when he was a child, he wandered off. They found him asleep with a mother bear and her cubs."

"Will I be able to see Chief Little Bear like I see you?"

"Don't know Mabel, maybe. He's a spiritual guide. He was a medicine-man and a shaman. A shaman is a mediator between the supernatural and man, and the medicine-man is a curer of diseases through traditional ways."

"We could use more of that today." I was thinking of the rapidly growing list of medications I take.

"The strange thing is, he told me he finished his time in purgatory a long time ago, but he can't leave just yet."

"What do you mean? I thought when your sentence is up you go to heaven."

"There's something holding him back. It has to do with his death. I've met a few dead people like him, and something happened at the time of their death. It's as if they don't know they are dead. Best I can explain it."

"When was the last time you saw Chief Little Bear?"

"Mabel, I told you I'm not in your time zone. It might have been yesterday. It might have been a decade ago. But to answer your question, I feel like it was closer to yesterday."

"Why is that?"

"Something he told me. He mentioned you," Irma said and looked over at me.

"Me! Holy Smoke. I'm listening."

"He said you should keep a gun close by."

"Wait, a minute! We're not one hour out on the road and we're talking guns? Do you think this has something to do with your fast track program?"

"I'm sure it does. You did bring your gun?"

"Yes, I did."

"Well, make sure it's loaded. Chief Little Bear would not have delivered that message if it didn't mean something."

"Fine. Fine and dandy." Maybe the old farts home wasn't such a bad idea.

"Actually Irma, Bob helped me pick out a good one for the road."

"What did you get? A machine-gun?"

"Funny! They're illegal. A Glock."

"That's a good choice. The Magnum 44 I used on Walt's killer was pretty hard to handle. My son still has that gun."

"Well, let's hope I don't need it."

But the look she gave me told me she thought otherwise.

CHAPTER 11

As I followed Bob and Lili, I got into a rhythm. From time to time, I got a glimpse of Bob's Harley sitting in the bed of his pickup.

Lili had no problem with the Harley and was very comfortable riding in the queen's seat. Bob insisted they wear helmets, and she agreed. He even offered to teach me how to drive the Harley, but I figured he was joking.

"Well, let's take one day at a time," I said the last time it came up in conversation, and Lili gave me her famous *are you crazy* look. The thought of driving a Harley through the national parks we planned to visit out west was tempting, though. Under Bob's guidance, I was now comfortable with Betsy.

"Mabel, you're a natural," Bob said the night before we left, He could see I was getting last-minute jitters. "Just remember, never come to a quick stop. Slow and easy does it. That's your mantra."

I wasn't afraid to learn to drive the Harley any more than I was learning to tow my camper or even shooting a gun. What scared me, what I was more afraid of, was the future. What did it hold for me?

"Remember what I told you. Fear will get you killed," Bob reminded me when we were at the gun range and he wanted me to get comfortable shooting the Glock. Lili was going to join us, but her back was acting up.

"All those years of housework, plus I saw enough of guns when I was growing up. I know how to shoot one if I have to."

I grew up in Brooklyn at a time when you had to develop a thick skin. Nobody coddled me. If I won, I won. If I lost, well, I lost. The trophy went to the winner, not the loser or anyone in between.

"They call that bullying," Bianca said when I told her the story about the older kids in the neighborhood who had pummeled me with snowballs. "We don't condone that today."

"Bianca, bullying, or whatever you want to call it now, was part of growing up back then. It made me stronger and it gave me a backbone. It's like eating dirt. It builds up your immune system."

Meg, on the other hand, agrees with her sister on this point, but then, she is a bit paranoid.

We were now on I-95. The transition was smooth. According to the GPS, we were getting close to the campground in Daytona. The walkie-talkie came to life. I eased up on the gas as Bob started with instructions.

"We're going to stop at the next truck stop. Just drive the pickup and the camper will follow behind you. Slow and easy does it."

Betsy followed along with no problem. Still, I wanted to make sure I didn't get myself backed into a tight spot, but it was nice to know I had Bob to get me out of a jam. I was soon to learn that I also had Irma to help.

"Remember, I drove an 18-wheeler."

She guided me into the truck stop and up to the gas pumps.

"Thanks, Irma. That did help."

I hopped out of the pickup and was gassing up Thor when I noticed Irma was standing next to me.

"What are you doing? Wait in the pickup for me."

She was now wearing jeans and a ball cap that read Peterbilt.

"I'm admiring that Peterbilt."

I watched as she walked close to the large truck next to us at the gas pumps.

"That's a beauty, a sort of vintage, like Betsy. The first one built was in 1939."

I took a deep breath when I saw the owner of the truck making his way back. He was a good-looking guy wearing the same cap as Irma.

"Howdy, ma'am," he said as he tipped his cap.

Irma was standing next to him, looking directly into his face.

"Irma, leave him alone."

The truck driver turned back to me, "Did you say something to me, ma'am."

"No. Yes. I mean, I said to have a nice day."

"Same to you, ma'am."

"Hmm, he looks familiar. I better get back inside."

As the Peterbilt pulled away, I saw Bob and Lili stretching their legs.

"Everything okay?"

"Fine, just fine."

I hoped he hadn't seen me talking to Irma. We finished pumping gas and were back out on the road. Not only was it the first day of the trip west, it was the first day of Irma's backseat driving—from the front seat. She sat next to me with the TripTik suspended above her lap. I could see her hands flipping through the pages, literally.

"Don't worry, Mabel. I've got your back, me and Trixie, here."

Irma had named the GPS Trixie. Bob asked me what voice I wanted, and I said I didn't have a clue. I turned to Lili, and she suggested a British female voice. She knew I was a big fan of the actress who played M in the James Bond movies. We both watched those movies more than once.

"Who's Agatha Christie?" Irma asked when I explained why Lili suggested a British accent.

"A writer of whodunits. Lili loves to read whodunits or cozy murders as she calls the books. They usually involve a murder and amateur sleuths who solve the mystery."

"Like Murder She Wrote," Irma said.

"Exactly."

We rode along, and I could see Irma looking at me from time to time as if she wanted to tell me something but held back. I had come to know that, even though Irma swore she couldn't see the future, Irma had what she called *feelings*.

"It's not something I picked up in purgatory. I had them before. I had a feeling the night I went to my son's rescue. I just felt like it would be my last one on earth."

"What is it?"

"Not sure. I don't want to scare you, but remember Chief Little Bear said that you need to be careful."

"Yes. What else?"

"Yeah, well, just prepare yourself, Mabel. This trip may very well turn into one of those Agatha Christie books. We may find out that we're the amateur sleuths, and we may have to solve a mystery."

With that, she spoofed out into thin air and left me alone with my thoughts.

CHAPTER 12

Daytona Beach, FL

According to Trixie, we were getting close to Daytona Beach. A two to three-hour drive in a car was something I was used to, but towing a camper seemed to take forever. Irma popped in and out. I saw the signs for Daytona Beach, and sure enough, Trixie's proper British voice came to life.

"In two miles exit the highway."

She was programmed to give us a heads up two miles before an exit. She was also programmed to politely tell us to turn around if we missed the exit.

"Turn around when possible."

She didn't stop and would continue with the 'turn around when possible' until you turned around or got to a point where she gave up and reprogrammed the route, all very calm and proper, like a Brit.

"Irma, it's a good thing we don't have a Brooklyn accent like my mother's.

Whatd'a yah–deaf? Turn this rig around now! Not next Hanukkah…"

"Nice of her to do that," Irma said when Trixie gave us directions. "She is very polite, just like I trained my girls. You need to pay attention to Trixie. Might learn a few tricks." She winked and I half smiled back.

We took the exit off I-95. The campground was located on International Speedway Blvd. Bob had been there before. It was a nice campground and convenient to the Daytona Speedway and a famous honky-tonk called the Boot Hill Saloon.

"Isn't that across the street from a cemetery?" Irma asked.

"You've heard of it?"

"I didn't spend all my days in Vegas, Mabel. Of course, I've heard of it. I think I'll check it out." She had a wicked smile on her face. "See if I recognize any names."

I followed Bob and Lili and soon we were in the campground. We made our way to the office and parked out front. Bob hopped out of his truck and headed into the campground office. A few minutes later, he came out with an older man who loaded the three of us onto a golf cart. He was wearing a Hawaiian shirt and knee-high black socks and a name tag that said his name was Jim.

"You're here at a great time since it is off season. Not crowded with all those snowbirds." Jim showed us our campsites and then drove us back to the office. "Holler if you need anything."

"Let me go with you this first time," Bob said as he got in the passenger side of my pickup.

I had no problem parking my camper. The campsite was a pull-through and long and level. This campground had full hookups, which meant water, electricity, and sewer. I watched Bob make quick work of it.

"Next time I'll watch, and you do the hook up."

"Copy that."

I knew I'd have to learn how to hook up Betsy, but I've been watching YouTube's so I felt ready. I cranked the awning down, and in no time, we set up our lawn chairs and sat down for cocktail time, the first of many to come. This was the first time Lili and I had had a chance to talk. Bob got up and went to say hi to our neighbors a few spots down.

"Well, how do you feel?" Lili took a sip of her beer. "There's nothing like a cold beer to welcome a warm summer evening." She clicked my beer and we toasted.

"Oh, Lili, this is stupendous. I feel like I belong here, Lili—I feel free."

"Well, wake up, Martin Luther," Lili said with a belly laugh, and we toasted the future.

Bob returned, and we made plans for dinner. We were heading over to the Boot Hill Saloon for burgers and fries. Bar food sounded really good to me. We gave each other a little time to spruce up till our Uber arrived, and then off we went. I found myself looking around for Irma, but she was nowhere in sight. That is until we were sitting down to our beers and waiting for our burgers.

The jukebox was playing a slow song that Lili and Bob recognized, and while they danced in popped Irma.

"I just checked out the cemetery across the street."

"Find any old friends floating around?" I whispered, making sure no one saw me talking to myself. The bar was getting crowded.

"Nope, I have a feeling those folks went straight to heaven or straight to hell. See you later, alligator."

Off she went as Bob and Lili returned to the table. I could see that Lili looked concerned. She had probably seen me talking to myself. I fiddled with the beer koozie and read the words out loud: "*YOU'RE BETTER OFF HERE THAN ACROSS THE STREET.*"

Before Lili could ask me anything, I turned to Bob. "So, tell me—what's the story with the cemetery? Lili said you come to Daytona for Bike Week."

"It's the Pinewood Cemetery. Just a few feet from their final resting place, during Bike Week, the nation's largest motorcycle rally, hundreds of bikers gather at this landmark bar. You can hear the distinct sound of Harley engines for miles. I'm sure it wakes the dead."

"He was a pirate in his past life." Lili took a swig of her beer and finished it.

"Ironically, the biker crowd is Pinewood's saving grace. It was abandoned for a long time. But now, thanks to the money raised during Bike Week, it is being well maintained. There are some really historic graves there."

"There's a legend about that place," Lili said.

"So, tell me."

I loved history and planned to learn as much as I could at each stop along the way. Lili was the same way. We're avid history channel buffs, and we loved trivia.

"A guy named William Smith moved here in the 1800s. He bought 5.5 acres right here where Boot Hill and the cemetery sit." Bob continued with the local lore.

"Legend has it that his daughter, Alena Beatrice Smith, died at age 24 and was buried over there, under her favorite tree, and in time, the land became the Pinewood Cemetery. After that, it became the graveyard of choice for many pioneer families."

"What's the history of this bar?" I asked.

"A watering hole across from the cemetery dates way back. During the 1930s, motorcycle and drag racing on the beach became popular. The bar attracted the racing crowds and took its name from the Old West, where cemeteries were often called 'boot hills' because the old boots would sit atop the cowboy graves. Thus, the Boot Hill Saloon was born." Bob lifted his beer to toast the historic bar.

"If you will excuse me, ladies." Bob got up and Lili turned to me.

"Are you okay?"

Uh-oh, I thought. Lili might have seen me talking to Irma when she and Bob were out on the dance floor.

"Why?"

"Earlier, you looked like you were talking to yourself. Bob said he saw it, too."

"Ahh, Lili, I guess I've started doing that—it just helps to say it out loud. My memory is not what it used to be."

She gave me a look like she didn't buy that malarkey but dropped it as our food arrived and Bob returned with more beers.

"Later," Lili whispered to me.

Just as well, because I came pretty close to spilling the beans about Irma even though I had planned to wait a little longer into the trip. I didn't need Lili to start worrying about me like Meg, who had texted me no less than three times during the day (which I saw when we arrived at the campground). Not to mention Louie texting to remind me to text him. I was going to be spending all my downtime texting Meg and Louie if this kept up.

Just the same, I knew I had to talk to someone about Irma, and Lili was my choice. She was my best friend, and I know she had seen a lot in her life and maybe even a ghost or two. We finished our burgers and beers and talked about what we would like to do in Daytona.

"When I get back from an early morning ride on my Harley, we'll head over to the beach and then the Daytona Speedway."

"Is there a race?"

"No, much better," Lili responded. "You're going for a spin."

"Me? Yah, sure."

Lili loved to play cards. It was well known on Long Island that if you wanted to be hired to work in the households Lili managed, you had to pass her card test.

"You can tell a lot about a person's character by playing cards."

"I know that you can drive on the beach here, but I didn't think they'd let you drive on the speedway."

"Yep, around the track," Lili said.

Normally she has a great poker face, but right now she was grinning. Not a good sign. I must have looked like a deer in headlights as it dawned on me that there was a race car in my future.

"No way!"

"You'll love it."

"I don't think so!" I was looking from Lili to Bob.

Bob shrugged his shoulders. "It's up to you. Your one and only chance to experience the magic of speed up close and personal."

"The professional drivers are cute," Lili chimed in.

"I'll stick to the sand. It's softer."

"The beach opens to vehicles at dawn and closes at dusk. Let's get there early before the crowds. After that we'll grab lunch and head to the Speedway," Bob said.

"You're really going to do a ride around the racetrack in a race car?"

"I am, and I do so whenever we're near a speedway or racetrack. We'll also check out the museum at the speedway. Did you know that car racing first started on Daytona's wide beach of hard-packed white sand in 1902? Since then, driving a car on the beach has become a local institution."

I could see Bob was in his element. We finished our beers, paid our tab, and took an Uber back to the campground.

"Give it some thought," Bob said as we said good night. "You're starting a new life on the road. What better way to christen the event?"

I knew he was talking about the lap around the famous racetrack in a real race car. Well, what do I have to lose? Oh yeah, my life! I fell into a sound sleep after I easily converted the dinette to my bed. Irma was quiet for a change.

CHAPTER 13

The next day we were in Bob's truck and headed over for our check-off-the-bucket-list beach drive.

"The reason Daytona Beach is called the "World's Most Famous Beach" is the twenty-three miles of hard-packed sands that make it the perfect place to drive on," Bob said as we drove to the beach.

It was a beautiful day, and we were early so the beach wasn't crowded. By mid-day it would probably be packed. Bob drove a little way onto the beach, and then we switched places.

"Mabel, you're driving the same sands that racing was born on over a hundred years ago. But to conserve natural resources, beach access is limited to specific sections of the beach."

"You do have to watch out for the sea turtles and people on the beach," Lili added. "Plus, you don't want to drive in soft sand. You'll get stuck just like we did up north driving in snow."

I gingerly started driving. It was an amazing feeling. A part of history was beneath my wheels. We drove along the beach with the windows down. I stopped for a moment. We were silent as we enjoyed the incredible view. The Atlantic Ocean on one side and on the other side was the famous Daytona Beach Boardwalk.

Lili was next. This was not her first time, but she loved it just the same. Bob got back in the driver's seat and soon parked the truck, and we went for a walk on Daytona's famous boardwalk.

Our walk took us past stores, restaurants, gift shops, and bars until we came to an arcade. We followed Bob, who made his way past dozens of pinball machines crowded with kids of all ages.

"He's like a kid again," Lili said as we watched Bob.

"Where's he going?"

"Skee-ball," Lili said.

Bob was standing in front of a game that looked like miniature bowling alleys. I remembered it as being a lot of fun. He was as excited as a kid as he tried his luck.

We watched as Bob took turns rolling a ball up an incline to a row of rings labeled with numbers. He was shooting for the big numbers for coupons to cash in for prizes. When he scored, he grinned like he had won a big jackpot.

"Just watch, on the way out he'll give those coupons to one of the kids who are too little to play the games," Lili said.

Sure enough, a cute little toddler was the big winner of the day. Bob asked his parents if it was okay, and then he handed the stack of coupons to Lili, who stooped down and handed the prize to the little guy.

"Thank you," said the dad, smiling at us. "We'll get him a teddy-bear."

"And we'll name him after you. What's your name?" added the mom.

"Bob."

"Bobby the Bear," said the mom, "I like it."

"Thank you again, Bob," said the dad, and winked, "I still like to play, too.

As we left the arcade, Bob grinned. "I let Lili do the honors. When I do it, they usually start crying."

After we grabbed a quick bite, it was time to head over to the famous Daytona Speedway.

Lili imitated gripping a steering wheel and turning it back and forth.

"Ready for a thrill?"

I rolled my eyes. "No, I'll be just fine watching."

"We'll see about that. It's fun."

"How about you?"

"My back won't let me, but yours is just fine with all that martial arts training."

"What do you mean?"

"You have to be able to crawl through the window of the race car. The doors don't open."

"Well, that settles it. I'll stand next to you, and we'll take pictures."

I did have a new camera. Old school, I know, but I was more comfortable with a camera. I still had not figured out how to print the pictures I took with my new cell.

We left the boardwalk, and the next thing I knew we were at the famous Daytona International Speedway. We parked and started walking toward the entrance. I read the signs along the way:

- *Race car ride-along experience at Daytona International Speedway*
- *Ride shotgun of a real NASCAR race car during an exciting 3-lap run*

- *Hold tight as your professional driver reaches speeds of up to 145 mph!*
- *All safety gear provided*

At the entrance, a young girl dressed like a race car driver was handing out brochures:

"Get a real taste of car racing on an exhilarating ride around the world-famous Daytona International Speedway. Hop in the passenger seat of a genuine NASCAR race car and brace yourself as an expert driver makes three laps around the track, reaching speeds up to 170 mph! Perfect for die-hard DAYTONA 500 fans who want the racing experience, but not the responsibility of self-driving at extreme speeds."

Lili poked me in the ribs.

"I think you should do it This will be your baptism and the start of your new life."

I gave Lili my best evil eye but when we arrived at the racetrack and I saw the race cars zipping around the track, I found myself considering it. We watched Bob suit up and crawl into the race car with his professional race car driver.

"Gentlemen, start your engines!"

The checkered flag waved, and in a flash, the car rumbled and was gone. As it zipped around the famous racetrack, I had to admit it looked exhilarating.

"Aren't you afraid they might lose control?"

I asked Lili as the car sped by, clocking close to 170 mph. I snapped pictures as fast as I could.

"He's a grown boy. We only have today. Tomorrow is not promised."

I looked back down at the brochure:

What to Expect

"Your adrenaline-filled race car ride takes place at the famous Daytona International Speedway in beautiful Daytona Beach. First, enjoy a meet and greet with a professional instructor who will give you a quick safety lesson and fit you with a driving suit, helmet, and neck guard. Then take the shotgun seat in a real Sprint Cup-style stock car for your extreme ride.

Buckle up and brace yourself as your driver kicks up the gears, zipping around the track in a qualifying run simulation. Experience what it would feel like to be a DAYTONA 500 competitor as you make three laps around the speedway, hitting a top speed of 170 mph."

Before I knew it, Bob was back.

"Okay, Mabel, it's your turn."

"It was a hoot to see you out there, Bob. But I don't…"

"Now or never," Lili said.

"What would Meg do if I sent her a picture of me?"

"It's your life, Mabel. I think a picture of you with that good-looking race car driver would be a hoot to send to Meg?" Lili responded.

Before I chickened out, I heard my voice say in a whisper, "Okay, I'll do it."

Lili winked at Bob. "Good for you."

In the end I'm not sure if it was the good-looking race car drivers, but I decided to take that leap of faith and while I was suiting up, I felt like crossing my fingers and toes.

As my driver helped me crawl through the window, I felt the start of a panic attack, but when he got in the car with me and looked over and said, "You'll be fine." I relaxed. No turning back now. Buckled in for the ride of a lifetime, I looked over to Lili and Bob standing on the side of the track. Thumbs up!

And what a ride it was. For the first lap, all I could really feel was the incredible G-force of the acceleration. The second whizzed by in pretty much a blur. And then, for the finale, my driver banked up on the wall, and for a split second, we were completely vertical. I did not even close my eyes. I wanted to remember this for a long time.

Three laps went by in a zing, and then—we came to a stop. My driver helped me out and shook my hand. "Welcome to racing," he said with a big grin.

"Roger that, young man."

Lili rushed up to give me a hug.

"Well done, Mabel. Now you're officially a race car driver. Can't wait until we get west, and you try those zip-lines" Bob said with a broad grin. "Wait until you go zip-lining over a canyon!"

What? Zip-lining. Was he nuts?

"And Mabel," giggled Lili, "I would love to see Meg's face when you send her that photo."

"Me too, Lili. Me too."

CHAPTER 14

Savannah, GA

By the time we made it to Savannah, I was comfortable driving Thor and towing Betsy. I found Irma was a big help. She was a quick learner.

"I had to be Mabel. I was always quick on my feet."

"So, did that have something to do with your clientele?"

"No, we were a high-end cat house. We always had mob muscle to make sure nothing happened to the girls."

"Did anything ever happen?

"Oh yeah. But it never happened again."

"What do you mean? My recollection of mob taking care of business involved swimming with the fishes."

"Like I told you, Mabel, we did not ask questions. If you asked the wrong question, you might not like the answer."

I got the message loud and clear. All was good. Irma kept me company but also kept a respectful distance when Bob and Lili were nearby.

"Don't want them catching you talking to me," she said after I told her about their concerns. "We have a long trip ahead of us, and frankly, Mabel, I would like you to enjoy it. Remember what I said. You only get one life, so be sure and live it."

We left Daytona at the crack of dawn, Bob's time zone. Natalie had routed us around Jacksonville to avoid the trucks and bridges. Although Jacksonville was the capital of Florida, it was also known as South Georgia. It had beautiful beaches and a busy port.

"Lots of insurance companies here in Jacksonville." Irma commented as we made our way past Jacksonville.

"How do you know that?"

"They all came to Vegas on conventions and meetings. I got to know quite a few of them. I run into some of those insurance guys from time to time in purgatory."

Bob's driving agreed with the TripTik, so I pretty much knew where we were going. It was a straight shot. I just had to watch when we got off the highway that I didn't turn the wrong way.

I had started my photo album, and the first pages were the Daytona Speedway pictures. My favorite was me sitting in the race car suited up and ready to go with both thumbs up. I also had one with me and the cute race car driver. I must have looked at the picture of me suited up and sitting in a race car a thousand times last night.

Of course, I had my navigator giving me directions as well. How could I get lost?

"From I-95 South: Take Exit 94 (GA 204) East toward Savannah. Turn Right onto Truman Parkway. Take Whitefield Avenue Exit. Turn right on Whitefield Avenue. Turn Left onto State Park Road. The park office will be 1/2 mile ahead on the right."

"Thank you, Irma," I said as Trixie gave us the proper heads up to exit in two miles.

I followed Bob and Lili into Skidaway Island, Georgia State Park, a scenic campground nestled under live oaks and Spanish moss while Irma read from the Triple A tour book.

"It is located near historic Savannah, the park borders Skidaway narrows, a part of Georgia's Intracoastal Waterway. Trails wind through maritime forest and past salt marshes, leading to a boardwalk and observation tower. Visitors can watch for deer, fiddler crabs, raccoons, egrets, and other wildlife. Skidaway Island State Park provides scenic camping, picnicking, and hiking opportunities. Visitors come to Skidaway to visit downtown Savannah only a short 20-minute drive away or to enjoy the peace and quiet of being in nature."

"Wowser. This is going to be fun, Mabel. I've heard from my pals in purgatory that Savannah is the most haunted city in the country. A lot of them come from here."

"Oh, great. Just what I need. More ghosts. Maybe you can organize a reunion?"

I pulled up behind Bob's camper in front of the State Park Ranger's office. I waited while Bob went into the office. He had reserved four campsites, two for us and two for the rest of the group. Irma continued reading from the tour book while we waited.

"The trails lead you through a mix of live oaks, cabbage palmettos, southern red cedar, and pines, over salt marshes and tidal creeks, out to views of the Intracoastal Waterway. The campground is nestled in a wooded area…"

When I looked over, she had changed. She was now dressed in fatigues.

"How do you do that?"

She just smiled as the drill sergeant spoke.

"You need to get out and walk, Mabel. Need to keep your exercise up. Lose a little of those extra pounds off your hips. Give Louie a surprise next time you see him?"

"Actually, Irma, on that point, we agree. I plan to get in shape on this trip out west. I love to walk, and Lili is a big-time walker. We're going to walk and get in shape for hiking in the mountains when we reach Colorado."

"I can't wait." Irma was grinning from ear to ear.

"You remind me of my kids on Christmas morning."

"I thought you guys didn't do Christmas."

"Remember we're hybrids, half Jewish and half Catholic. Oh boy, we did Christmas. My mother-in-law made sure. Looking back, I have to thank her for that, but not much more. She was a thorn in my side. Have you run across her?" I was wondering if Big Stella had a layover in purgatory.

"Nope. I can't say that I have."

"I can't imagine her going straight to heaven."

"Rule number three—no gossiping, Mabel. Figure it out yourself."

Bob and Lilli's campsite was the designated happy hour location, and then after that, we would head into Savannah for dinner on the riverfront. We had made it. This was our first official stop on our trip west. Lili and I were having drinks outside my camper and waiting for the rest of our group to arrive. I did fine on parking and setting up my camper.

"You pass, Mabel," Bob said.

Bob had slipped into military mode and reported that the first couple in our group, the schoolteachers, ETA was 30 minutes. Bob got busy with a few chores and left Lili and me a little time for girl talk.

"So today we get to meet the new campers who will join us on the trip west," I said. "Has Bob found out any more about the couple from Fort Lauderdale?"

"Nothing he has shared. Bob has heard from the schoolteachers constantly, though. The wife, Peggy, called and texted several times today to let us know where they were and when they would arrive."

"Peggy, hmm. What did she teach?"

"High school and she was the principal."

"Oh, well, then she is used to running the show."

"Both couples have traveled west before. We'll have to see how it goes, but today we meet and greet and get to know each other. I'll be right back; I want to check on some happy hour food."

Lili loved to cook and entertain, which was a good thing because I didn't. Taking care of five kids was plenty for me, and luckily, being married to a doctor with patients who liked to keep a low profile, didn't call for a lot of parties or entertaining. While Lili was checking on the food, Irma popped in and sat down in the chair Lili had just vacated.

"I don't like them."

I still wasn't quite used to her appearance and disappearance.

"Who are you talking about?"

I looked around to make sure we were alone, and Lili was still inside her camper. "Don't like who?"

"One of the new couples that will be joining your caravan."

"You haven't met either one."

"I got another message from Chief Little Bear. He told me you need to be careful of the man from the cavalry."

"Cavalry?" It took me a second, but then I knew what she meant. Well, Chief Little Bear came from a different era.

"Bob is checking him out. His cop radar is turned on. His name is Oscar. He is retired military, not cavalry."

"He's bad news. He might be our first challenge, so be on your toes."

"What do you mean our first challenge? I'm hoping we only have one challenge to tackle on this trip and that it'll be enough to scoot you all the way up that Rainbow Bridge. Can't you talk to Saint Peter about that?"

"You don't talk to Saint Peter. He talks to you, and you listen. Pay attention, Mabel."

Irma vanished just as Lili came back.

"You okay, Mabel?"

"Yeah, just a little heartburn."

No sooner had she sat down when two Airstreams rolled past us. I got up to look and saw that they were pulling into the two spots on the other side of Lili and Bob's Airstream.

"Well, shall we go meet our new neighbors?"

"Let's give them a few minutes to get settled. Bob will come fetch us," Lili said. "We'll relax and enjoy our drinks and then do the introductions once Bob gets a nice fire going in our fire pit."

It was getting chilly, so it would be great to sit around their fire pit and enjoy a drink with new friends.

I zipped up my Boot Hill Saloon jacket. Bob bought one for Lili.

"The jackets will give you something to remember the beginning of this exciting adventure. You'll need them on chilly evenings."

It was nice and snug. Before long, Bob came for us, and I followed Lili to the roaring fire pit. She went inside to get the happy hour food, pigs in a blanket and mini-egg rolls.

Josh and Peggy joined us. Retired schoolteachers, they looked pleasant enough in a dull sort of way. I looked at Peggy's retro 1950s frames and as I looked closer, I almost thought they could be originals because I had a pair just like them in high school. Josh wasn't bad looking. Dressed like a college professor, a jacket with worn patches, khaki pants, and boat shoes. Within a few minutes of casual conversation, they started lecturing us.

They knew all about Savannah, and pretty much everything else. A couple of walking encyclopedias. Peggy did most of the talking and self-appointed herself as our guide for the evening. It didn't seem to bother Bob or Lili. I'm not much for small talk, so if they liked to talk and fill us in on local trivia, I had no problem. That was just fine with me.

"So, what do you do, Mabel?" Peggy the former school principal asked.

I knew the question was coming, and I wasn't prepared. It's the—*what do you do?*—question, so the person asking can size you up.

In the past, I answered I was married to a doctor. That put me in the category of women who married well. I certainly wasn't going to tell her that I had been married to a doctor, but he dumped me for a 20-something barfly. That would put me in the loser category or in the *oh, you poor dear* category.

She was standing with Lili and me around the fire pit. Bob was chatting with her husband. We were still waiting for the mystery couple to appear. I was stuck for an answer, and that was when Irma came to the rescue.

"Tell her you're a writer." I could see Irma out of the corner of my eye.

"I'm a writer."

"You are?" Peggy said with a note of surprise in her voice.

Lili gave me her poker face look. I looked over at Irma, and she gave me a wink and buzzed off to let me fend for myself.

Well, I've always wanted to write, and I planned to check that off my bucket list while on the trip. That part was true. Along with climbing Mount Everest and going back to school to get a college degree. I have a lot on that bucket list; most of it will just stay on the list.

"Oh, I'd love to read your work! Do you have a good editor? I taught English."

"You go, girl," Lili whispered.

While Peggy took a minute to clean her glasses, I whispered to Lili, "Well, it's better than telling her I'm divorced and why I'm divorced."

Lili was still giving me *the look*, but she was discreet, came from all those years working in Downton Abbey.

"Just remember that the truth is always easier. It's just the way you say it. You could have said you were a widow and left it at that. It would have been what we call a white lie, not the big fat sucker you just told her.

Now you are a writer, and you are going to have to become a writer and add to that story because trust me, this woman will not leave you alone."

Well, Irma will have to come up with a few chapters. She certainly had plenty of stories to tell. I was saved from having to embellish my story with the arrival of Oscar and Eleanor. Oscar was tall, and so was his wife. You could tell from the way he held his shoulders that he was ex-military. Eleanor was a solid looking woman, not as outgoing as her husband.

After introductions and drinks and finger food, we were silent for a moment. So far, they hadn't shared much, but it soon became apparent that Oscar did the talking.

He was one of those men who liked to hear the sound of his voice. He talked, and then he laughed with a distinct ha-ha. Like he'd just told us a joke, but we didn't get the punch line, so he followed it up with a ha-ha. I didn't like him from the start. And I don't think it had anything to do with Irma's warning.

He reminded me of some of Jack's mob patients, and Eleanor reminded me of their wives. Eleanor was quiet, a mouse, but then I've known a few mousey women in my day, and you had to be careful because sometimes, they turn out to be rats.

Peggy jumped in to ask her pop quiz question, "What do you do?"

"Retired military," Oscar told the group. This time he didn't add a chuckle. "Now, I'm in sales and investments."

Peggy tried to ask what type of investments, but he was too smooth for the schoolteacher. He wasn't her student, and he subtly let her know it. She figured that out quickly and was quiet after that, but I soon had his MO or modus operandi. Oscar was a deal maker, a wheeler-dealer. He could lay on the bull.

I had met my share of men like Oscar over the years, colorful and personable. Jack had lost his share of money to men like Oscar. Hold on to your wallet. For some reason, doctors think they know business because —well, they are doctors. Once Jack got burnt on some tax shelters he was talked into and after that, he became more cautious. Now that I'm divorced, I seem to be a magnet for men like Oscar. They find out I was married to a doctor and assume I got a tidy settlement and are more than happy to help with investing that money.

Lili and I had heard our share of stories from the women in the book club. They didn't know what to do with the money from a divorce, and so it sat in the bank. They fell for a guy like Oscar and lost it all.

The fact that they were married never got in the way of these men. In fact, they used that to get to know lonely women. Made them feel safe. I planned to keep my distance from Oscar and Eleanor; they were bad news, just like Chief Little Bear had warned.

I got the feeling they were checking us out. I looked over at Lili, and I could tell from the look on her face she was thinking the same. Well, it's going to be a long trip, and I needed an attitude adjustment, so I traded in my beer for a Cosmo.

"Since Savannah is known for ghosts," Bob announced to the group. "We'll be taking a ghost tour after dinner."

This gave Peggy the opening she was waiting for and jumped right in with our lesson. "Savannah is the oldest city in the state of Georgia, besides one of the most haunted cities in the US."

Peggy was in her element. She was on comfortable ground with geography and history and most school subjects we had forgotten a long time ago. I had zoned her out while I deliberated on whether it was wise to drink another Cosmo, and the schoolteacher picked up on that and asked me a pop question.

"Mabel, as a writer, you must know that The Garden of Good and Evil is set in Savannah."

Luckily, I was familiar with the movie. "Yes, I do, and I'm looking forward to seeing the house it was based on while we are in Savannah."

That seemed to placate Peggy, and I decided to fix one more drink in case Peggy came back with a pop quiz. Bob had decided on a walking tour at night through Colonial Park Cemetery. Peggy continued her lesson. Josh had closed his eyes like he was taking a nap.

"The Colonial Park Cemetery was the city's main burial ground for the last century. It's a historic cemetery right in downtown Savannah."

"Mother of God, will that woman ever stop!" I heard Irma say. "Ask her husband if he's ever been to Vegas."

"Well, we should all hear a lot of creepy stories and haunted history," I said.

I decided I had enough to drink. Peggy had given me a look when I had made the last one. What was she, a nun back in the day?

Lili, who had been quiet up till now, spoke, and when Lili spoke, you listened. Unlike Peggy, she was commanding and captivating, and you found yourself wanting to listen.

"Actually, the cemetery was established in 1750, when Savannah was the capital of the British Province of Georgia, the last of the Thirteen Colonies. By 1789 it had expanded three times to reach its current six acres. It was Savannah's primary public cemetery throughout its 103 active years. Burials ceased in the cemetery in 1853."

"Well, that's interesting," Peggy said. Her feathers were ruffled, and she looked like she was trying to come up with something to put one over Lili. You don't challenge Lili.

"More than 700 victims of Savannah's 1820 yellow fever epidemic are also buried there, including my great-great-grandmother. I'll show you her headstone if you are interested."

Peggy started to say something but decided wisely to drop it. Well, she wasn't dumb.

Oscar and Eleanor decided to pass on the outing, but the rest of us took an Uber to Riverfront Plaza, where River Street's restored nineteenth-century cotton warehouses included shops, bars, and restaurants.

For dinner we boarded a riverboat. The red and white Savannah Queen, with its bright red paddlewheel, was the perfect place for a dinner cruise to get a glimpse of the city past and present.

Over a dinner of shrimp and grits and sweet potato casserole, we started to get to know each other. Once they were relaxed, Peggy and Josh stopped being so pedantic. They realized they didn't have to impress us with facts and figures.

During the cruise, I caught sight of Irma a few times. Singing with the live band was one time. Later I think she was dancing on the paddlewheel as it went around and around.

But it wasn't until we were waiting to start the ghost tour that she made an appearance right behind me as I waited for the group. They were circled around Bob, who was handing out tickets for the ghost tour.

"Gee whiz, Irma, stop that! You scared the bejeebers out of me. Can't you just appear like a normal person?"

Irma came to stand in front of me. Her face came within an inch of my nose. We squared off like two fighters.

"Really? Mabel? A normal person? I'm dead."

"I noticed that. What are you doing here?" I moved from being directly under a streetlight.

"I'm along for the tour. Get used to it, honey. I want to find out about ghosts."

"You?"

I looked around to make sure no one was watching me. It was already dark, and I stood in the shadows. "You are a ghost?"

"Mabel, there are different types of ghosts." Irma mimicked Peggy's schoolteacher tone. "Some ghosts are a lot like me, stuck in purgatory, and then there are those who are stuck on earth. Those are the ones who haven't come to terms with being dead. They keep trying to come back to the land of the living. You usually find them in the house or location where they died."

"Like you in my camper?"

"No. I didn't die in the camper. I died outside. I just like the camper because it reminds me of Walt. I've accepted that I died in my beautiful mink coat on the ground in a puddle. I'm not trying to come back! I'm trying to go up in the world, so to speak. You just happen to be my ticket since you have the power to see me."

"Mother of God," I said a little too loud and then lowered my voice. "You mean, I'm the reason you can get out and about?"

"Yep and Mabel, my friend, am I glad *you* bought the camper. I've spent many a decade in storage waiting for you."

I kept an eye out for our group. A few people nearby were staring at me. I covered my mouth with the brochure in my hand.

"They think I'm crazy talking to myself. Lili has already caught me several times."

"Well, work it out. Anyway, you are going to have to tell her. Even Bob."

"Oh, yah. Sure. Bob was a homicide detective. Before that Special Ops."

"Chief Little Bear told me we are going to need his help."

"Crap, Irma, what else did Chief Little Bear say?"

"I would rather he tell you himself."

"No, please! I can't take two of you, Irma."

I groaned and put my hands on my hips. "Okay, so when do I get to meet him?"

"Probably tonight, he's on the tour."

"What do you mean? He's on the tour."

"He's buried in this cemetery."

"Mother of God," I said again. I looked over my shoulder and saw the group now heading toward me. I needed to figure out a way to chat with Irma and not arouse suspicion.

"They're on their way back. Scram. Float away. Leave me alone. I don't need Lili telling Meg I'm talking to myself."

Irma gave me a very serious look.

"Oh, just calm down. Use that phone you carry. I was one of the first to use a BlackBerry."

"You had a BlackBerry?"

"A pink one."

"I liked my flip phone, but Meg insisted on a smartphone. It's smarter than me."

The tour started, and we had a great guide, and, of course, Peggy had to stick in her two cents because she had no faith in our young tour guide, who was dressed as a Goth with black fingernail polish and dozens of piercings. Our tour guide led us through the historic cemetery and told us ghost stories along the way. It was dark, but not that scary. We were surrounded by dozens of other tourists on ghost tours. I felt like we were all on some kind of reality show.

"A lot of dead people here," I said to Lili, who gave me the look.

"Well, it is a cemetery, Mabel. Are you okay?"

"Why?"

"Because I saw you talking to yourself a few minutes ago."

"I'm fine, but we do need to talk."

I might as well open the door a crack. Irma was all over the place. Zooming in and out and telling me little tidbits about some of the dead people buried in the cemetery. I walked ahead and almost tripped over a tombstone covered with leaves.

"Hey, be careful. Oh, my lord, looky here! It's Amos."

She disappeared and popped back in within seconds.

"Where did you go?" I whispered. It was a good thing it was dark.

"I went back to purgatory and found Amos and told him I found his grave." Irma was beside herself with glee. "Sometimes they don't know where they're buried. Death happens fast."

As we walked along, I could see her up ahead or behind me. It was making me dizzy. Lili was looking at me curiously. I shrugged my shoulders with an—*I don't know*—look. She gave me the—*yes, you do*—look.

Maybe now wasn't such a good time to broach the subject of Irma. Luckily, the tour guide distracted her.

"Here is an interesting tombstone," she said as she stepped in front of a grave site with a large tombstone.

I looked at it. No need to read the name carved into it. I knew immediately that it belonged to Chief Little Bear because he was standing right behind the tombstone and staring straight at me. He was wearing a colorful turban on his shaven head and had a blanket over one shoulder. Across his cheeks were stripes of color: yellow, red and white.

When he turned to look to his left, I saw that there were two feathers stuck in his scalp-lock at the back of his head. I looked at what he was looking at—Irma strolling toward me dressed like a nun with a wooden rosary hanging around her neck.

"I'm praying for you, Mabel. I've never seen him like this."

Chief Little Bear was holding a tomahawk which he was tapping against his muscular thigh. The tour guide shined a flashlight on the gravestone.

"Chief Little Bear was a native American Cherokee

leader. His tribe fought on the side of the Confederate Army in the Civil War. They did so on the promise that when the South won, they would not take any more of the tribal lands.

"Is he going to say something?" I whispered to the nun. The rest of the group was intent on the guide's story.

"He's talking to me right now."

I looked up, but all I saw was a figure slowly slipping away. He raised his hand and held the tomahawk to his chest. Was it a way to say goodbye or a threat? I wasn't sure.

"Irma, what did he say?"

"That there is going to be a death."

With that, she disappeared. I jumped when Lili came up behind me and put her hand on my shoulder.

"Hey, girl. What's up with you? You look pale. You look like you've seen a ghost."

"Ha-ha! No, just talked to one."

"What? Are you okay? You haven't been taking too much meds? Or dipping into that antique stash of yours?"

She was referring to a little tin of marijuana I had been saving for years for an emergency. Anyway, I had left it in Boca Vista.

"I'll explain later. I promise."

Although, along with my concealed weapon permit, I did have a medical marijuana card just in case of an emergency. Lots of the book club members got their cards when Florida begrudgingly passed the medicinal marijuana law. They took hits off of something that looked like what Marilyn Monroe used to smoke in the movies wearing her long white gloves.

Between the time and the lateness of the hour, I was exhausted. By the time we piled into the Uber to take us back to the campground, I was yawning and just wanted to close my eyes. Peggy was a little chatterbox all the way back. I was glad I was sitting next to Lili and not Peggy.

I was very thankful when we finally got back, and I could make a quick exit. Before Lili could ask me any questions, I said goodnight and headed for Betsy. No nightcaps for me. I was exhausted. I fell sound asleep as soon as my head hit the pillow, but in the middle of the night, Irma woke me up.

"We need to talk."

"Now? Can't it wait?"

"I spoke to Saint Peter. He called me up… for a chat."

"He did?"

Irma's time was different. It was like we were in outer space.

"He told me some more about the fast track program. He said the time is near and that I will be tested on this part of your trip."

"What does that mean? The test will be while we are here in Savannah, the ghost capital of the world?"

"Mabel, he's not a fortune teller. He's a saint and a big one at that. He guards the entryway into heaven. You know, like a goalie."

"You know about soccer?"

"Hockey, Mabel. Remember, my cat house was in Vegas. The hockey boys loved it there. Now pay attention. Saint Peter runs the joint. I'm already being tested with you as far as I'm concerned. I should be getting extra credit since I've got to deal with you and this fast track program of his."

"I understand that, but didn't he tell you anything? Chief Little Bear's warning was in code. 'There is going to be a death.' What does that mean? He just stood there staring at us with that angry look on his face. He's scary."

"Well, Chief Little Bear has a right to be. He was angry when he died and still is. He has anger issues. Maybe that's why he's still here. Anyway, he did give me another message. That's why I woke you up."

"Oh, great. I'm listening."

"Someone in your group is going to die soon."

"I think I like his first message better. Soon? From what? A stroke? A heart attack? It's not me, is it? It's not a murder?" I asked, not really wanting to know the answer.

"The Chief is not a big talker. You probably picked up on that. My feeling is that it involves Oscar and Eleanor."

Irma and her feelings! She did her disappearing act, and I did my best to fall back asleep. It was a restless night, to say the least. Oscar? Was he going to kill Eleanor? Or her, him? I could see that. Mousy women have hidden depths. It couldn't be me. I didn't even know them. Well, I couldn't quite figure it out. A brain fog, exhaustion and a headache from the Cosmos and wine we had on the dinner cruise sent me back to sleep.

No sooner had I dozed off I woke up and sat straight up in bed. I knew where I had seen Oscar. I had seen a picture of him in the Jack-in-the-box in my safe deposit box. He was either connected to the mob or the CIA.

"Crap," I said loud enough to wake the dead. I was going to put my money on the mob.

CHAPTER 15

The next day I decided to start walking. I needed to air out my head after last night. I had my Fitbit and had a goal of 10,000 steps a day.

Bob mentioned last night that he was going to get up and take his Harley for a spin around Savannah. Lili was going with him. He would check back with the group a little later and let us know what our plans were for the evening. We were free for the day, which suited me just fine. Irma was nowhere to be seen. The rest of the group was still in their campers. I knew Lili and I would talk. Lili was patient. Something I was not. I was more than ready to let her in on Irma. Lili was from New Orleans, so I didn't think she would be all that shocked.

As I headed out on my walk, I saw a camper parked close to our group. It was a canned ham, and a young man was sitting outside drinking coffee. I had looked at these before I bought my Airstream. This vintage camper resembled a canned ham or a toaster on wheels. He smiled as I was walking by.

"Good morning," he said, and then nodded toward our campers. "Nice campers. They are well built."

"Yes, they are. As well as yours."

I guessed he was about the same age as my daughter Cecilia. He was wearing a plaid shirt, jeans, and boots with a baseball cap on his head that said, *I love Nashville*. He had that look young men have today, a day-old beard look. He was good looking, but not in a movie star way. He was more rugged. Well built. I could see the biceps under that Blake Shelton plaid country shirt. Lili and I follow The Voice and were excited we were going to visit Nashville. Who knows? Might even see Blake Shelton if we were lucky.

"My name's Mabel."

"I'm Joe." He stood and tipped his hat and offered a handshake. He had a solid grip.

Just about that time, Bob and Lili roared in on his Harley. We watched as he parked, and they removed their helmets. They saw us, and they both headed over to where I was standing with Joe.

"Nice Harley," Joe said to Bob.

"My name's Lili and this is my husband Bob."

"Ma'am." Joe shook her hand and tipped his hat and did the same with Bob. "I'm Joe."

Good old-fashioned manners, I thought.

"Nice rig," Bob said.

"Thank you. You have a nice one too. I like vintage campers. Don't make them like they used to."

Bob and Lili started to head back to their camper. "Nice meeting you. We meet later in the day for cocktails," Lili said. "Why don't you join us?"

"Thank you, ma'am, I'd be honored," Joe said, with another tip of his *I love Nashville* ball cap.

"Nice truck you have ma'am" Joe pointed at Thor. I could see he was trying to make polite conversation. We were both still standing.

"Thank you. Call me Mabel, I insist."

"Well Mabel, why don't you have a seat?" He pointed to a seat under the awning of his rig. "Coffee?"

I decided my walk could wait for a bit longer. Coffee sounded inviting after my restless night. I sat down while Joe went inside and returned with a hot mug of coffee.

"Thank you, Joe"

The ladies in my book club would-be all-over him. With the howdy-do's out of the way, we made small talk. I felt comfortable talking to Joe. Pretty soon, we knew almost everything about each other. Interesting how you don't mind sharing information with someone you just met. Just like talking to your hairstylist. You already have that bond because you trust them with your hair.

He refilled my coffee, and I sipped on it while he talked. The coffee tasted delicious, and it felt good sitting in the warm, morning sun. He had a natural charm with respectful, southern manners. He'd been born in Georgia, and his parents, brothers, and sisters still live nearby. He was currently living in the campground with ambitions of making it big in Nashville.

I knew within a few minutes that he was a dreamer, just like my daughter Cecilia. Could be why we hit it off so well. I told him all about my daughter on Broadway, and he told me about his time in Nashville.

"I work as a mechanic to pay my bills. On older campers and such."

He had tried Nashville for the last couple of years and had recently returned to recharge. He was taking a break but planned to head back to Nashville.

"If that doesn't work out, I plan to head out west to figure out what to do next with my life."

"Really? We're heading that way, Nashville and then west to the national parks. We might see each other on the road."

We had connected on a deeper level in a matter of minutes. It was like I knew this young man for a long time, not less than an hour.

"You know, it's funny, Joe. I'm also here because I need to decide what to do with the rest of my life. Unfortunately, I don't have as many days left as you."

I found myself telling Joe my story. He listened attentively. I saw an older pickup truck, and a newer Harley parked next to his rig.

"Can't afford both truck and bike payments," Joe said. "I keep the truck in good condition but it has a lot of miles."

"When were you planning on heading out to Nashville?"

"Soon, if I'm going to do it."

"Well, why don't you join our caravan?" I said out of the blue. "We could use someone a little younger with your mechanical skills, and it sounds like we're going the same way."

Joe was silent. I could see he was thinking it over. After all, we were older, a lot older.

"Give it some thought."

I knew Bob would be okay with his tagging along. Plus, I enjoy talking to young people like my grandson Sid. After all, they were young with fresh ideas and a different outlook on life.

"I will. Hey, why don't you guys drop in at the place I'm playing tonight," Joe said. "I'm singing with a local band. It's called Earl's Bar."

"Well, we were planning on hitting some local honky-tonks along the river. I'll talk to Bob. We might see you there. Country music?"

"Yes, ma'am," Joe said and tipped his hat.

We finished our coffee and said goodbye. I decided to go back inside for a minute before I resumed my walk. I looked out the window where I could see Joe. He was getting ready to head into town in his old pickup with his guitar and equipment. I ran outside and hollered at him. He stopped and came over.

"Ma'am, are you okay?"

"I'm fine. Say why don't you take my pickup?"

"Ma'am, are you sure?" Joe said as his eyes lighten up.

"It's Mabel, and yes, I'm sure. We plan to Uber while we're here in Savannah. It's just going to sit here. That way you'll put less miles on your truck."

"Thank you, ma'am—uh, Mabel." Joe tipped his hat once more as I handed him the keys.

I had a feeling that this was the beginning of a good friendship. Not the cougar kind, but one where you found someone you could trust and help each other. I watched as he headed out the campground.

"He's a good kid," Irma said as she took this moment to pop into view. "You're going to know him for a long time."

"How would you know? I thought you couldn't see the future. One of your feelings?"

"Yep, I just know. I can't see the future, but sometimes things come to me. He and your daughter Cecilia will become good friends, real good friends. I know that."

With that, she was gone. Funny thing, for some reason I had the same feeling about Joe. Not so sure I liked knowing that Irma could sense things, but that ship had sailed. No turning back now.

CHAPTER 16

We took an Uber to dinner. We decided tonight we would check out the honky-tonks. Peggy and Josh decided to go shopping instead of joining us for dinner. They were not big drinkers. That was another reason why I didn't warm up to them. Oscar and Eleanor begged off. Said they had friends to visit. They were staying to themselves. Not very social.

It was a warm evening and we were making our way to where Joe was playing. We walked by a bar and stopped. It had a flyer and menu out front, and it sounded like a Coyote Ugly saloon. It advertised female bartenders and bar top dancing.

"Let's go in," Bob said.

"You sure you can handle this big boy?" Lili said with a wide grin.

I knew that Coyote Ugly was known for their sassy waitresses and a movie by the same name. My daughter Cecilia considered working for Coyote Ugly when she first arrived in New York. Luckily, she didn't need to as early on she landed jobs on Broadway as a dancer. Of course, luck really means hard work meeting opportunity. She'd always been a hard worker and always wanted to be on the stage ever since she was a kid when

I took her to a Broadway play. She was still waiting for that break out part.

"I hope life doesn't pass her by," I told Lili a little while back.

"Wrong, Mabel, she is living her life."

For this evening's fun, Lili was dressed country. Complete with tight jeans, boots, and a sparkly top. Bob usually wore jeans anyway and for the evening had a shirt with rolled up sleeves.

"You look like you are getting ready for dinner on a cruise," Lili said when we met for dinner.

I was wearing white pants and a black top and black sandals. She was right. I needed to look at my wardrobe. I was still dressed for Boca Vista or little Palm Beach, as Lili called it. I didn't own a pair of jeans. Meg had once commented that older women shouldn't wear jeans. But like Lili said, I had to start living a new life.

We walked in, got seated, and ordered drinks. Before long, Lili had made friends with all the waitresses. People just gravitated to her. She's a large, boisterous woman with a sharp tongue and a wit to match. While she and Bob were chatting it up at the bar, Irma decided to drop in.

"My girls always had manners. Listen to these tarts."

I looked around and made sure no one saw me talking to Irma.

"Some men like feisty women. They get a kick out of it. They're not rude. Later on they'll dance on top of that bar."

"You're kidding."

I now watched with apprehension as Irma evaporated, and the next thing I knew, she was on top of the bar. One of the gals decided to give Bob and Lili an impromptu peek at the show. The place was getting busy, and the bar was filling up.

Irma was trying to follow along with the hips-don't-lie routine, but her hips didn't quite work that way. Obviously, her Vegas showgirl days may have been more strutting than dancing. I was afraid she was going to push the waitress off the bar, but so far, she had kept her poltergeist antics in check. Finally, she disappeared and reappeared right next to me.

"What's up with these women? Not the way I ran my establishment."

I breathed a sigh of relief when Bob and Lili returned and suggested we leave to find a restaurant.

"Bye, Bob," the girls all said as we left. Lili gave them thumbs up. I just smiled.

We made our way along the riverfront. We stopped at a quaint restaurant that served up southern cooking. Lili and I shared some home-cooked fried chicken. Bob had chicken and dumplings. So much for my plans to get in shape.

"We'll do a double walk tomorrow," Lili said as I finished all my mashed potatoes.

After dinner, we made our way to Earl's Bar, where Joe saw us come in and joined us. He led us over to a table near the stage that had a *"Reserved"* sign sitting on top.

"Usually, this is only for family, but I told the manager, Selma, you were my Aunt Mabel and were visiting from out of town."

He gave me a wink. Well, he was cute, and for a minute, I could see why the cougars were cougars, but I attributed that to the booze. I watched him in his tight jeans setting up on the stage. We ordered drinks, and Joe made his way back to our table.

"I want you to meet someone."

He went up to the bar and brought the bartender back to our table.

"This is Selma, everyone. Selma is the best bartender in town. She also happens to live at our campground."

As we said hello I recognized Selma because I had seen her talking to Oscar earlier in the day. I'd noticed because it looked like they were having a serious chat.

"Nice to meet you folks," Selma said. "I think we talked in the campground office today," she said to Bob and he nodded.

She was probably about my age, but up close, I could tell life had not been easy on her. She had a slight accent that Lili immediately picked up on.

"Where are you from?"

"I'm from Louisiana, a little town near New Orleans."

"Me too, it's a small world."

Selma made a quick exit back behind the bar, and Joe made his way to the stage. I turned to Bob. "Do you know her?" Bob was silent.

"I've seen her in the office," Lili said.

"I saw her talking to Oscar today. It looked like they were having a serious discussion."

Bob had been quiet during our exchange, but we could tell he had something on his mind. Lili and I waited to see if he was going to let us in on his thoughts.

"She stopped me today when she saw me in the campground office. She said she heard I was a retired cop, and there was something she needed to tell me."

"Really," both Lili and I said at the same time.

"She wanted to talk about Oscar. She said there was something we needed to know about the guy."

"What did she say," Lili now asked Bob.

"That he was a con man. We didn't really have a chance to talk much more."

"Well, that's a coincidence. Meeting Joe today, and here she works at the same bar and lives in our campground."

I was thinking about the possibility of Oscar's picture in my safe deposit box and Irma's warning.

"Yeah, in my former line of work, we didn't believe in coincidences."

"You might have to find out more about Oscar," I said. Lili nodded her head in agreement.

"Oh, I'm on it. You'd better believe I'm on it," Bob said.

Before long, the place was packed. Joe did a lot of songs most of the crowd recognized. We were all baby boomer age and loved the rock-and-roll from our era. Lili and I got up and danced, and Bob did the slow dances with Lili. Joe had a great voice and could really play the guitar. He knew all the popular country songs.

"He's very talented," Lili said.

"He seems like a good kid," Bob said.

I had filled them in on Joe and our conversation back at the campground.

"I might need his help on a few things on my rig before we head out. Something is going on with the wiring and might keep us here in Savannah a few extra days," Bob said.

"So, do you think he might take you up on that offer you made? Decide to join us and travel with us this summer?" Lili asked.

"Maybe. I'll mention it again tomorrow when he's looking at my propane tank."

As we were leaving, I left Joe a Ben Franklin. I hoped that would seal the deal, and Joe would think seriously about joining us on the road. I had a good feeling about him, and I think he needed a break from his life, plus we could use someone young with his skills. We might need those muscles for more than one reason.

CHAPTER 17

Bob's rig, as it turned out, did need work, so we were staying in Savannah to get the work done.

"This usually happens when we first head out. The rig does sit during the winter months," Bob said. "Don't worry; we'll be out on the road before you know it."

Bob kept his Airstream at a marina in Fish Camp. I'll probably do the same when we return to Florida. MC, my CPA who helped me with my IRS problems and her husband live on their boat, *The Mary Catherine,* in a slip at that marina. Louie told me he rents her condo in the same complex as her two aunts. Ernie, the bartender from Hotel Florida also lives in that marina.

"What's the name of the marina?" I asked Louie.

"Davy Jones' Locker."

"That's an interesting name. I wonder if some of Jack's patients live in that marina."

"Could be Mabel, could be. To be honest, it's a place that's perfect for hiding. I'll take you over there one day. We can look at all the big yachts."

"That's okay, Louie. I'll take a pass." The idea of bumping into any of Jack's old patients wasn't really something I relished.

Bob hired Joe to do the work. Apparently, it needed some parts, so Bob informed the group that we would be waiting for the parts. Lili was going to join me for a morning walk. It was time to have that talk.

I was having my morning coffee when my phone buzzed. I looked down, and it was a call coming in from my daughter, Cecilia. We took a few minutes to chit-chat and catch up on mother-daughter stuff.

I had invited all my kids to spend some time on the road with me. The only one who had shown any real interest was Cecilia. I already knew Meg would never set foot in my camper. My son Henry said he might surprise me and asked if it was okay to bring a friend.

"Absolutely. I would love to meet him."

"Mom, I might fly out for a few days when you get to Nashville," Cecilia announced.

"That would be great."

I told her all about Joe. I felt like a matchmaker, just like my Aunt Sadie.

"Well, I'd like to meet him. Is he good looking?" She asked sheepishly.

"Well, let's just say he's easy on the eyes."

Cecilia's first love was her dream to make it big on Broadway. But she was getting older, and I knew she was reflecting on her life. Her biological clock was ticking. Unlike my millennial daughter, she was more conservative. Husband first and then a baby.

I knew those two would hit it off. They had a lot in common. If I listened to Irma, it was in the cards. Cecilia needed a break from New York. She was finishing up a part in an off-Broadway show. Her knees and an old Achilles tendon injury were acting up. The doctors told her she needed to give her body a rest. I also knew the dancing jobs were not coming as frequently as in the past.

"I might have to get a part-time job. I could teach dance. Maybe even open my own studio."

"Listen to your doctor and give those legs a break. If you tear your Achilles tendon, you are out for a good year."

Cecilia knew that. At her age, a torn Achilles could mean the end of her career.

"I'm hoping to land an acting part to give my legs a break. Waiting to hear back."

The doctor had told her six weeks off and physical therapy, but I knew it would be more like a week. She was at a fork in the road. Younger dancers were getting the best parts. That's show biz. She had to decide if it was time to hang up those dancing shoes, but she kept putting it off. She just hadn't figured out where to go next. Broadway is a strong magnet. It would be hard to give up her dream of seeing her name in lights.

"I'm waiting for a good acting part. Once I land that, I'm set. I'll give up dancing parts." Unfortunately, those acting parts were also going to the younger actresses.

"Or I might head out to LA."

I could hear from the tone in her voice that LA was her last chance.

"Got to go, I'll call you when I have more news."

I finished my coffee and was getting up for my walk when my cell buzzed again. I thought it was Cecilia maybe deciding to come on down to Savannah and take that break, but I could see it was Jack. We already had our check-on-the-box call at the beginning of the month. I decided to answer. Make sure the grandkids were okay.

"All safe in the Jack-in-the-box?"

"All safe, Jack."

He came up with the code name for the box of pictures.

"This is your second call this month." He was quiet, and then he asked.

"How are you doing?"

"Jack, I am doing fantastic." And I meant it.

"Good, I'm glad for you, Mabel," he paused, while I waited for him to get to the point of his call.

"Are the grandkids okay?"

"Yes, yes. They're all fine. Jack Jr keeps me in the loop. Not so much Meg. She hasn't forgiven me."

He was referring to the divorce. This was not like Jack at all. What was going on? Was he about to tell me he didn't have long to live?

"I've been meaning to call you and tell you something for a long time."

I took a deep breath. Oh, boy, this sounded ominous.

"I'm sorry, Mabel, for what happened."

I couldn't believe what I was hearing. But I knew this day would come—I had been waiting for it.

"You mean leaving me for someone the same age as our youngest daughter?"

"Yes."

I could hear something in his voice that in all the years I knew the man I had never heard before. I heard sorrow and regret. I never saw Jack display emotion. Not even when his beloved father died. He was not one to show his emotions.

"I lost it, and now I'm going to pay for that." I heard a deep sigh. "Talk to you later. I hope we will always be friends."

I sat for a long time and thought about what just happened. Later, during our walk, I told Lili about it.

"Forgive, Mabel. But don't forget. Just move on."

CHAPTER 18

Irma popped in right after I got back from my walk with Lili and, of course, had her two cents to say about Jack and the safe deposit box. I still hadn't told Lili about Irma. I had planned to, but we talked about the call from Jack instead. I figured that was enough news for today's walk.

"Don't forget. All your baggage came along when you became the new owner of Betsy. I think you should give Jack the key to the Jack-in-the-box and let him deal with. I don't want you swimming with the fishes. I'd be back in storage, and you'd probably be stuck in purgatory with me."

That was not a comforting thought. I thought of what Louie had told me one day. "Mabel, politics is just another way to launder mob money. They keep it pretty well hidden with PACs and offshore accounts."

From time to time, he reflected on his days as a lawyer with mob clients before he left Miami and settled in Fish Camp.

"Do they ever ask you to represent them?"

I knew when he needed to make ends meet, he drove his Cadillac limo for Uber.

"All the time and it would be a lot easier financially, but I like my life the way it is now."

My small flat screen was on, and the news was reporting that the governor of Florida was going to throw his hat in the ring for senator from Florida, and the spin was that he looked good for even higher office.

"Do you think Vito knows about the pictures?" I asked Irma.

Irma stuck her nose right up to the screen. If she were human, it would have left a nose print. Technology really fascinated her. She would occasionally remind me that she left this world in 1998, and this modern stuff amazed and bewildered her.

"Get your nose out my TV. How about asking your contacts in purgatory? They might know a thing or two about the governor."

"Those guys went straight to hell, Mabel."

"Not the mob guys. Trust me; I know they went straight to hell. I'm talking about their wives. Some of them, I might even know. They, surely, didn't go to hell, but most of them wouldn't have gotten a straight shot to heaven either."

"I'll ask around. There's a bunch of them passing time in purgatory. Sort of like your book club gals. If they weren't Jack's patients, then some of their relatives might have been."

"Like who?"

"You remember Little Stella?"

"Oh my God, yes!"

Little Stella was actually the ringleader of the mob wives after my mother-in-law, Big Stella, passed on. Those two were best friends. After some serious pestering, Irma shared that Big Stella was not in purgatory.

"So that woman got into heaven!"

"No! But Mabel keep that in the vault. Her husband eventually did, though. He did a lot of good deeds while he was alive. I heard he was happy he wasn't going to share his days in eternity with that woman."

Karma was alive, and I smiled.

"You're probably right, Irma. I should give that box to Jack. If Vito found out about those pictures, he would not be happy. Neither would his mob friends backing him for higher office."

"Besides, I suspect Jack is not worried about swimming with the fishes. No, he's more worried that his contract with the alphabets will be terminated, and he'd be placed in witness protection. I doubt that Tiffanie would go along and she would clean him out. I guess I have no choice but to play the cards I've been dealt Irma, for now."

"Let me track down Little Stella and the rest of those mob wives and a few folks I knew from back in my day. In the meantime, I want you to think about giving that box to Jack and his government friends. I'll be sure and give Little Stella your best."

"Thanks. We were always cordial like Meg is with Jack Jr's wife."

"What about Oscar?" Irma now asked.

"What about him?"

"I think his picture might be sitting in your safe deposit box."

"How do you know that?"

"I told you. Your baggage came with the camper when you bought it."

I just looked at her. "So, you get daily updates? Like the evening news?"

"Sometimes it just comes to me."

"A feeling?"

"Yes."

"I think Bob is working on it. Selma, who bar tends in town and lives in the campground, stopped Bob to talk the other day. She wanted to warn him about Oscar. She told Bob that Oscar was a con man."

"He is," and poof, she was gone.

CHAPTER 19

The part for Bob's rig arrived, and Joe got to work on it. Bob was looking at the day after tomorrow to make our way to Nashville. Cecilia was going to fly into Nashville and join us. I mentioned this to Joe and showed him a picture of my beautiful daughter.

"Wow," he said, holding my cell and looking at her picture. "Sorry. No disrespect, but she is beautiful. I look forward to meeting your daughter."

He looked at her picture a little longer before handing back my cell.

"Good."

I smiled and gave Joe a wink. He looked relieved. He knew I had just given him my approval.

"I think I might join you for the leg of your trip to Nashville. That is if the offer is still open," Joe asked shyly.

I guess the possibility of meeting Cecilia helped him make up his mind.

"It's open, and that would be great. I'm sure Bob will be thrilled to have you join the group."

It was time before we left Savannah to talk to Lili about Irma. I knew she wanted to talk. She had caught me a few more times chatting with Irma. Roll the dice and see what happens. I just had to figure out a way to tell her and make sure she didn't think I had lost it. We were sitting around the fire pit and having a cocktail before the rest of the group joined us. I took a sip of my Cosmo and began.

"Lili, you remember I told you when I was a kid, I could see things."

"Dead people," she said as she took a sip of her drink. Well, she did have a photographic mind.

"Lili, I know this might sound nuts but I think my camper is haunted. In fact, I know it is." I took a swig of my Cosmo.

"Mabel, how many have you had today?"

I held two fingers up.

"Well you remember I told you I grew up in New Orleans. And I'm sure several of the houses I managed on Long Island were haunted. Doors opening and closing, lights turning on and off and dogs barking at something only they could see."

"Her name is Irma. I can see her. She speaks to me, and I can hear her." I downed the rest of my Cosmo. "And I also saw a friend of hers, Chief Little Bear. His tombstone was on the ghost tour. But mainly I see Irma." I knew I was speaking fast, but I just had to get it all out before I lost my nerve.

"Irma?"

"Yes, and she was a show girl in Vegas and then a madame of a house run by the mob. Her son, a cop like Bob, lived in my camper. The mob had a hit out on him, and she took a bullet to save his life. She's stuck in purgatory and stuck in my camper."

I stopped to take a breath.

"There must be a reason why you can see her, Mabel. Trust me on that." Lili made the sign of the cross.

"I thought you were Baptist?"

"I am. But it doesn't hurt. So, what's her story?"

"She told me that if she does good deeds for the living, it will help to get her out of purgatory sooner. Saint Peter gives her extra credit for those good deeds. When she got pregnant, she decided it was best to give up her son for adoption. She named my camper Betsy after her sister, who raised her son."

"Well, from what I know about spirits, I would say you are here to help her to get into heaven. It sounds like you're going to be part of those good deeds, whatever they might turn out to be."

Then in a whisper Lili shared something with me.

"I can see them sometimes, too."

"Dead people?"

"Yes, usually out of the corner of my eyes. I think I've seen Irma. Is she a flashy dresser?"

"Oh yeah, she was a hooker, and apparently she has a large wardrobe."

"I'll keep this in the vault."

Lili got up to check on the happy hour goodies.

"I'm glad you told her," Irma said as Lili went into the camper to check on appetizers. She plopped herself in Lili's chair.

"So, you eavesdropped?"

"I was in stealth mode."

"I do feel better now. If anybody would understand about you, I knew it would be Lili."

"Some of my friends in purgatory are from New Orleans. But most of them were fortune tellers. I think we are going to need her help on the fast track program, Mabel."

"You do? What do you mean?"

"It goes along with what Chief Little Bear said. Someone in your wagon train is going to die, and I will be called on to find out why."

"Did Chief Little Bear happen to mention who was going to die?"

"Nope," Irma said. "But relax, it's not you."

"How do you know that?"

"Because that's why you can see and hear me, Mabel. I get it now. We're going to have to work together. I have a feeling it's going to be like those Agatha Christie books or those detective movies you and Lili love to watch."

I looked over, and she was gone. "Great," I said out loud. "That old folk's home is looking better and better."

It was then I heard voices. I looked across the way, and I could see Selma and Oscar talking. It sounded like they were having a heated conversation. I could see Selma was visibly upset. Oscar looked like he was listening and attempting to calm her down.

As I looked at Oscar, I thought he resembled John Wayne. I remembered that sometimes Jack's patients wanted him to make them look like one of their favorite film stars. I watched as Selma stomped off in a huff leaving Oscar standing there. From a distance, he looked like John Wayne. I will have to find out more about Oscar, probably starting this evening because he and his wife were going to be social tonight. They were going to join us for dinner.

CHAPTER 20

Joe and Selma joined us for happy hour. I could sense Selma was on guard. Peggy and Josh, the schoolteachers, were busy teaching. Tonight, the lesson plan was all about roasting marshmallows over a fire.

"There's an art to roasting a marshmallow. The best ones are burnt at the edges," Peggy said.

Before long, the booze clicked in, and Oscar took center stage and thankfully interrupted the history of marshmallows. We learned a little more about Selma. It turned out that Selma had known Oscar and Eleanor for several years as they had frequented both the campground and Earl's Bar.

"Even after Selma won the lottery she stayed living here in the campground," Oscar said. "And still works at Earl's and also volunteers in the campground."

"I can't sit still," she explained.

"But you won the lottery?"

Surprisingly, it was Josh who asked. He seemed to be intrigued about her winning the lottery. My guess is if he won, he would put some space between him and Peggy.

"I never had that kind of money. My son's in the military. His dad never came home from Vietnam. He never met his father. He has dedicated his life to a military career. I like my life and don't feel the need to run away from it."

That didn't seem to satisfy Josh, but it was an honest answer. I liked Selma.

"What do you do in the winter?" Peggy asked.

I noticed that Peggy was drinking wine tonight, and Josh was having a light beer. Good. I thought. That'll relax them both a bit.

"I usually rent a room over Earl's bar, but this winter, I may go to Florida. My doctor said it would help my bones. The cold really does a number on my arthritis. All those years standing on my feet, it's getting worse every year."

"Come to Boca Vista," Lili said.

"I know that area. I might, although I'm leaning toward the west coast near St. Petersburg. They have a few campgrounds I've been looking at for the winter."

"How much did you win?" Peggy asked. Well, so much for the booze relaxing her. The wine was working, but not in a good way. Josh gave her a look, but we had all figured out that Peggy wore the pants in the family.

"A lot," Selma said and looked directly at Oscar. That was when Oscar took his cue and spoke up.

"Selma won a power ball."

"I only bought one ticket. Can you imagine? For someone like me who paid my bills in cash or money orders to come into that kind of money was a shock. Oscar helped me with investing."

"He did?"

Peggy now turned her attention to the mystery couple. Eleanor was quiet. She didn't strike me as timid. It was almost like she wished she were somewhere else. I was still trying to figure out what they were drinking.

You can tell a lot about someone from their drinking habits. They both seemed guarded. They were dressed in what Lili calls casual rich. I noticed a gold Rolex on Oscar's wrist. I decided to speak up.

"My son Jack and my son-in-law are financial planners. They have a firm on Long Island."

"I'm not a financial planner. I am more of an advisor and help my friends, like Selma," Oscar said.

"Yes, Oscar invested some of my winnings" I noted a hint of sarcasm. I looked over at Lili. Her eyes told me she picked up on that tone in Selma's voice.

"In what?" Peggy asked.

Maybe a few drinks for Peggy wasn't a bad thing.

"Oil and gas wells. Right, Oscar?"

"Oh," I said and then quickly took a sip of my drink. Jack had lost his shirt in oil and gas well tax shelters when they were hot back in the day. Doctors always were an easy mark.

"My ex-husband invested in oil and gas tax shelters. He lost lots of money." Like Peggy, the booze was relaxing my tongue and my brain.

"Those were tax shelters, and a lot of people lost their shirts." Oscar, the personable salesman, explained. "Times have changed. What does your ex do?

"He's a plastic surgeon."

"I see," Oscar said. "Well, I have a number of friends who are doctors. They are not always the best businessmen."

"I'd have to agree with you on that," I said.

"So, you are divorced?" Peggy cornered me as happy hour was breaking up.

"Yeah, I'm divorced, Peggy."

The cat was out of the bag. Lili was right. The truth will trip you up if you try to dress it up with a lie. Kind of like buying a dress you intend to wear once and take back to that fancy mall store. They always take it back. No questions asked. Somehow that price tag always pops out, and someone like Peggy catches you. Not worth it. Well, at least I figured out the connection between Selma and Oscar.

At dinner, Oscar managed to sit right next to me. After some polite conversation, he got down to business.

"If you don't mind me asking, what is your ex-husband's name? I spent some time in New York, in my younger days."

"Jack Gold."

Oscar gave me a long, calculating look. Probably the same look Meg's clients give her when they decide to tell her what really happened.

"I knew your husband, Mabel."

"Is that so?" I tried to sound surprised, but not really sure that it worked.

"Did you meet him with one of your deals?"

I was born and raised in Brooklyn. I had my Aunt Sadie's quick tongue. Oscar just smiled, and then he chuckled. That nervous laugh he probably uses to give him time to think. I had never developed that trait. Foot in the mouth was my way. Not always helpful.

"It was a long time ago. I was young and got caught up with some bad men, really bad men. If you know what I mean."

"I might." He now had my attention.

"I was heading to jail, and instead, I was recruited to become an informant for the FBI. In return, the FBI helped me change a few things," Oscar said. "I think you know what I mean. I hope you will keep it between us. I joined the military, and the rest is history."

"Of course. We've been divorced for a few years. I had a feeling you knew who I was."

He just smiled. I could tell he wasn't going to show all his cards just yet.

"I appreciate your discretion. I'm telling you this because, since we arrived, I think I've seen a few ghosts from the past. You might want to be careful."

I looked at Oscar. For a second, I was wondering if he could see Irma. I took a quick look around, but she was nowhere to be seen, probably out in space somewhere.

"Ghosts from the past? Is that why we are having this cozy chat?"

"Next time you chat with Dr. Gold, you might mention Willie Nelson."

"Willie Nelson?"

"He'll know who I'm talking about. Let's just say the person I'm talking about liked country music. Kind of like me and old John Wayne movies."

I looked at Oscar now, and there was that hint of John Wayne. Maybe if he were wearing jeans and a cowboy hat, it would be more noticeable.

"I see. Well, it's a small world, Oscar. Jack and I don't talk much."

"Thank you, Mabel."

"Roger that."

Little did I know that it would be one of the last times I would hear Oscar's boisterous and infectious laughter.

CHAPTER 21

Selma and Lili hit it off and became fast friends. It seems like the two women had a lot in common, both from towns in Louisiana, and both loved to read. That link bonded them, and she opened up like a flower.

"Did she say any more to Bob about Oscar?"

"No, even backtracked a little when Bob brought his name up. That man has Bob's radar way up. I can tell you that."

Our getting out on the road and heading to Nashville was further delayed. Now it was Peggy and Josh who needed work on their rig. Joe was being kept busy. Lili and I went out for a walk on one of the campground's beautiful hiking trails, enjoying the glorious May weather.

"Selma told me this trail will take us through a maritime forest." Lili pulled out a brochure with a map. "She gave this to me. She has learned a lot about the area from working in the office."

Lili held out the map for me to see. "It says here that the campground is nestled in a wooded area mostly shaded with a mix of hardwoods and pines. Along the trails, you will find a mix of live oaks, cabbage palmettos, southern red cedar, and pines, over salt marshes and tidal creeks that lead to views of the Intracoastal Water-way."

"It's beautiful, Lili. Just between us, I really don't mind the delay in our trip west," I said, breathing in the fresh air. "I understand why Selma lives here."

I told Lili about the conversation I had with Oscar at dinner. I was still thinking about it. I guess Oscar also did background checks on who he was traveling with over the summer.

Lili was not a gossip, but she decided that I needed to know some information about Oscar that Selma had shared with her.

"Selma told me that she invested part of her lottery winnings with Oscar. She is a widow, and like she told us the other night, she had never had that kind of money. She gave her son a portion of her winnings, but didn't know how to invest, so she turned to Oscar. That might have been a big mistake," Lili said as we walked along a beautiful trail.

"So, what happened to her money?"

"When she's asks about her investments, all Oscar says is that investments take time."

"Did they have a romantic relationship? There seemed to be something more to their body language. They have to have a history."

"Yes. She told me Oscar and his wife were separated and talking about divorce when she won the lottery. That's how he got close to her. They were romantic, but when Oscar and his wife got back together, Selma broke off the relationship. But by then she had given him a chunk of her winnings."

"Oh Lili, That's not good."

"By the way, his pet name for his wife is the Bar-racuda because she's always snapping at him."

"Well, she is a little odd. She reminds me of some women I knew back on Long Island. She hasn't said much socially, but I don't think it's because she is shy. I get the feeling she doesn't want to have anything to do with us."

"Especially Selma," Lili said. "Might be why she is cool to the group. She might know that Oscar had a fling with Selma while they were separated."

"Could be, Lili. Maybe she thinks they're still having an affair? He doesn't come across as a trustworthy guy."

"Selma's son thinks Oscar has used her money like a Ponzi scheme. He robbed Peter to pay Paul—or more likely vulnerable women. Selma saw him talking to some nefarious looking characters one night when she was working at Earl's."

"Nefarious? Mob nefarious?" I was thinking about my chat with Oscar.

Lili just shrugged her shoulders. "From her description, it sounded like muscle."

"Well, we both know what that means. You could say from our past lives."

Lili knew all my secrets, including Jack and his prior and current patients. She was a keeper of secrets and I could trust her.

"Did she say how much she gave him?"

"No, but I'm guessing it was a lot. Not all at once. He kept coming back. For someone used to paying her bills from paycheck to paycheck, it must not have been easy for her to suddenly deal with that kind of money."

"Hmmm." I tried to imagine a seven-figure bank account.

"She paid taxes on her cash tips, out of respect for her son's service and his father, who gave his life for this country."

"Well, I respect that. How did she get to know Oscar?"

"At Earl's. Oscar and the Barracuda have a condo in Fort Lauderdale, but they spend the summers traveling. They stay in Savannah for a few months."

We had arrived at a beautiful spot along the Intercostal waters. We stopped talking to just enjoy the beauty. People who don't get out into nature are missing so much. I again felt so happy that I had decided to hit the road. I don't think they serve Cosmos in old folks' homes.

"They have alligators in these waters," Lili said, pointing at what I hoped was a log.

With that thought in mind, we turned around and headed back to the campground and continued our conversation.

"Well, Lili, that explains why they've had some heated spats around the campground. What does Bob make of Oscar?"

"He's been in touch with some of his law enforcement contacts. Oscar apparently is well known in the Las Vegas and Atlantic City casinos. Good chance that he gambled away Selma's money."

"Could explain the nefarious characters Selma saw at Earl's."

"Bob plans to sit down with Selma and tell her what he has discovered. She needs to know before we head out to Nashville. Not that he could to anything about getting her money back, but he may suggest she talk to Louie. You know Bob recently got his private detective license and Louie has talked to him about doing investigative work."

"I know that his law firm is picking up thanks to referrals from our book club members. They always have friends going through a divorce and need help to find money and assets their rich husbands are hiding. Did Selma tell you how much she won?"

Lili was quiet for a moment and then she told me, "Two million after taxes. She took the lump sum payout."

"I wonder how much she gave Oscar. Two million after taxes can go fast nowadays."

Lili shrugged her shoulders. "Her son still has most of the winnings she gave him. When she talked to Bob about a new camper, she told him she has enough to pay cash for a camper and a pickup, but I don't think she has that much left. That's why she asked Oscar to cash out."

"I guess it's a good thing she kept her bar tending skills sharp." We were close to finishing our walk and could see our campsites.

"I don't like that man," Lili said.

"I don't either, and just between the two of us, neither does Irma."

CHAPTER 22

It wasn't long after our walk that Bob talked with Selma. Our trip was still on hold until Peggy and Josh got their camper fixed. They decided since they were getting one thing fixed and Joe was so reasonable, they would fix a few more things.

Bob told Selma about Oscar's gambling and his suspicions that Oscar was in over his head and maybe in debt to some mobsters from Vegas.

"She broke down crying," Bob told Lili and me.

We were at Earl's for happy hour. Selma was working. She came over and sat down since it was early and slow.

"I think he lost all my money. He keeps telling me he's working on getting it, but it will take time to find a buyer for my oil and gas wells. I was such a fool. I could kill that man." Selma was visibly upset.

"Do you know his wife paid me a visit? She acted like she was my best friend and spent the whole time complaining about Oscar. She said if it wasn't for his military pension and some good deals along the way, they'd be broke."

We were all getting to know the Barracuda. She was a real pain and had a sharp tongue.

"The Barracuda cornered Lili and me the other day and joined us on our walk. We cut our walk short because she spent the whole time complaining about Oscar."

Selma got up and went back up to tend bar.

"What is it?" Lili asked Bob. The two of them sometimes communicated like mentalists.

"I talked to one of my retired FBI contacts. The FBI has a file on Oscar from a few years back when they were looking into a money-laundering scheme out of Vegas. They talked to him but couldn't get anything on him. Oscar might be a gambler and a wheeler-dealer, but he has offshore bank accounts. That's all he shared."

"Offshore bank accounts, well, you're preaching to the choir," I said, looking at Bob and Lili. They knew my story of Jack and his hiding cash in offshore accounts when we were going through the divorce. That's when my CPA, Mary Catherine Mahoney, found the accounts and saved me financially.

"Sounds like Oscar might be saving for the future if they divorce," I said.

"Might be there are two women who have it out for Oscar," Bob said.

CHAPTER 23

The next day, the Barracuda reported Oscar missing to the local police. He had not come home the previous night. She told them that Oscar had told her he was meeting with some investors at Earl's.

Lili had checked in on the Barracuda and brought her some food. "She's sleeping and wants to be left alone."

It didn't take long. A few hours later Oscar's body was found on an isolated trail at the far end of the campground.

Tom and Jerry, from the Savannah police department, showed up and interviewed everyone in the campground. Tom was tall and slender and Jerry was short and the opposite. They asked us to stay close by our campers and not leave town.

At happy hour, we were shell-shocked when the news came out that the police had arrested Selma for the murder of Oscar.

"Bob, you used to be a cop?" Peggy, true to form, jumped right in and cut to the chase. "Do you think Selma murdered him?"

We all looked at Peggy. "Silence is a good response," Lili reminded me over the years.

We were quiet, but it didn't work. Peggy was eager to tell us what she knew about police work. Apparently, more than a homicide detective from LA and the local cops. She continued talking while she handed Josh her glass for a refill. He poured her another wine, and he popped a Budweiser. No more light beers. They had become a little more relaxed about their drinking. Especially Josh.

We were brainstorming. All of us had been questioned, and we all had picked up bits and pieces about Oscar's murder. Peggy made it sound like she had successfully obtained inside information out of Tom and Jerry. Well, they might have not been a match for the school principal. She could come on like a nun, a mother superior.

"It's my understanding that the Barracuda told police that Selma had an argument with Oscar earlier in the day," Peggy said.

"How do you know that?" Bob asked.

"I heard Selma talking to Oscar. My window was open."

Yeah, your friendly nosy neighbor. Every village had one. I had heard on a TED Talk that people are nosy because they want to feel good about themselves. The same applies to gossip.

"Selma was talking to Oscar before she went to work. They had a big fight right outside his camper. The Barracuda heard them, too. They were loud enough."

"Did you see the Barracuda," Bob asked.

"Yeah, she had her window open and was listening too. We both heard Selma threaten to kill Oscar if he didn't get her money back. She said she was almost broke, and then she left in a big huff. Oscar went into the camper and told the Barracuda that he was going out. That he had a meeting with some investors later at Earl's."

"How do you know all this," Bob asked Peggy, who seemed to be auditioning for the star witness at the murder trial.

"When Oscar left, I popped in and talked to the Barracuda. Just to make sure she was all right."

"I see." Bob now turned his attention to Joe. "Did you see Oscar at Earl's?"

"I did and told the police that Oscar had stopped in Earl's later in the evening. I was getting my equipment together to leave. Selma left early. She didn't feel well. Earl was bar tending. I saw Oscar at the bar talking to Earl when two men showed up."

"What did they look like?"

"Like guys you wouldn't want to meet in a dark alley."

"Did you notice anything else about them? Anything that seemed peculiar?"

Joe was quiet for a moment before he spoke. "Yes. It looked like Earl knew them. The four of them were talking, serious like."

"Did you tell Tom and Jerry this?"

"No, sir, I did not," Joe said.

"It's okay, son. No worries."

"My mom always told me not to volunteer information until I was asked."

"You have a very smart mother."

"So, did Tom and Jerry tell you what happened? Why they came back and arrested Selma," I asked Bob. I knew Tom and Jerry would talk with Bob and share information.

"Well, what they did share with me was that Oscar showed up at Earl's to meet with his investors, just like Peggy told us."

"See," Peggy said and smiled at everyone.

"When Oscar was heading into Earl's, he ran into Selma on her way out. They got into a very loud fight in the parking lot. She threatened to kill him in front of a number of bar patrons."

"Good grief," I said.

"Joe, do you remember if Oscar left the bar with those two guys?" Bob asked.

"Yes, sir, he did. I told the police that they talked, and then the three of them left at the same time."

"Well, that was the last time Oscar was seen alive." Bob took a long drink from his Budweiser and then spoke to the group.

"As we all know, the police have arrested Selma. Tom and Jerry told me that when they found Oscar's body, they found a gun next to his body. That gun was registered to Selma. If it turns out that it was her gun used to kill Oscar, then Selma won't be coming home anytime soon."

CHAPTER 24

We broke up after happy hour and decided to eat in for the evening. Most of us didn't have much of an appetite. Irma was waiting for me when I returned to my camper.

"Where have you been? A lot has happened lately. I thought for sure you would be buzzing around with all the commotion."

"I was around, in and out, but in stealth mode. I didn't want to distract you. This was the death Chief Little Bear foretold."

"Yes, well, he didn't see Selma being arrested for murder. That would have been a nice head's up," I said to the ghost who was dressed in workout clothes for the evening.

She was wearing neon green spandex tights with a black leotard with a wide headband and black leg warmers. I think I had an outfit just like that back in 1980.

"You look like you just got back from a Jane Fonda workout class."

"I kept in shape, Mabel. I had to in my line of work. My girls did the same. We even had a regular boot camp with a drill sergeant whenever he came to town." She smiled at that memory. "Anyway, I'm ready to solve this murder and get myself on the fast track out of purgatory. Someone murdered Oscar and I don't think it was Selma."

I thought about that for a moment. Irma, out of purgatory, would mean Irma out of my life. I pretty much had no choice but to go along.

"What if Selma did it? She had plenty of reasons to shoot the guy. Her gun was found next to Oscar, and they had a big fight right outside of Earl's where a lot of people heard her threaten to kill him. The evidence is stacked against her."

"Well then, Selma better hope her oil rig strikes oil because she's going to need a good criminal lawyer. Like your daughter, Meg."

Irma was standing in front of me with her hands held out in front of her as she did squats.

"Meg did say she was thinking about getting back into law. Perhaps I can convince her to handle it pro bono. That's Latin for free."

"I know what pro bono means, Mabel," Irma said in a deep squat in front of me with the spandex outfit from a 1980s aerobics class.

"Of course you do. Did you ever do yoga? My son Henry is a yogi."

"No, remember I left at the end of the nineties. Step class was my favorite." She continued with the squats. "I think that's a good idea, Mabel. With Meg as her lawyer, it will go a long way in aiding our investigation. Saint Peter reminded me that I have to find the murderer for it to count as a good deed."

"It seems too cut and dry. It's almost as if Selma is being framed for this murder. I guess we'll have to see if the bullet that killed Oscar came from her gun."

"Since they found his body on a hiking trail in the campground, anyone in the campground could be a suspect," Irma said.

"True. The Barracuda also had plenty of motives to kill Oscar. Oscar had that offshore bank account. She might have found out, and I bet he had a life insurance policy. She was awful quick to point the finger at Selma."

"Do you remember anything else, Mrs. Gold?" Irma asked in an official voice as she appeared to write in the notepad. She now was dressed like a cop, and I could see a gun in a holster.

"You changed your outfit."

"Just stick to the facts, ma'am," Irma said with a twinkle in her eye. "It gets me in the mood"

"Well, when Joe was packing up to leave the bar, he saw Oscar talking to two men he said you wouldn't want to meet in a dark alley. The three of them left together. The Barracuda told the cops that Oscar had a meeting with investors from Vegas. They could be disgruntled investors like Selma. Maybe even mob?"

"Why do you say that?" Irma, the cop, asked while taking notes as best as she could with those specter fingers.

"Selma told Lili she had seen Oscar talking to 'nefarious characters' at the bar. Sounded like mob muscle to us. He did like to gamble."

"If that's the case, Oscar was in debt to those guys. You never want to owe the mob. They start by breaking your legs or your fingers. Had to set an example, or everyone would have a free ride. What else?"

"Well, officer, just what Oscar told me a few nights ago at dinner? He knew Jack from the old days. Someone who looks like Willie Nelson had him worried. He told me to be careful and told me to ask Jack about Willie."

"Have you?"

"No, I have not."

"Is that it, ma'am?" Irma said in a voice that sounded like Sergeant Joe Friday from the old Dragnet TV show.

"Just something Joe mentioned. That when the two mob guys showed up at the bar, it looked they knew both Oscar and Earl."

"Hmmm, now that is interesting. What do you know about Earl?"

"Only that he is the owner of the bar, and he and Oscar were friends."

"You and Lili need to talk to Selma. When you do, you need to ask her about Earl."

"I don't know if I want to get Lili involved in this."

"She's already involved. She and Selma have become fast friends. The way it happens when you meet someone you knew in a past lifetime."

"Is that why sometimes you meet someone and you feel like you've known them forever?"

"Yup, that's the way it works."

"Do you think we knew each other?"

"Nah, Mabel. I'd remember you."

She was back in her neon aerobics outfit. My head was getting dizzy with all the wardrobe changes.

"Maybe I should make a trip back to Boca Vista and look at those pictures in my safe deposit box. See if Oscar is in there along with someone who looks like Willie Nelson."

"Mabel, we need to find out who murdered Oscar. It might be all I need for Saint Peter to let me through those pearly gates. Keep thinking about that. I'd be out of your hair, and you can spend the rest of your life in peace."

I woke up in the middle of the night, thinking about my chat with Irma. She was right. We had to figure out who killed Oscar and for more reasons than getting her out of my hair. If Oscar's murder was tied to those photos sitting in my safe deposit box, then Jack and I might end up in witness protection, and, like Jack, that was not how I wanted to spend my golden years. I really liked camping.

CHAPTER 25

Tom and Jerry were now holding interviews in a back room in the campground office. Since Joe lived at the campground and worked at Earl's, he was at the top of their list. He had been called first and spent a lot of time with them. When they were done with him, he joined Lili and me at her camper where we were having coffee. Lili went into the camper and came back with a mug of coffee and a piece of homemade coffee cake.

"Here, Joe. They kept you a long time."

"They did. They called Bob in when they were done with me." He put the plate on his knee and took a gulp from the mug. "They sure had lots of questions."

Lili brought me another piece, which I didn't turn down.

"Bob said Tom and Jerry interviewed all of us but now want to circle back around to talk to us more in depth," Lili said. "Mainly want to know where we were the night of the murder and if we have an alibi. We were in for the night."

I had Irma. I don't think they were going to buy that as an alibi. I had no motive, and neither did anyone else in the group other than no one warmed up to Oscar, but that's no reason to shoot him.

"I told them all I know," Joe said. "After Oscar and those two guys left, I came straight back here and went to bed. They asked me if I saw Selma when I came home. She usually closes the bar and is the last to leave but that night she left early. Wanted to know if the lights were on in her camper."

"Were they?" I asked Joe.

"No. I told them her camper was dark when I drove past. Earl called me to talk. Earl said the police talked to the waitresses who were working the outside patio. A lot of people heard them fighting. They said it got very loud."

"Did Earl say what they heard other than she was going to kill him?" I asked Joe.

"Earl said they argued about her money. She wanted it back. Then she hit the roof when he told her that there would be no money if she cashed in on the oil rigs now. He kept saying she should wait because it could still turn around. She accused him of stealing her money. That she knew he was a gambler, and he had stolen her money and lost it gambling."

"Well, unfortunately, that could very well be true," Lili added. "Oscar had a serious gambling problem. He spent a lot of time in Vegas and could have been deep in debt to the mob."

"Those two guys Oscar met the night he was killed didn't look like old army buddies. They looked shady."

"So, Joe, can you tell us a little about Earl?" It was almost like I could hear Irma prompting me.

"He's had some hard times as of late. His wife had cancer and died. He and Oscar go way back. They served in the military together."

"So, they were friends?" I asked.

"Yes. Earl doesn't share a lot. He stays in the background and lets Selma run the bar. Selma told me that Earl was afraid he was going to have to sell the bar to pay for her his wife's cancer treatments. Eleanor and his wife were good friends. She was there with her every day at the end."

"So, Joe, you felt like Earl knew those two guys who were meeting Oscar the night he was killed."

"Yes. I saw them talking. The more I think about it, I think they were there to talk to Earl *and* Oscar."

"Why is that son?" Lili asked.

"You notice things working in a bar. You're cordial to your patrons and fans, you pay attention to them. After all, they pay my bills, and I want them to be happy and return. Earl was talking to them and it didn't look like friend bar chatter."

"Do you remember anything else about those men?" I asked Joe, who thought for a moment.

"Yes, one was wiry and skinny with a ponytail. He was the spitting image of my hero, Willie Nelson."

"Are you sure?"

"Yes, ma'am."

I sat there thinking about that. He was describing the guy Oscar warned me about. I didn't like asking Jack if he worked on someone who was a fan of Joe's favorite singer. But it was either that or visit my safe deposit box real soon.

"It still doesn't explain how Selma's gun showed up next to the body," Lili said. "If she shot him, why would she have left the gun?"

"Earl keeps a gun at the bar under the counter. The last one was stolen, and Selma told Earl she would bring her gun in until he replaced it. She liked having a gun nearby," Joe said.

"Did he replace the gun?" I asked Joe.

"As far as I know he did not."

"The Barracuda has become a real social butterfly lately," Lili added. "Selma told us she stopped by to visit and spent the whole time complaining about Oscar. She could have killed Oscar. She had as much motive as Selma."

"But she would have had to get her hands on Selma's gun. Do you think the Barracuda knew the bar kept a gun under the counter?" I asked Joe.

"It wasn't a secret. All the help knew. Earl told me about it when I was hired. Just in case he wanted us to know about the gun and where it was located. It's possible she knew."

"But how would she have known the gun under the bar belonged to Selma?" Lili pointed out the elephant in the room. We pondered about that for a moment.

Joe got up to leave. "I have to get ready for work. I'll chat with you lovely ladies a little later. Thank you for the coffee, ma'am, and that delicious coffee cake."

"Bob told us about the offshore bank accounts. If the Barracuda found out about those accounts, she may have told Selma during her social visit. That would have added fuel to the fire and got her all stirred up, so the next time she saw Oscar, she'd let him have it." I said.

"I hear you. You don't know about people, Mabel. I've been surprised more than once with the families I worked for, really surprised."

The mouse had turned into a rat as far as I was concerned.

"We need to talk to the Barracuda," I said. "Let's bring her some comfort food. After all, she is a grieving widow."

Although so far, we had not seen any tears. Not even crocodile ones.

CHAPTER 26

"That woman killed Oscar, I know it," the Barracuda shouted as she threw open the door to her camper.

Lili walked in with her tuna casserole and I followed. You can't go wrong with a tuna casserole when you're paying your respects. Or so we thought. Her camper was newer, larger, and spotless. I could see it had two twin beds in the rear. Although it was roomy and had a modern interior it didn't feel as cozy as my camper.

"I made a tuna casserole for you. You have to keep up your strength."

"Not hungry."

"Oh, I'll just put it in your fridge."

Lili stuck the tuna casserole in the fridge, and we sat down. That's when I saw Irma. She was dressed like a police officer, only she was wearing a miniskirt, knee-high boots, and she was holding a long black whip. I watched Irma raise her hand and crack the whip. I nearly jumped out of my seat.

"Did you hear that?" The Barracuda jumped up.

"Hear what? I didn't hear anything. What about you, Lili?"

Lili rolled her eyes. "No, Mabel, I didn't hear anything." Lili leaned toward me and whispered. "Is Irma here?" The Barracuda was walking back and forth, checking out everything that might be the source of the source of the sound. She turned the radio on and off. She opened the refrigerator.

I leaned closer to Lili. "Sssshh. She's dressed like a meter maid on Halloween night, with a whip in her hand."

"Hello, Irma," Lili whispered. "I think I can see you in the corner of my eye."

"Tell Lili I said hello."

"Irma says hello."

"Yikes!" I said as Irma cracked the whip right next to the Barracuda's ear.

"Stop it," I said to the ghost with a big ol' grin on her face.

"You heard that?"

The Barracuda looked all around her. We watched as she stooped to look under her chair. "Do you believe in ghosts?" She said looking up at us as she sat back down.

"No," both Lili and I said at the same time.

"Well, I do. I got up this morning, and those pillows were all over the floor."

She pointed to a dozen small pillows on the sofa where Lili and I were sitting.

"You've been through a lot," Lili said. "You sure you don't want some of that tuna casserole?"

"Might be Oscar," the Barracuda said in a barely audible whisper.

I guess she wasn't hungry, but I sure was, and I was thinking of taking Lili's prized tuna casserole home with me. The Barracuda got back up to do another sweep around her camper.

"Okay, Irma, what the hell are you doing?" Lili sat next to me calmly.

"I know what she's doing," Lili said as we heard the Barracuda close the door to the head.

"You can't even see her."

"Don't have to. She's trying to scare a confession out of her."

"Is that it?"

"Damn right, I am," and then Irma realized the word damn would add a minute or two to her jail time. "Dang it. It's good Lili is here to help. She's smart and you're going to need all the help you can get, sister."

"What'd she say?" Lili asked.

"In her best Humphrey Bogart, she said she's glad you're here. Welcome to my world."

"See what you can get out of her. I'll be back." Irma vanished, sounding a lot like the Terminator.

"She wants us to find out what the Barracuda knows."

When the Barracuda returned, she didn't look well.

"I'm ready to get the hell out of here. Truth is told I hated traveling in this rig. I'd fly back to Fort Lauderdale today if the cops would let me. I'm going to check into a hotel in Savannah. It's right down the street from Earl's Bar."

"What about your camper," I asked.

"Don't care. I'm going to put it up for sale. I'll let it go cheap. Maybe that singer Joe might want to buy it."

"Well, you've told the police everything you know, and they have arrested Selma," I added.

"I'm sure she killed Oscar, but they asked me a ton of questions about Oscar and those two guys he met with at Earl's."

"Do you know them?" Lili asked.

"They're from Vegas, mobsters. Oscar owed them a ton of money. I'm sure he took Selma's winnings and gambled it away, trying to pay down his debt. I tried to warn her about that."

"You did?" I said.

"Sure. I had enough of Oscar. I watched him con people out of their life savings. I went over to talk to Selma and she just about blew a gasket."

"Why did you do that?" Lili asked.

"Because that louse asked me for a divorce," she gasped.

She probably regretted sharing that morsel with us.

"I was curious to see if they had hooked back up. We were separated for a while, and I know they had a fling. That's probably when he talked her into investing her winnings. Oscar was no saint, but I loved the man, and I stood by him. We argued about his gambling. Just couldn't kick the habit. I told him someday it would get him killed, and it looks like I was right."

"Had they? Hooked back up?"

I could hear my stomach grumbling. I was tempted to get up and grab some tuna casserole.

"Nope, but I could tell by the way she looked at him, she still had feelings. That's why she fell for everything he told her. He could charm the paint off the side of a barn. She told me straight to my face that he had told her he was asking me for a divorce. She told him to get the hell out of Dodge. I have to give her that."

"So, are you okay?"

"Financially?" Lili finished my sentence. "Hell, no. Right after the louse asked me for a divorce, I hired a lawyer, and they hired a private detective."

"Did they find anything?" I jumped in. "Maybe they can shed some light on those two mob guys who visited Oscar that night."

"Well, that's up to the cops now," the Barracuda said. "But lucky for me, they found some bank accounts in Panama. Oscar flew down there a lot. He probably had a girlfriend waiting for him. It turned out that the louse had stashed some money away."

Lili and I gave each other a look. So, the Barracuda had found out about the offshore accounts. More motive as far as I was concerned.

"Selma actually did me a big favor killing that rat. May he rest in peace."

The Barracuda made the sign of the cross and Lili and I joined her.

"Now, if you'll excuse me, I need to pack a few things and get out of here."

We left as the widow started packing. I discreetly grabbed the tuna casserole on the way out. Since she was leaving why let it go to waste? As I shut the door, I heard the distinct sound of a whip cracking.

CHAPTER 27

Lili and I were back in my camper. Irma was waiting for us, absent the whip.

"She's here." I warned Lili.

I scooped out two plates full of tuna casserole and placed them on the dinette table. My stomach sounded like an angry cat, so I dove in. Lili started talking to Irma.

"Well, Irma, we talked to the Barracuda. Oscar was a rat, and he was about to divorce her. She hired a lawyer, and they found offshore bank accounts in Panama."

Irma was looking at me as I scarfed down a mouthful. I was now eyeing the other plate. Lili didn't look hungry.

"Tell Lili to talk to Bob and tell him about this chat with the Barracuda. I think she was the one who killed Oscar. Also sounds like Oscar didn't lose everything gambling."

Lili looked over at me. "Irma said you need to talk to Bob."

"I plan too as soon as he gets back from talking to the police."

Lili moved her plate of food over to my side. I went to work.

"I keep coming back to Selma's gun."

I was getting full and pushed the almost empty plate away.

"I wonder if the police know if the bullet that killed Oscar came from Selma's gun."

"I'll ask Bob. You didn't like my casserole, did you?"

"I should probably go for a walk. Hey, I've got an idea. How about I walk over to the campground office where they're interrogating everyone? Irma, you come along and see what you can find out."

"That's brilliant Mabel, let's go."

Irma shot out the door, or should I say right through the door.

"Lili, I'll be back. It might be a good idea to take the casserole with you?"

"Good idea seeing you didn't care for it." Lili raised an eyebrow as she picked up the half-eaten casserole.

I had just stepped into the campground office when I saw Bob next to a man dressed in a suit and tie. It wasn't Tom or Jerry, the local cops.

"Bad timing," Bob whispered to me as he left the campground office.

The man in the suit introduced himself and flashed his FBI credentials, Lt. Daniel Kirk. He was on the short and stocky side. Lt. Dan fit the part. Just like in the movie Forrest Gump. That's how I remember names anymore. I associated them with a movie. I looked around; Irma was nowhere to be seen.

"Mrs. Gold, since you're here, why don't you come in and we can get your interview out of the way."

Lt. Dan pointed the way. I followed him into a room set up with computers, and a host of electronic devices and a long table with chairs on both sides. It looked like the room had been used for storage by the campground. Boxes and supplies were stacked high all around the perimeter of the room.

"Please have a seat."

He was joined by another man, also dressed in a suit and tie. "This is my partner, Agent Bill Grove."

Agent Bill reached over and shook my hand. He was tall and lanky and looked younger than Lt. Dan.

"It's nice to meet you. Can I get you anything?"

"A Cosmo?" Neither one smiled. "No, thank you, I'm fine."

I now saw Irma. She was standing behind Lt. Dan and Agent Bill. She had changed into Black: jeans, T-shirt, leather gloves. Her outfit was accessorized with a large whip.

Now that the niceties were out of the way, Lt. Dan got right to the point.

"We're with the organized crime division and would like to hear if you can shed some light on what is going on here."

"What happened to Tom and Jerry, the local police officers?"

"They oversee the murder investigation. We have questions on a different case," Agent Bill said in a *'that's all you need to know tone of voice.*

He took over the interview, "How well did you know the victim?"

"Not very well, we just met a few nights ago."

"Did your ex-husband know him?"

I caught my breath and looked at Irma. I didn't see that coming.

"Careful," I heard Irma say as she walked back and forth behind the two G men. Irma raised the whip, and I heard it crack like lightning. Lt. Dan and Agent Bill did not. Unless they had the room wired for ghosts.

"What do you mean?" I asked Irma.

Lt. Dan answered. "Your ex-husband, did he know Oscar?"

They thought I was talking to them.

"Feds," Irma said. "Be careful."

"Ask him yourself. We've been divorced for several years. Or try the CIA. You guys rub shoulders with them, don't you?"

They sat there quietly, looking at me. Silence designed to make you squirm and say something you would regret later. I just smiled. What could they do to me? I'm an old lady from Brooklyn. Plus, Jack and these guys work for the same company, just different divisions.

"Or better yet, if you need to know anything about my ex-husband, I suggest you talk to his friend, Cliff." They didn't bat an eye when I mentioned Jack's handler's name. "Who are you guys?" I was born at night, but not last night.

"Ma'am, we are asking the questions here," Agent Bill said. I guess he was the bad cop and Lt. Dan, the good cop.

"Don't say anymore," Irma said.

Before I could say anymore, Irma cracked her whip and a stack of boxes fell and landed right behind the two. They were boxed in.

I jumped up as Lt. Dan and Agent Bill tried to shove the boxes back so they could stand up. The manager of the campground office heard the commotion and ran in the room.

"I heard a loud noise," he said, and before he could say anymore, another stack of boxes fell. It was like a game of dominoes.

"We'll talk later, Mrs. Gold," Lt. Dan said as he shoved a box aside and stood up. "Don't leave town."

As I backed toward the door, I left Irma in the middle of the room, standing on the table and cracking her whip as more boxes continued to fall. I scooted out of there and headed back to my camper. Lili and Bob were outside waiting for me.

"Who are those guys?" I asked Bob. "They wanted to know if I knew Oscar and then started asking me questions about Jack."

"FBI out of the Las Vegas office," Bob said. "Probably threw that out to shake you up and put the scare in you."

"They said they were with organized crime. Do they think someone else killed Oscar? Mob from Vegas?"

"Don't know. Could be why they're here, but I don't trust them."

"That might point the gun at the mob and not Selma?"

"That's usually not the way it works, Mabel. They might be here to keep the lid on whatever case they've got going. They are always after bigger fish. I saw that all the time in LA."

"But what about Selma?" I asked.

"As far as they are concerned, the murder case is under the jurisdiction of the local police, not their investigation."

"But if they know something, they'll share it with the locals, right? Any information that proves Selma is innocent?"

"Not if it impacts their case. That's why Selma needs a good criminal lawyer. Tom told me this morning that the feds are putting pressure on them to transfer Selma to a state penitentiary to await trial."

"Why would they do that?"

"Intimidation? Protection? My educated guess is it has something to do with their case."

Bob and Lili returned to their camper, and I went inside to get out of the heat. I sat down and poured a cup of coffee and added ice and a shot of Kahlua.

"Well, as they say in Florida, it's always five o'clock somewhere."

CHAPTER 28

We met later at the fire pit for cocktail hour. The Barracuda, to our surprise, showed up. She already had a few drinks by then. Josh and Peggy were not going to join us for drinks but would see us at dinner. They were a little spooked and told Bob they were thinking of heading out and would meet us in Nashville. Joe had wrapped up the work on their camper. All they were waiting for was to get the green light from Tom and Jerry so they could leave.

"I'm leaving this damned place," the Barracuda said. "My camper's haunted and full of bad vibes. I'm checking into a hotel in town." She gave us the name of the hotel and left to finish packing.

"I know that hotel. It's within walking distance of Earl's," Joe said.

I thought about that for a second. "You might see more of her. Since she and Oscar were friends with Earl and his wife."

"Maybe, but after his wife died, Oscar was the only one I saw at Earl's," Joe responded.

"Keep an eye out," Bob said. "Let us know if you see her. I'd like to know if she leaves town."

"I will. She gave me the keys to her camper. Said she was selling it. If I took care of it and found a buyer, she would give me a tip." Joe got up to head into work. "Thanks again for the loan of your pickup."

We had a nice dinner along the riverfront. Peggy told us that the police said they could leave town and so they were doing exactly that, tomorrow morning bright and early. They were going to Ashville and then to Nashville. Bob suggested we spend the next day at Tybee Island. I had not heard back from Lt. Dan or Agent Bill. Maybe they were still picking up the boxes. Irma was quiet, too.

"Tybee Island is a small coastal community about 18 miles away," Bob said the next morning as we drove to Tybee Island. "Tybee Island Light Station is the first lighthouse on the southern Atlantic coast. The name Tybee came from a Native American word for salt."

At the Visitor Information Center, we picked up some brochures.

"Get ready for our workout, Mabel. We are going to climb all 178 steps and take pictures at the top of the lighthouse," Lili said.

"So, we can go inside the lighthouse?" I asked, looking down at my sandals and Lili's walking shoes. I really needed to go shopping.

"You can and you will," Bob said. "The lighthouse is the oldest and tallest lighthouse in Georgia."

It took some time, but we made it to the top of the lighthouse, and it was well worth the effort. The bird's-eye view was spectacular. We could see massive ships navigating the Savannah River. There even was a wedding taking place on the beach. I took a ton of pictures, and later, we had lunch on the island while admiring the beauty of Tybee. It was just the break we needed from the chaos at the campground.

When we returned to the campground, we stopped in the office and found out that the FBI had left, and so had Josh and Peggy. Bob reported she was texting that they were almost to Ashville.

"I'll let her have the last word, or otherwise she will continue to text," Bob said.

Since we had a big lunch and had brought back doggie bags, we decided to stay in and call it an early evening.

"We'll talk to people in the campground tomorrow and then go visit Selma," Lili said as we parted for the night.

Just as I was about to doze off, I heard Irma's voice, "I'm coming along tomorrow."

I sat up and looked at my roommate. She was wearing a long pink satin nightgown, and she had on pink and gold sequined slippers with a fuzzy pink pom. It was from a bygone era.

"I'm still looking for Little Stella." Irma said as she floated around my camper in her vintage lounge wear. "I'm beginning to wonder if she made it out of purgatory. We don't exactly get word when someone leaves. They check in, but eventually, they check out."

I yawned. It had been a busy day.

"Night, Irma. See you tomorrow."

"Good night."

I heard an echo from somewhere across the shore as my Aunt Sadie used to call the great beyond.

CHAPTER 29

Lili and I were up. Had our coffee and we were out on our walk and were planning our day.

"So, we're just going to walk around the campground and knock on camper doors?"

Lili had turned on her *I'm in charge here* mode. I hadn't seen this for a while, since our last book club meeting.

"We'll walk around the campground. Most of the campers sit outside and have coffee. Engage them in casual conversation. You know what I mean, small talk."

"I do. But I'm not good at that."

"Your friend Irma is," Lili said with a grin on her face.

"That I am."

It was Irma, and I could see her walking alongside Lili and me. She was dressed in a hiking outfit, but more for a mountain, not the flats of Savannah. I just shook my head.

"Morning, Irma," Lili said.

"Morning, Lili."

"She says good morning."

"Irma, is there any way you can arrange for Lili to see you or at least hear you?"

"Nope, not my department."

I shook my head no in the direction of Lili, who continued to explain our marching orders.

"Those we miss on our walk; we'll catch by hanging out in the campground office. Here's our first interview."

I looked up ahead. I could see a couple sitting outside their Prevost RV.

"These people have money," I said to Lili. "I saw that rig at an RV show before I bought my camper. A Prevost has a million-dollar price tag. A lot of rock and country stars travel in one when they are on tour. We'll see plenty in Nashville—if we ever get there."

"Howdy," Lili said as we stopped in front of their impressive rig.

"Morning," they said in unison. They looked to be middle age, but like Peg and Josh, serious and bland.

"Nice rig," I said, sounding stupid. They just smiled and took a sip of whatever they were drinking.

"Ask them if they are roadies," Irma said. "You are as engaging as a wasp stuck on a fly trap."

"You folks roadies?" Lili asked with a smile. I looked her way. She and Irma were on the same wavelength. The husband made a smirk, but the wife smiled and opened up.

"No, a lot of people ask us that question." She stood up and came over to join us. "My name is Joyce, and this is my husband, Frank. Joyce remained standing next to Lili and me. Frank just nodded and picked up a newspaper and started reading. The Wall Street Journal.

"Hope my stocks are doing well," I said to Frank.

"Me too," he said. "Otherwise, we may have to sell this rig and head home to Wyoming."

"Wyoming? Ask him if he lives near Laramie," Irma said. "Walt is the sheriff of a small town nearby."

I looked over at Lili, who knew Irma was talking to me.

"What part of Wyoming?" I said. I watched Irma as she sat down in the empty chair next to Frank.

"A small town outside of Laramie. You probably never heard of it."

"Ask her if she knows Sheriff Walt Long!" Irma jumped up and was back in my ear. "She might know Walt."

"My parents left me a ranch when they passed. We own it free and clear. It's between Laramie and Cheyenne. We plan to settle down there once we finish traveling around the country."

Irma was standing very close to Joyce. As if by standing that close, she could read her mind.

"You don't happen to know a sheriff by the name of Walter Long, do you?"

"No, I don't. But a lot of small towns have sheriffs who, along with their deputies, are the only police for miles around. I remember that from growing up in Wyoming."

"Dang," Irma said.

I could see a look of disappointment on her face that made me sad for her and her predicament in the after-life. I made a mental note to talk to Bob about visiting the town where her son lives so she could see him one more time. That's providing she's still stuck in my camper when we make it that far.

"So, what do you think of the murder that took place in our campground?" Lili jumped right in when the opportunity presented itself.

"What murder?"

Whoops. That didn't go too well, I thought as Lili went over the details of Oscar's murder.

"Really," Joyce said. "Goodness, Frank, did you hear that? Someone was murdered right here in this campground. Maybe we should think about moving out?"

"No, no," I said. "This is probably the safest campground around now, with the local police and the FBI in the campground."

Both Frank and Joyce gave Lili and me the deer in the headlights look.

"FBI?" Frank said.

"They didn't talk to you?"

"No. We've just got back. Rented a car and went off antique hunting for a few days. As a retired judge, I know the FBI doesn't show up for nothing."

"They were talking to everyone in the campground about the murder."

"About a local murder?" Frank said firmly. "Whoever was murdered must have connections to a federal case."

"Oh. Is that how it works?"

"Well, they packed up and left," Lili added. "The FBI, I mean."

"Good," Frank stuck his nose back in the Wall Street Journal. Joyce took that as her cue to sit down next to Frank.

"Well, nice talking to you," Lili said, as we moved on down the lane.

Irma walked in front of us. She turned and gave me a look. "Neither one of you would have made it in my business." With that she spoofed off."

"What did she say?" Lili asked.

"At our age, it's not important. That didn't go that well."

"Let's keep moving. Anyhoo, they were a little strange. Most people traveling are a little more social."

"They sure weren't. Joyce started to warm up until we mentioned the murder," I noted.

"Let's talk to Gordy." Lili waved to a man up ahead. I could see he was getting up to come talk to us.

"Why? He and Kari show up right at happy hour and drink your booze and stay for dinner. Not sure they have anything to add to what happened?"

"Be patient, Mabel."

"Hey Gordy, how are you and Kari doing?" Lili said as we approached him.

Gordy had on a T-shirt from Tybee Island and a pair of Hawaiian shorts and dark knee-high socks. He looked like he lived in one of those senior enclaves in Florida. The kind Tim Dorsey writes about in his Serge Storms series. He was just missing the golf cart.

"Well, my arthritis is acting up, and so is Kari's bursitis."

I gave Lili the *see I told you so look.* If they had anything to add, it would be after we spent ten minutes hearing about their ailments. Gordy and Kari were way past traveling on the road. In fact, they lived in Atlanta and just getting here was a big trek for them.

"Try some whiskey," I said and got a look from Lili. "I'm sure Lili has some back at her camper."

"Tried it," Gordy said, moving a little closer since he was hard of hearing and didn't like wearing his hearing aid.

"And?" I said loud enough so he could hear me or read my lips.

"Kari fell the last time we self-medicated. A broken hip at our age is a trip to the snake pit. Might be time to move to Chicago, where our son lives."

"Chicago, I don't know. I think I'd stick to the whiskey," I said to Gordy, who either didn't hear me or chose to ignore me.

"So, they arrested that nice lady who works in the campground office, what's her name?" Gordy was talking loud enough so everyone in the campground dead or alive could hear us.

"Selma," Lili said.

"Say that again?" Gordy was cupping his good ear like a bullhorn and pointing it toward us like it would help.

"Selma," I said louder than needed.

"Oh. Selma. Nice lady."

Lili and I waited patiently to see if Gordy had anything useful to add.

"She told me all about her son, who is in the military. Same branch as I served."

"Thank you for your service," Lili said.

"Did the police talk to you?" I asked. You need to keep Gordy focused.

"Yeah, they were here talking to everyone. I told them we met the man who was murdered one evening at happy hour at your camper. Other than that, we didn't know him. They must have scared some folks off. After the cops left us, we got a knock on our door from the driver of the Bluebird motorhome that was parked next to us. He asked me what was going on. I told him someone in the campground was murdered. Guess the cops spooked them good. Went right back, and they headed out in the next hour."

"Who were they?" I asked loud enough so he could hear me. "In the Bluebird?"

"Didn't say, seemed odd, two foreign guys in business suits with a driver. Just between us, I could have sworn I saw the guy who was murdered talking to them one evening. Yeah, I'm pretty sure he was here one evening talking to them."

"Did you mention that to the police," I asked.

"Nah, I forgot, but I will if I see them again."

We thanked Gordy and said we would see them later and continued our trek around the campground.

"I wonder who was in the Bluebird," I asked.

"Not sure, but it sounds like they took off as soon as they heard about the cops."

"I'm not so sure his eyesight is any better than his hearing."

We made our way to a section of the campground we had not been to before. I didn't see any campers up ahead, mostly tents and a few pop-up campers.

"Tents," I said to Lili.

"Yeah, people call it primitive camping. It attracts young folks and bikers passing through minimal amenities. You camp in a remote location, and you fend for yourself."

"No one's around?" I said as we started our walk through this part of the campground.

"Probably not up yet. You'll see more primitive camping in the National Forests as we make our way west.

"Hold it right there."

Lili and I stopped dead in our tracks. A guy was standing next to a pop-up camper and an old pickup. He was bald and he was lean and muscular. He didn't look friendly. We might have woken him up. He was holding a long rifle. It wasn't pointed at us, but I had a feeling he kept it loaded.

"Whoa, hi there," I said. "We're campers. We're just out for a walk."

"Well, ladies, no offense, but I suggest you take your walk back where you came from."

"Sure," I said and was turning around quickly, but not Lili. She had decided to engage this dude in conversation.

"We didn't mean any harm. Why the long rifle? Looks like something my dad used to hunt with back in Louisiana."

"I keep it for protection," he said as we watched him place the rifle inside his truck on a gun rack. "Sorry if I scared you two ladies, but in case you didn't know, there's been a murder in this campground. There have been cops and FBI everywhere. May have to pick up and move. The campground is going downhill."

"My name's Lili and this is Mabel."

"My name's none of your business. No offense."

"No offense taken," I said and smiled. "Maybe we should go, Lili. Leave this gentleman to his business or whatever."

I guessed he was a small-time drug dealer. I was sure there were a lot of buyers here in the primitive camping zone.

"Yeah, cops everywhere. Have they been back here to talk to you?" Lili said to Mr. None-of-Your-Business.

"Yup, two locals and then two feds. Talking to everyone, but I think they found a lot of people were not home."

As he leaned next to his truck, he lifted out a cane. "I'm a veteran. Staying here since it's not too far from my doctors at the VA."

"Thank you for your service," both Lili and I said.

"The name's Daryl."

We shook hands. He had a strong grip. "What are you ladies doing back here? Hiking trail doesn't lead back here."

"We thought we'd go a new way. See what's back here," I said to Daryl, who wasn't buying my story.

"The man murdered was traveling with us," Lili said. "To be completely honest, we were out talking to folks to see if they saw anything the cops might have missed. They arrested our friend Selma, who works in the campground office. Do you know her?"

"Selma? Are you kidding me? She was arrested for that murder. She wouldn't hurt a flea. She always gives me a couple extra days to come up with the rent. In turn, I look out for suspicious stuff. Sort of informal security," Daryl said as he nodded his head at the long rifle sitting in the gun rack.

"Did you see anything?" I asked, picking up on Daryl's reluctance to talk to cops. "Maybe we could get it to the police without involving you?"

"Might help Selma," Lili said. We could see Daryl was thinking it over. We waited.

"Look, you keep me out of this, but I did see something the night that guy was killed. Maybe you can get it to the cops without involving me, especially if it helps Selma. Those cops! They grab somebody as quick as they can and then stop investigating. Good people get caught in the cross hairs."

"Sure," Lili said. "My husband's a retired homicide detective. I'll make sure he keeps you out of it. He can talk to the officers handling the investigation."

"I saw two guys carrying something heavy. Wrapped up in a tarp."

"A tarp? Did you see what it was," I said.

"Just between us, my guess is a body."

"You need to tell the police," I said and then realized by Daryl's reaction that it was the wrong thing to say.

"No, I don't, and after today, I'm out of here. This place is getting too noisy and nosy for my tastes. But I'll tell you what I'll do," he said as he reached for his shirt pocket and pulled out his cell phone.

"I'll text you this picture I snapped that night. There was a full moon. A little hard to see, but you can make out the two guys and what they were carrying. They walked right past my campsite. I was out doing my business."

Lili and I took a look at the photo, and it showed two men carrying something wrapped up in a tarp. It looked heavy.

"What's your number?"

He was looking at me, but Lili got out her cell. I watched as he texted the photo.

"Done," he said. "I deleted the photo and your number."

As we walked away, we turned back and saw that he was putting chairs and an old bike in his pickup.

"Looks like he's packing up. I'll show this to Bob. Let's go visit Selma at the jailhouse."

"Yeah, he'll probably be out of here by this afternoon and we won't see him again."

CHAPTER 30

Selma looked drawn, and both Lili and I could see she had lost weight.

"Are you eating?" Lili asked.

"I seemed to have lost my appetite. It might have something to do with being arrested for Oscar's murder. Plus, the food here stinks."

"I can attest to that," Irma said. "Jailhouse food stinks."

Selma was behind a glass window and didn't use the phone on the wall to talk to us. We could hear her fine. No one else was in the visitor's room, and the guard left us alone.

"Taking a smoke break," Selma said.

"So other than the food are they treating you okay?" I asked.

"Oh sure, I know most of the local cops from Earl's. The FBI wants me transferred to a state penitentiary. The locals are doing their best to stall the feds because they know it is a rough place. I need a lawyer to get me out of here on bail, or at least stop the Feds from sending me away. My son can put up the money. He still has the lottery money I gave him. Thank God."

We both could see the fear in her eyes.

"He's deployed overseas and telling them that his mother is in jail for murder doesn't exactly qualify as a good reason to ask for leave. He has a friend in Atlanta who is a lawyer and is working on it but he's not a criminal lawyer."

Lili looked over at me.

"My daughter Meg is a criminal lawyer. Well, she was before she took on a bigger job as a stay-at-home mom. She's in New York. Let me call her and talk to her. See what she can do."

Lili nodded her head in agreement.

"I don't have much money left."

"Don't worry about that right now. I'll talk to Meg about representing you pro bono. My grandson is a teenager now and Meg was just telling me that she wanted to get back to work. She's a great defense lawyer."

"Trust me, I didn't kill Oscar. I thought about it a lot, but I could never do it, even though the guy was a rat."

"Ask her about the gun," Irma said. She was standing right next to Selma. "Come on, we don't have all day."

"Selma, can you tell us about the gun they found next to Oscar's body? They say it's yours?"

"That's what they told me when they arrested me. I don't know how it got there. Earl kept a gun behind the bar. When it was stolen I brought in mine until he replaced it. He had just fired someone, and he figured he stole it. I always check the gun when I start my shift, and when I end my shift. I got to work, checked for the gun, and it was gone. It had been there the night before."

"What day was that?" I asked.

Selma sat there with a serious look on her face. "It was the day I was arrested for his murder."

"So, your gun was under the bar the night Oscar disappeared?"

"Yes, I left early that night, but I still checked."

While we let that sink in, rapid-fire Irma moved on with her questioning.

"Ask her about the Barracuda and their last visit."

"So, the Barracuda came by to visit you recently?" I continued as Irma gave me a nod of approval and thumbs up.

"Yeah, she stopped by to tell me she and Oscar were getting divorced and wanted to know if I had hooked up with him....again."

Selma rubbed her forehead.

"It's giving me a headache just thinking about it. That woman had Oscar killed. I'm sure of it. Now she's trying to frame me."

"Selma, have they determined if your gun was the murder weapon?" Lili asked.

"No, they're still working on it. That's why I need a good criminal lawyer to make sure nothing falls through the cracks."

"We met a guy out back in the primitive camping area. He greeted us with his long rifle. Do you know him?" Lili asked.

"Oh, that's Daryl. He lives there on and off. He keeps an eye out on that section of the campground, so we list him as a volunteer. Like me."

Selma paused for a moment, took a deep breath, and looked down at the floor.

"He's messed up from his time in Vietnam. Another *Fortunate Son* like my husband, who never came back and never got to meet his son."

"I'm sorry, Selma," I said.

Selma refocused on me and asked, "Is Daryl causing trouble?"

"No, but he told us that he saw something the night Oscar was murdered."

"He did? What?"

"Two men carrying something wrapped in a tarp," Lili said.

"Did he tell the police?"

"No, he seems to have an aversion to them," Lili said.

"Damn. Anyway, they wouldn't believe him. He's been busted for possession of drugs and for dealing. Poor guy has PTSD issues. That section where Daryl lives backs up to the place where they found Oscar's body."

Lili got out her phone and held it up so Selma could see the photo.

"Daryl took this the night he saw two men walking past his campsite carrying something in a tarp," I said.

"Did you show that to the cops or those FBI guys?" Selma said studying the picture.

"I'd like to suggest we hold off showing it to law enforcement until I've had a chance to talk to my daughter about representing you. We might want to give it to her first."

"Why?" Selma asked.

"Cops look at the facts like looking at a black-and-white photo. I know I'm married to a cop," Lili said.

"Lawyers, on the other hand, look for the gray in a photo. Might cast doubt on that black-and-white version. Not everything is as it appears to be. Always some gray, my daughter has told me."

"Mabel, Lili, thank you both. I'm forever grateful. I just want this nightmare to be over."

On the other side of the glass, Irma gave her a virtual hug. Our time was up, and we watched the guard escort Selma back to her cell. She smiled and waved goodbye. She now had a flicker of hope in her eyes instead of total despair.

CHAPTER 31

Lili and I returned to my camper. Selma wasn't the only one with a headache. Mine was banging away, and it didn't help to find Irma sitting on the couch waiting for me. I must have groaned because Lili asked if Irma was there.

"She's on the couch."

"Tell Lili I said hello and then call Meg."

"She says hello. She wants me to call Meg."

"Hello, Irma," Lili said. "I agree. It's time to call Meg."

"Meg will give me a sermon about getting involved in a murder. You know how she feels about my camper and this trip. Yeah, that will go over like a lead balloon."

"Just start by asking for her opinion. Make it hypothetical."

"Meg was a particularly good criminal lawyer. That's her element. She'll get it out of me."

"Call her," Lili said. "Selma doesn't have a lot of time, and I don't trust the FBI. They have a stick in this fire. You heard what Selma said. They want to move her to the state pen. That makes her situation much more complicated."

After Lili left and Irma popped out to find a new outfit, I took two aspirins and sat down and closed my eyes. I was just getting the courage to call Meg when she called me. For once, I didn't mind that she had gotten in the habit of calling every day to check on me. We chatted for a minute, and I assured her all was well. Then I decided to just to spill my guts and told her about Selma and the murder.

"What! Mother, what have you gotten yourself mixed up in? Driving that trailer was bad enough. Now a murder! I told you…"

Once she finished scolding me, I gave her the Cliff's Notes version of the case against Selma.

"Wow," Meg said. "That's quite a story for a sleepy campground in Georgia."

"They've told us to not leave town. One of the couples in the group got permission to leave. Guess they can't really hold us."

"No, they can't. But if they do want to keep you, they can arrest you. Who has talked to you—the police?"

"Well, yes, and the FBI."

"The FBI? Mother, really, you should have called me. Why is the FBI involved? That would make it more than a crime of passion. If they are involved, it's connected to a federal matter. I never trusted the FBI. They lie," she said. "I'm not saying that lawyers don't lie, but the FBI often lies to make a case. That's why I'll never go back to the prosecutor's office. They all go to the same church."

"Well, Oscar, the guy who was murdered, may have gotten himself involved with a group of shady people. He had a gambling problem."

"You mean the mob?"

"Seems that way, from Las Vegas where he liked to go to gamble."

"I hope your friend Selma has a good lawyer. It sounds like she is going to need one. The FBI will let her hang for this if it has something to do with a mob or a cartel case. Did you see any DEA agents?"

"No, but then they all look alike. Military crew cuts, it's hard to tell. Do they wear those jackets with big lettering on the back?"

I heard my daughter take a deep breath. Irma popped in as I was talking. I watched her dart around my camper. She was getting animated. Like a cartoon character.

"Tell her," Irma said. "We need her to stall Selma's transfer to the state pen. That will give us time to figure out who killed Oscar. I'd like to get to the bottom of this before I get called into a parole hearing with Saint Peter."

I just shook my head and whispered. "I'm getting to that. I can't rush her."

"Mother, is someone there?"

"No, I was just thinking out loud. Look, Meg, I just know Selma is innocent."

"How do you know that? From what you've told me, they have her gun, and it was found next to the body. Evidence doesn't lie."

"Lili and I think she's being framed. It was either a mob hit or his wife, Eleanor, whose nickname is the Barracuda. She had a good reason to kill Oscar, he asked for a divorce and she found out he was stashing money in offshore accounts."

"Really, Mother, you and dear Lili need to stay out of this. Let the police do their work. Haven't you learned from all the movies you watch that it's not a good idea to get tangled up with the mob?"

It was all I could do to not bite my tongue in two, and Irma was not helping zipping around my camper like the Roadrunner.

"If she were my client, we'd be talking a plea deal."

Irma stopped dead in her tracks, "Now, ask her now."

Well, I knew I couldn't tell my daughter that a ghost, by the name of Irma, who haunts my camper, and I had to figure out who the murderer was so that she can get some time lopped off her sentence in purgatory. So, I tried the next best thing, manipulation. I begged her as her mother.

"Meg, can you help her? She has nobody, I believe her, and so does Lili. She needs a good lawyer, someone like you. Lili's husband thinks that for reasons of their own, the FBI is pushing the local cops to transfer her to the state pen. Her son can't help. He's in military and deployed. A lawyer friend of his is helping, but he's not a criminal lawyer. You said you wanted to get back into law. Just see if you could get her transfer stalled so she can stay here in Savannah."

"I'm not a lawyer in Georgia."

"She's thinking it over," Irma said, clapping her hands. "Mentioning the FBI helped."

"Well, would Florida be close enough?"

"Why?"

I knew my daughter had kept her license to practice law in both New York and Florida, where they had their condo.

"I can call my friend Louie, and he can file whatever paperwork you lawyers file for this kind of thing. You remember him. You met him."

"Isn't he the lawyer who operates out of a limo? The big Cadillac with a bar in the back? Picked us up at the airport a couple of times?"

"Yeah, but Louie's got an office now. It's in Boca Vista. A lot of the women you met at the book club use him. Plus, you remember Bob, Lili's husband, he just got his private eye license, and he is going to do work for him. Business is picking up."

"I liked the guy. He was… colorful. He told me all about his practice in Miami on one of those airport trips."

Irma was now making the sign of the cross and thanking all the saints above.

"He's a good lawyer, Meg. But not as good as you when it comes to murder and stuff like that. Please, will you help Selma?"

I could almost hear my daughter's brain working. She wanted to get back into law but hadn't made up her mind yet. This might be what she needed. Then, just like she did at the book club, she surprised me.

"Okay. I'll do it. Now, Mom, I want you to listen to me."

"I'm listening," I said, and so was Irma, who had her ear right up next to my cell. "Can I put you on speaker? I think the connection is a little spotty." I put her on speaker and then she made her closing argument.

"I'll do this on several conditions," Meg said. I rolled my eyes at Irma. Well, she was a darn good lawyer.

"You need to stay out of this. I'll call your friend Louie. He can file the paperwork, so I can come on board as an associate. Then I'll call Selma and talk to her. She'll need to agree to my representation."

"Oh, she will. I told her I would talk to you and I was confident you would do it." Whoops, I whispered to Irma, who was shaking her head and throwing her arms up in the air.

"Yeah, I thought as much," Meg said. I kept quiet. "I'll start by stalling her transfer. I still have a few contacts with the FBI. Female agents and moms like me. We keep in touch on social media. I want to find out what the FBI's connection is with this murder before I talk to Selma," Meg said, and for the first time in a very long time, I heard something like excitement in her voice. "Like I said, I don't trust them."

"Thank you, Meg."

"I'm not done. There is another condition."

I whispered to Irma. "Damn, here it comes."

"What's that?" I asked sweetly.

"I want you to reconsider this whole camping trip. You've had a nice trip to Savannah. Go on to Nashville, visit the national parks and then when you return, I'd like you to think about moving back to Long Island. I've picked out some nice senior living locations nearby. You can fly up once you are back. We have the condo in Florida if you want to go back for the winter."

"No way," I whispered to Irma.

"Just go along," Irma said.

I couldn't believe she was now dressed like a referee in a football game.

"Okay, Meg," I said, closing my eyes and shaking my head and crossing my fingers. "I'll give it some serious thought. Thank you."

When I was off the phone with Meg, who apparently had learned some manipulation tricks from her mother, I texted her Louie's number and Bob's in case they needed his private eye skills. I figured she'd call Louie and bring him up to speed. He'd be calling me soon enough. I just didn't need to talk to another person who would be worrying about me or trying to stick me in a retirement home.

"No way in hell, Irma, will I move back to Long Island. I don't want to go back to that life. I like my new life."

"The sooner we figure out who murdered Oscar, the sooner you can head to Nashville, and the sooner I can get out of here," Irma said. "I hope this will do it. Fix yourself a drink and me one too. I'll do you a big favor and switch to vodka."

CHAPTER 32

We decided to head to Earl's to catch Joe with the band. "I'll invite the Barracuda. Let's see if she shows." I sent her a text. She had checked into the hotel close to Earl's Bar. When we walked in, we saw Earl was behind the bar with a new bartender.

"I had too Selma might not be coming back anytime soon. Whenever she does, her job will be waiting for her."

The three of us found a table where we could see who came into the bar. I put my phone on silent since the texts from Louie and Meg were blowing up my phone. He had called earlier, and we talked.

"I'm worried about you, Mabel. I heard you got yourself mixed up in a murder investigation. I just got off the phone with your daughter Meg; it seems she is coming to work for me."

I spent some time with Louie putting out that fire. I suspect he had seen a murder or two in his prior life as a lawyer in Miami. Louie was level-headed, and I liked his calmness. He would be good for Meg. He had filed the paperwork, bringing her on board as a lawyer with his firm. He said that part was easy since she had a license in Florida and New York, and somehow, all that will allow her to represent Selma in Georgia. Louie went on with the legal jargon, but it was over my head and way above my pay grade.

"That's great, Louie," I must have repeated a bunch of times. Meg had called me too.

"I talked to Selma."

She had become Selma's attorney of record. Any move to transfer her to a state penitentiary would have to go through Meg, and that wouldn't happen without a fight.

I looked down at another group text from Louie and Meg. They were putting their heads together. It seems like the collaboration was working. I texted back I would call tomorrow. I took a swig of my Cosmo.

"Your daughter Meg called me earlier," Bob said.

I hadn't had a chance to talk to Bob. It was all happening fast.

"I asked her to represent Selma. She needed a good criminal lawyer. The FBI was getting ready to ship her out. Meg will be able to stall the transfer."

"I also heard from Louie. It seems like Meg is now working with his firm. He might need me on board as a private eye for this case. He wanted to know how you got yourself involved in a murder, the both of you. He's worried that you and Lili will go all gangbusters. Like a Thelma and Louise tag team."

"What did you tell them?"

"Just the backstory," Bob said while he took a sip of his beer. "Meg assured me that Thelma and Louise would stay clear of this murder investigation."

Lili and I just smiled. Joe had arrived and was setting up the stage. He sent over a round of drinks and joined us.

"What's new?" Joe asked.

"Lili and I paid Selma a visit at the jailhouse. The FBI was pushing to transfer her to a state penitentiary. I talked to my daughter Meg, and she agreed to help stall the transfer."

"That's great. I'll be sure to let her son know that. He's been calling me for updates. He'll be relieved."

"Have you seen the Barracuda?" Bob asked Joe.

"Actually, I have. That's what I wanted to tell you. She's been dropping by the bar and spending time with Earl."

"She has?" I said.

"Maybe Oscar's murder has brought them closer," Lili said.

"That could be. They seemed to be deep in conversation."

"How deep?" I asked.

"Deep."

"Well, she has no one to turn to, now that they are both widows," Lili said.

"Keep an eye on her," Bob said.

"I will, but speak of the devil," Joe nodded his head toward the front door.

The Barracuda walked up to the bar and said something to the new bartender. She didn't see us at first, but when she did, she made a beeline to our table.

"Evening folks."

She was dressed like she was going out later. Lili and I recognized the look. We call it the 'I'm available, come on over here and talk to me' look. Joe excused himself, and the Barracuda took his seat. A waitress came by for our drink order. "Vodka Martini," the Barracuda said. "Grey Goose. Not that cheap stuff."

She turned her attention to us. "Anything new with that woman who murdered Oscar?" She didn't waste time and was looking directly at Bob for answers.

"The FBI may have a lead on those two guys Oscar left with the night of his murder," Bob said.

Lili and I looked at him. I was wondering where he was going with this, but the Barracuda was about to tell us.

"The FBI needs to get their noses out of this murder investigation. Those two were here to talk to Oscar about his gambling debts. They had no reason to kill him. They were muscle sent here to collect from Oscar. He usually found a way to pay or get more time. I told all this to the feds. Selma murdered him. My God, her gun was found right next to him, and the bullet matched."

"How do you know that?" Bob asked.

The Barracudas' eyes darted around the room and she leaned in.

"Earl told me."

"How did he find out?"

"Don't know. You'll have to ask him. He's been in Savannah a long time, and he's friendly with the local cops. They all hang out here. He may have heard it from them. Just came by to say hello."

The Barracuda picked up her Vodka Martini and gulped it down before making her way to the ladies' room.

"Looks like she's got a hot date," I said.

"I spoke with Tom and Jerry this afternoon," Bob said. "I told them I've been hired as a private investigator by the law firm representing Selma. I asked them if the autopsy report was back. That's the only way to know if the bullet that killed Oscar matched Selma's gun."

"What did they say," I asked.

"Not yet."

"That's odd. How would Earl get that information if Tom and Jerry didn't have it?"

"He wouldn't," Bob said. "However, like she said, Earl's been here a long time. He may know someone in the coroner's office. I'll ask Earl tonight if I get the chance."

We looked over at the bar and I could see Earl talking to his customers with the new bartender. It would be hard to replace Selma.

"I'll be right back," Bob said.

We watched as Bob made his way to the bar. Within a few minutes, he was talking to Earl. The conversation was short. Bob headed back our way.

"What happened?" Lili asked when Bob sat down.

"He said he never told the Barracuda any such thing. He said she's just anxious to collect on Oscar's life insurance policy and is spreading rumors. Called her a name I won't repeat."

"Does it rhyme with stitch?" I said.

"Life insurance," Lili said. "I wonder how much."

"Don't know. I'll look into it after I talk with Meg," Bob said. "It's one more thing to add to the list, so the police start taking a closer look at the Barracuda as a suspect. That'll take the heat off Selma."

"Roger that," I said.

I looked over at Lili, and she seemed to read my mind. She reached down and got out her cell phone.

"Bob, there's something you need to know," Bob looked at Lili and then me.

"I'm listening, ladies."

Lili handed her cell to Bob, and he looked at the picture.

"Who is this? Or should I say what is this?"

"When Mabel and I were out walking the other day, we wandered around and we met this guy by the name of Daryl. He knew Selma, and it sounded like they were friends. She's helped him out when he was a few days short on the rent. In return, he's kept an eye out on the back section of the campground, where they have tents, pop-ups, and bikers," Lili said and paused so Bob could digest what she was about to tell him. "He was shy about talking to the police. But he gave us this picture he took on his cell the night Oscar was murdered. There was a full moon, and he was standing next to his camper when he saw two guys in suits walk by carrying something wrapped up in a tarp."

"A tarp?" Bob said as he took Lili's cell and stared closely at the picture.

"Yeah, probably one of those you see after a hurricane has made landfall," I said for no good reason at all.

"So, what else did Daryl tell you two sleuths?"

"He thought it looked like it was a body," I said. "That's why he snapped that photo."

"I can't see much. I can't make out a face. But yeah, it could be a body rolled up in that tarp."

"The spot where they found Oscar's body is not far from Daryl's campsite."

"Lili, text me that photo and then delete it from your cell, please."

I watched as Lili did as Bob requested.

"Who else knows about this?"

"I told Meg," I said.

Bob looked at us and took a deep breath.

"I'll take this up with Meg. In the meantime, you're both off the case, got that?"

"Yes, Bob," once again we answered in unison.

Lili looked at me and smiled. He didn't tell me to delete it off my cell, so we were safe there. We watched as the Barracuda came out of the ladies' room and joined a man sitting at the bar. He finished his drink; they got up and left the bar together.

"I wonder who that was," I said as Joe returned to our table.

"Did you just see who left with the Barracuda?" Bob asked Joe.

"Yes, sir."

"Do you recognize him?"

"Well, I can't swear on it, but he sure looks like one of the men who were here the other night talking to Oscar."

"The night he was murdered?" Lili asked.

"Yes. He looks a lot like the guy who was here with the one who looks like Willie Nelson."

Joe went back up to do another set with his band, and while Lili and Bob were chatting Irma arrived and sat down next to me. I tried to make eye contact so that she could read my mind: "Not now. Get lost."

"You are going to have to talk to your ex."

"No," I said discreetly to Irma.

"I'm afraid so, Mabel, afraid so."

"I have a better idea," I said to the ghost. "Later."

CHAPTER 33

On our way back to the campground, I was thinking of making a quick trip back to Boca Vista to peek inside my safe deposit box. Bob made his way into the camper, and I pulled Lili aside.

"I need to make a quick trip home."

"You do?"

"I need to look in my safe deposit box."

Lili knew all about the saga of the safe deposit box. "Why?"

"It has to do with what Oscar said to me the night he sat next to me at dinner. When he was a lot younger, he got mixed up with the wrong crowd."

"What does that have to do with the box?"

"He said he thought he had seen some ghosts, and he wanted me to ask Jack about someone he called Willie Nelson. I really don't want to ask Jack, to be honest."

"Okay. Bob is spending some time with Joe tomorrow. They're going to work on his camper."

"Good. We'll leave early, and we should be back by happy hour."

CHAPTER 34

Lili and I left bright and early the next morning. She decided to tell Bob I needed to make a quick trip home.

"You know my opinion about lies. They aren't worth the trouble. Truth is always easier."

"Did he buy it?"

"Not sure, but the good news is that he didn't ask any questions. I told him I'd text along the way."

We headed out, and no sooner had we got on I-95 than I looked in the rear-view mirror and there was Irma. Today, she was dressed like a showgirl. She looked like something from an old 1940s movie, including the big head-dress which was sticking through the roof of my truck. I tried to keep my eyes on the road.

"We have company."

"Hey, Irma."

"Howdy gals," and then she was gone.

"She just took off—dressed like a showgirl—looking like she was in one of those old Fred Astaire and Ginger Rogers movies."

Traffic was light as we made our way to Boca Vista.

"When was the last time you looked in that box?"

I kept looking in the rear-view mirror, but so far, no Irma.

"After the divorce when I moved to Florida. When I opened the safe deposit box in Boca Vista, I looked. There's just an envelope with a bunch of old pictures. There's only one photo that Jack is really concerned about."

Lili wasn't one to pry, so I didn't share that the picture that concerned Jack was the current governor of Florida. When we got to the bank I parked, and we took a minute to stretch our legs. It was a small branch office of a well-known bank with offices all over Florida and east coast.

"Mrs. Gold, how are you?" I recognized the bank manager as he greeted us.

"Hello. I'm just here to check on my safe deposit box. This is my good friend Lili Young."

"My pleasure, Mrs. Young," he said as he shook Lili's hand and escorted us into a small room lined top to bottom with safe deposit boxes. It was about the size of a walk-in closet. There was a table in the middle.

Only people my age still had safe deposit boxes. I asked Bianca one time if she had one, and she looked at me with that look you get from young people. They don't even walk into a bank, let alone have a safe deposit box.

"I was going to call you, Mrs. Gold," the bank manager said.

"You're not closing the safe deposit boxes, are you?"

"No, no, although this bank is one of only a handful that still offers safe deposit boxes. The FBI was in here asking questions."

"They were?"

The manager described the two agents from Savannah. Obviously, Lt. Dan and his side-kick Agent Bill. Lili gave me a knowing look.

"Actually, we've met them. They are looking into an FBI investigation in Savannah at the campground we're staying at. Did they say what they wanted?"

"No. They asked questions, but it was more about your ex-husband."

"I see."

I handed the manager my key, and he used it and his key to open the tiny door and pulled out a steel box that he placed on the table. After asking me if I needed anything else, he promised he'd call me if they came back.

As soon as we were alone, Lili asked, "Why were they here?"

"Who knows with those two? It looks more and more like Oscar may have had dealings with the mob." I looked up, and there was Irma.

"Our friend is back."

Irma was still dressed like a show girl. She had on a pair of black stilettos.

"I wish you could see Irma's outfit. Loaded with sequins, and it's as bright as a Christmas tree. I might have to get out my sunglasses. Lili, I'm thinking it's probably not a good idea for you to see what's in the box. If it ever came down to it, I want you to be able to say you never saw the contents."

Lili nodded. "I'll go wait in the lobby and leave you and Irma alone."

"Here goes nothing."

I looked at the steel box. Like a slab in a morgue. I lifted the lid. There was the manila envelope. Irma was watching me, and for a change, she was quiet. I opened the envelope and took out a handful of photos and laid them out like a deck of cards on the table.

"These are really old, Irma."

"You can say that again. Polaroid cameras were popular back in the 1970s. We had them in the cat house."

I didn't ask anything further. Too much information, but I suspect her cat house had more than a few on hand.

"Most of these guys are dead, Irma. That is except for this one."

I held up two photos of the governor of Florida, one before and one after photo.

"Who is that guy?"

"His code name is Vito, like the godfather."

"Marlon Brando," Irma said. "Did you know that Marlon Brando wanted to make the godfather look like a bulldog, so he stuffed his cheeks for the audition?"

"So, you're a fan of the movies?"

"Oh, you could say that, Mabel. Remember what happens in Vegas, stays in Vegas."

"Right," I said. Didn't want to know about that either.

"Vito is the one that worries Jack and the reason he checks in with me each month. Now the governor is probably going to become our next senator. He was an accountant for the mob, years ago when Jack first opened his practice. I'm sure my mother-in-law, Big Stella, may she rest in peace, referred him to Jack."

I took a minute to shuffle through the old photos and placed them back in the envelope. "None of Oscar or Willie Nelson. A long time ago, Jack did shred a bunch of them. That was right about the time he started working for the feds."

"Let me look at that godfather one," Irma said.

I held them up so she could see them. She came really close and stared at them.

"You can put them back. I just wanted to make sure I didn't know the guy."

"Did you?"

"No. But I can spot evil when I see it, and that man is evil, Mabel, pure evil."

CHAPTER 35

I walked back to the lobby where Lili was waiting for me. Irma was nowhere to be seen.

"No, Oscar or Willie Nelson," I said as we left the bank and got in Thor for the drive back to Savannah.

"Now what? Run by your house?"

"Heavens no! I don't want to run into Louie just in case he's there checking on the house. He'd be worse than talking to Meg right now."

"Afraid you might have second thoughts about returning to your camper?"

"No, Lili! But I do want to make a quick stop. Then we'll hit the road and find a place for lunch. Ever been to the Hotel Florida? I know the bartender. His name is Ernie. I first met him when I moved to Boca Vista. He knows a lot of people. He introduced me to Louie. And he once worked for the feds."

"Bob has been there. A lot of law enforcement types hang out there, and a few spooks, too. Is he FBI?"

"Ernie tells everyone he's retired from Homeland Security. I asked Louie about that, and he told me that Homeland Security is code for government agencies buried very deep."

"Like CIA?"

"Yep, and some we probably never heard of."

As we pulled into a parking space at the tiki bar, I could see it was relatively quiet. We walked up to the thatch-roofed bar where Ernie, a tall man with long white hair tied in a ponytail, was joking around with two tourists.

I also saw Irma was waiting for us. She was sitting on a stool at the bar. She looked like a flower child with a peace symbol headband and flowers in her hair, which was long and straight. Just like mine used to be when I flattened it with my mother's iron. I sat down next to her with Lili on my other side. The minute Ernie saw me, his face lit up. After handing the tourists their drinks with little umbrellas, he walked down to us.

"I've been expecting you," Ernie said to me. Ernie extended his hand to Lili. "I'm Ernie. Any friend of Mabel's is a friend of mine."

"I'm Lili," she said.

I watched Irma extend her arm to Ernie. He looked her way for a split second. Good grief. Was he able to see her?

"Relax. He can't see me, Mabel, but I like this guy."

"Now, what can I get you, lovely ladies? It's on the house."

"Thank you Ernie we'll take a rain check on the drinks. We have a drive back to Savannah," I said.

Ernie brought us something non-alcoholic to drink and Lili and I took a few minutes to tell Ernie about our trip west and that I was here to check on a few things. This was the first I had been back to the bar since the night I met Ernie, and he introduced me to Louie.

"Your friend Louie is a frequent patron. So is your CPA, Mary Catherine Mahoney."

"Oh. Please say hello to MC for me. So, have you talked to Louie lately?" I looked around to make sure he wasn't going to show up here.

"The other night he talked about the murder at your campground and that your daughter was going to work with him."

"You haven't talked to my daughter Meg, have you?"

"No, not yet."

"Well, actually, I am glad he talked to you."

"Ask him about Oscar," Irma said.

I looked at her. "Shush," I said without thinking. Ernie gave me a look.

I watched as Irma walked over and gave Ernie an imaginary kiss. "He reminds me of my son."

"My husband, Bob is a retired homicide detective from LA. He is also retired military. Marines, you may have met him. He's been here for the camaraderie."

"Please thank him for his service, ma'am. I probably have met him. Yes, he would have a lot in common with the pirates that frequent this little bar."

"Have the FBI spoken to your husband, Lili? About the campground murder?"

"Yes, they have," Lili said.

"They had a few words with us too," I said.

"Well, they have been here and were asking me about your ex-husband, Dr. Jack Gold," Ernie said.

I just closed my eyes and took a deep breath.

"Is that what you meant when you said you were expecting me?"

"You might bring us that drink, Ernie," Lili said. "Make it a light Cosmo here for Mabel and I'll have sparkling water with lime."

"I just came from my bank, and they had been in there asking about Jack."

I had shared with Ernie the night we met that Jack was a plastic surgeon and that he did work for the feds after he shared with me that he was Special Forces and had retired from Homeland Security. There was something solid about Ernie. That if you were lost or in trouble, you would want him to come to your rescue. That was why I opened up to him that night about Jack. That and the several Cosmos.

"Would you just ask him?" Irma was now hollering in my ear. "Quick like a bunny. Remember, I'm not in your time zone. I don't have an unlimited visa to hang around."

"Did they ask you about a man by the name of Oscar Johnson?" I asked.

"You mean the man who was murdered in your campground?" Ernie nodded his head.

"Yes. Well, let's just say he might have been involved with some of the same people who were patients of my ex-husband, many years ago."

"Well, that might explain why the FBI was asking about your ex."

"It might be a little more complicated than that," I said.

Ernie was silent, but something told me he already knew the answer but wanted to hear it from me.

"So, Ernie did you know Oscar? He was retired military, a high-ranking officer."

"Let's just say I knew of him, and yes, he was a very high-ranking officer."

"Ask him if the mob was after him," Irma said in my ear like I was deaf, but Lili beat me to the punch.

"Do you know if he had ties to the mob? My husband talked with some of his associates, and they told him that he had some gambling problems with the casinos out in Vegas."

Ernie closed his eyes for a moment.

"What?" I said

"Déjà vu, you remind me of MC and the many times she sat right where you are and asked for my help. Only that usually involved terrorist plots. Okay, I want you both to listen."

Ernie looked around, and then he looked right at Irma. Maybe he could see her. After all, he was a spook.

"Oscar was involved with some serious made guys out of Vegas. He owed them a lot of money. You might say that they turned his bill over to a collection agency."

"He means a hit man," Irma said. "Ask him about Willie Nelson."

"Did that collection agency have someone working for them who looked like Willie Nelson?"

"He *is* the collection agency."

"Good grief." I finished my Cosmo.

"They have arrested a woman by the name of Selma. We think she is being set up for the murder," Lili said.

"Maybe by Oscar's wife, whom he called the Barracuda," I said.

"The Barracuda?" Ernie smiled

"It was his pet name for her. We think he was about to leave the country—without her."

"My husband is doing some PI work for Louie and discovered Oscar had some offshore bank accounts. Apparently, the Barracuda also found out and didn't like it."

"We need to find out who murdered Oscar."

"Why?"

"Do you believe in ghosts," Lili said.

"I do," Ernie replied with no hesitation. "I've been introduced to that world."

I watched as Irma walked over and gave Ernie an imaginary kiss. "He reminds me of my son."

"Well then you won't be surprised when I tell you that there's this ghost, Irma, who haunts my camper. If we figure out what happened to Oscar, it might get her out of my camper and out of my hair."

"I see," Ernie said.

I looked over at Irma, who was tapping her pointer finger on the bar and giving me the evil eye.

"You know Mabel; you do remind me of MC. Lili, why don't you give me your husband's number. Let me look into this, and I'll give him a call. I'll keep you both out of that conversation—if you promise to stay out of harm's way."

"Thank you, Ernie."

I watched as Irma gave him another imaginary kiss and "I love you" in sign language.

"I told you he reminds me of my son."

CHAPTER 36

We were just about to leave when I could see Ernie looking over our shoulders.

"What brings you two lovely ladies here?"

I turned around and immediately recognized the two women heading toward the bar. They were Mary Catherine Mahoney's two Greek aunts. I had met them briefly in her office one day when she was working on my IRS case. Another time I met a pair of Catholic nuns in her office.

"Out this way for a funeral," the shorter of the two said. She was the one who looked like a munchkin from the Wizard of Oz.

"Ladies, this is Mabel and Lili. They live nearby and stopped in for a drink."

"How do you do? I think we may have met at my niece's office one day?"

The taller of the two said. They were both dressed in black, the old school funeral color.

"Yes, how are you?"

I hesitated for a moment, trying to remember this distinguished-looking lady's name. I would have to think of a movie part for her. Maybe Aunt Voula from the Big Fat Greek Wedding.

"I am Sophia, and this is my sister Anna."

"Just call them Aunt Sophia and Aunt Anna," Ernie said. "Everyone does."

"Happy to meet the both of you."

I reached out to shake their hands. Aunt Sophia had a very strong grip.

"Likewise," Lili said and shook hands with the two Greek aunts.

"Can I get you ladies a drink?"

"No, we just came by to say hello, can't stay for long. Have office hours later," Aunt Sophia said.

"Office hours?" Lili asked.

"Yes, these two ladies are card readers," Ernie said. "They are pretty good at it."

Sophia and Anna sat on bar stools on the other side of Lili. Irma had vanished, for the moment anyway. After a little small talk, I jumped right in and asked Aunt Sophia my burning question. Might as well, it sure wouldn't hurt.

"What do you know about ghosts?" I looked around to make sure Irma wasn't nearby to cause a ruckus.

"What kind," Aunt Anna said. "They come in different flavors."

"The dead kind."

"Yes, well—typically—they are *all* dead," Aunt Sophia said. "Tell us a little more."

"Sorry, the kind that haunts the vintage camper that you bought to go out west and start a new life after your husband of nearly forty years divorced you for a woman the same age as our youngest daughter."

Not sure what prompted that, but I felt like sharing my story with these two women. You do that sitting at a bar or waiting at the airport for your plane. Tell perfect strangers your life story.

"Sounds like you've got a problem," Aunt Sophia said, looking at Ernie like she was telepathically sending a message to him. *"Ya, think?"*

"Yeah, those varmints are hard to get rid of. They are attached to something from their time on earth. Like your camper. Have you seen the ghost?" Aunt Anna asked.

"Yes, she has," Lili said. "She can hear her as well. Her name is Irma."

"The name Irma is derived from a German word. It means War Goddess," Aunt Sophia said.

"Good grief," I said. I looked at Ernie. He just smiled.

"That's very interesting. You obviously have the ability, Mabel. Did you have it as a child?"

"Yes, but it disappeared as I got older. It just came back when I bought my camper."

"How about you?" Aunt Sophia directed her attention to Lili.

"No, but I do think I catch sight her out of the corner of my eyes. Or if I squint my eyes."

"Then you can see her if you put your mind to it."

"Well, I'm okay, just catching a glimpse. She's quite a character."

"She won't leave until her time in purgatory is up," I said. "That's what she tells me."

"Well then, get used to her. Have you seen others?" Aunt Anna asked.

"When I was a kid, some relatives that had passed on. Now, only Irma and Chief Little Bear. A friend of hers. He's got anger issues. Can't blame him. He scares me."

"My educated guess is that you are stuck with her for the time being," Aunt Sophia said. "Maybe that's why you can see her."

"She thinks I'm here to help her out of purgatory."

"Yep, that would be my guess, too," Aunt Sophia said.

"Well, good luck with that," Aunt Anna said. "They're like bed bugs. You can't see them, but they bite and are really hard to get rid of."

"And watch out for Chief Little Bear. He appeared to you for a reason. Hopefully, next time, he'll be a little more cordial," Aunt Sophia said.

CHAPTER 37

Lili and I stopped for a sandwich on the way out of Boca Vista and still managed to get back to Savannah just in time for happy hour. We picked up Chinese take-out and had dinner back in the campground. About like a picnic.

"I got a call from Ernie," Bob said as we finished dinner. "I've met him before at Hotel Florida, the tiki bar on the water."

"He's in your line of work. Not bar tending, if you know what I mean."

Bob decided to drop the line of questioning when Lili suggested we call it an early night. I was relieved to let Lili do the explaining to Bob.

As I was getting ready for bed, Meg called.

"Good news. Just got word that Selma's transfer has been delayed."

"Oh, Meg, that's great news, and thank you."

"No. Thank you. To be honest, Mom, I am happy to be back in the thick of it. I like Louie a lot, and we work well together."

"Did you hear anything about the FBI and their involvement?"

"I did talk to my contacts. The FBI and the DEA are investigating a money-laundering racket. The usual stuff, ties to the mob and cartel, who target small businesses, like bars, to get them to launder their money. They muscle their way in and force the owners to sell cheap or just sign over ownership. Same with gas stations and grocery stores. Louie said something about a contact named Ernie. That he might be helpful. Do you know him?"

"I met him when I first arrived in Boca Vista. He's a bartender at a tiki bar on the water. Says he's retired from Homeland Security. Lots of cops and feds hang out at his bar."

"I see."

I could almost hear that mind of hers clicking away, like an old electric typewriter. I held my breath and bit my tongue, and I didn't say any more like by the way he might be a spook. Oh, and Lili and I saw him today at the tiki bar.

"We're lawyers, not cops, Mom. Got to make sure we don't cross that line, or it could come back and bite us."

"Right, I understand." Not really, because Lili and I had crossed that line and probably re-crossed it several times.

"Mother, don't forget what we talked about. When you get back from your camping trip, I want you to come up for a visit so I can show you some places I have in mind. There all nice. Some of my friends from the country club have their mothers at a few of these places. There is a lot to do."

"Like what," I stupidly asked.

"Arts. Crafts. Mah-jong. Bingo. Something to do every night if you want. And you'll meet some of my friend's mothers. They'll love you."

Oh yeah, love hearing about my divorce. I'll be the topic of gossip and entertainment for those women.

"I haven't forgotten, Meg. I'm giving it consideration," I said, thinking about a drink, but it was a little late.

After catching up with news about Sid, we said good night. She would probably spend all night planning the tour of old biddies' homes.

"Well, I'll blow up that bridge when I come to it." I said out loud after I said good night to Meg.

"No way, Jose Cuervo, I like camping too much."

CHAPTER 38

It was time for my check-in call from Jack. I was sitting in my camper trying to figure out whether I should just ask him about Oscar and Willie Nelson when I heard my cell playing the theme song from The Game of Thrones, which was my ringtone for Jack. He was right on time and Irma was nowhere to be seen.

"Hello."

"Mabel, it's me."

I just smiled. Jack was more challenged with technology than I was. The fact that he could skillfully wield a scalpel never crossed over to using modern devices. I guess Tiffanie was no help in that department, probably too busy shopping and spending Jack's hard-earned money.

"How is everything?"

"Same as last month, no problem with the Jack-in-the-box. How about you?" As soon as I said that I slapped myself on the side of my head. "Dang." I thought to myself.

"I'm okay, Mabel. Thank you for asking. I do cherish your friendship."

I was quiet.

"So, what's this murder at your campground all about?" Jack asked.

Jack had obviously talked to someone. More than likely, it was Jack Jr. or Cliff, his CIA/FBI handler. I decided to ask him about Oscar since he'd opened the door and I didn't find Oscar in the Jack-in-the-box.

"A man named Oscar Johnson was killed, and they arrested a woman named Selma who lives here in the campground. They had some history. He was a wheeler-dealer, and she'd won the lottery awhile back. He invested some of her winnings in gas and oil wells. It seems he also had a gambling problem, and he may have lost her winnings instead of investing them."

"That name sounds familiar," Jack said.

"He said he knew you from the old days."

Jack was silent on the other end of the line.

"He did? Did he know some of my old patients?"

I knew what he meant. Jack sometimes talks in code, too much time hanging out with the alphabets and spooks.

"Looks that way. He had some visitors the night he was murdered. They were from Vegas."

"Well, that was a very long time ago, a past life. I knew a lot of people back then, but most of them are dead or living out their days under the protection of a U.S. Marshall."

Since I had asked about Oscar, I decided to ask about Willie Nelson. What the heck. The door was wide open and all the windows.

"Do you remember someone who looked like Willie Nelson? You know, from the old days."

"Why?"

"One of the Vegas guys that paid Oscar a visit, the night he was murdered, looked like Willie Nelson."

"I might," Jack said. "He wasn't a patient, though. Mabel, you need to be careful."

I could tell by the tone in his voice Jack was dead serious.

"Why? Is he a friend of the governor?"

"Let's just say they all tend to know each other—if they live long enough."

"I checked the box, and neither Willie nor Oscar is part of the photo album."

Jack was quiet, taking all this in, and then he spoke.

"Willie Nelson was never in that box. If Oscar was, it was a very long time ago. Remember, I shredded a lot of those pictures when I went to work for the Feds."

"So, Willie is a friend of Vito?"

"Yes, he is Mabel. I am telling you this so that you watch your back. Be really careful. I'll look into things from my end."

That was code for he was going to talk to Cliff.

"If you find anything out, you might want to pass it on to Meg. She's representing Selma, the woman accused of the murder."

"Our Meg?"

"Yeah, she's getting back into law. It just happened."

"I see, Mabel. I will look into it and pass on anything of importance to Meg."

"Talk to you next month, Jack."

"Next month, Mabel, or maybe sooner."

I thought about texting Meg to give her a heads up but decided to hold off. Let Jack handle that call with our oldest daughter. Irma popped in while I was thinking about the conversation I just had with Jack.

"Well?"

"I think Willie Nelson and Jack have a history."

"What did he say?"

"Nothing. HIPPA Rules."

"What?"

"Something that came after your time. Anyway, Jack didn't say anything, but then that says a lot."

"So, Willie may have been a patient of Jack's."

"No, Jack said he wasn't. All those guys stick together. He said he would look into it. I'm guessing he is on the phone right now with Cliff, his handler."

"What about Oscar?"

"Jack said if he was a patient, it was a very long time ago."

"Hmmm," Irma said. "By the way, I'm still looking for Little Stella. It's a big place. Chief Little Bear must be busy because I haven't heard from him either."

"Jack told me to be really careful."

"He did? Well, that ship has sailed Mabel. The safe and secure life disappeared the day you stepped foot in this camper."

CHAPTER 39

Lili and I had settled into a routine. A walk around the campground in the morning before it got hot. On the way back, we stopped and had coffee with Joe. Bob took his Harley out for a spin. He returned early and joined us for coffee.

"I heard from Josh and Peggy. They're busy seeing the sights of Ashville, which like Savannah is rich with history. They toured the Biltmore Estate and plan to go back a second time," Bob reported.

"They are thinking of staying a little longer in North Carolina. There is plenty to see, the Great Smoky Mountains National Park, not to mention the Blue Ridge Parkway. Could actually spend a summer there and not see it all."

"How long of a drive is the Blue Ridge parkway?" I asked. "Can you do it in a day?"

"Not so sure you would want to and miss the beauty. The parkway is 469 miles long and runs from the bottom of the Shenandoah National Park Skyline Drive in Virginia to the Great Smoky Mountains National Park near Cherokee, North Carolina," Bob said wistfully.

I could tell he was anxious to get back out on the road. I looked over at Joe, who stayed quiet and out of this part of the conversation. Not his place.

"They were asking when we were going to join them," Bob said.

"What did you tell them," Lili asked.

"I told them soon and that we would meet them in Nashville. June is a big month in Nashville. I heard from Meg and Louie. They have stopped any transfer business, but Louie told me that it could be a long time before a trial."

"Trial? Has the investigation stopped just because they've arrested Selma?" I asked.

"The police will follow up on leads. But it's slow and meticulous work. Especially if they have a viable suspect on hand."

"So, what you are saying is that unless a real tip comes in, Selma will sit in jail. They move on to other cases."

"Meg and Louie will tell you that is when the lawyers take over."

Lili and I knew what Bob was saying. He was telling us that there is not much more we can do for Selma. We did have a trip out west planned, and the days were flying by. Before we know it, September will be on our doorsteps and winter right around the corner. Irma had other thoughts, of course.

"Nope, that is not going to happen, Mabel."

I could see her standing near Joe. I looked over at Lili and closed my eyes. She got the message. Irma was nearby. Today she was back in her meter maid outfit.

"You and I have more work to do. We're a team. We need to find the killer. The only way to do that is to stay close to the scene of the crime. Here! Not Nashville. I'll be back later. I'm still trying to track down Little Stella and have that talk with her."

I looked over at Joe, respectfully quiet. He was a good kid. I really wanted Cecilia to meet him when we got to Nashville. I might suggest they find each other on twit-face as I call social media. Always gives Sid a big laugh.

"Joe, have you seen the widow?" Bob asked.

"Eleanor is spending a lot of time lately with Earl."

He didn't call her the Barracuda. It was his upbringing and southern manners. He didn't grow up in Brooklyn like me.

"The Barracuda and Earl?" I said foot in mouth before I could stop it.

"Yes, ma'am. Last night after closing as I was driving back to the campground, I saw him walk into her hotel."

"Are you sure? The one where the Barracuda is staying?"

"Yes, ma'am."

Bob and Lili were quiet while we digested this information.

"Willie Nelson? Has he been back?" Bob asked.

"No," Joe said.

"Bob, I understand what you are saying, and we didn't start out to spend the whole trip in Savannah. But we need to find out more about the Barracuda," I said. "Just who is she? What is her relationship with Earl? Maybe it's developed from being friends with his late wife to something more. Sometimes that happens. Two widows hook up."

"The other day, he didn't have two kind words for her," Bob said. "We will stay a few more days and I'll see what I can find out. But then we will need to leave for Nashville."

"We understand," Lili said. "Mabel and I should head into town and do some last-minute shopping then before we leave Savannah."

Bob had that serious look on his face, but he didn't disagree with Lili. "Text me," he said.

I looked up, and there was Irma.

"Roger that," Irma said. "Roger that."

CHAPTER 40

Lili and I stood in the doorway of Earl's bar and looked around. There was a good-sized crowd for lunch. Lili poked me with her elbow. "Let's head for the bar. That's where we'll find the regulars."

"Good idea."

We found two stools near the middle and waited for someone to take our order.

"What can I get you?"

The bartender was a younger version of Selma. The second in a matter of days. But she might not be the last. It's not easy to find someone who clicks with long-time regulars.

Like my dad's bartender in his bar and restaurant back in Brooklyn. He was Irish and worked there for close to three decades. A good bartender was key in a bar where everyone knew your name, starting with the bartender. When he died, the gathering after his funeral Mass spilled out the door and out into the street. New York's finest stood guard out of respect. He was family to my dad's customers. Selma was that kind of bartender. You can't replace that.

"You can bring me a draft," Lili said, "and a Cosmo for my friend."

"Sure thing," the bartender said and soon returned with our drinks along with a menu. We looked over the menu and ordered burgers and fries, which the bartender brought promptly. While we were finishing our lunch, I looked over at Lili, who had been sitting next to a man who was quietly nursing his drink. He looked like a regular.

"It's five o'clock somewhere," Lili said as she took a sip and then placed her beer on the coaster. Where I knew it would sit. Lili wasn't much for daytime TV or daytime drinking. But to chat up the regulars, we needed to be one of them. The bartender brought us some napkins and turned to the guy.

"Need a refill on your whiskey, Gary?"

A good sign. Selma knew everyone by their name, just like my dad's bartender. This new bartender might make the grade.

"Ready and willing," Gary said as pushed his empty glass across the bar.

The bartender quickly brought Gary his refill.

"Cheers," Lili said, picking up her beer and clicked my glass. She held it and looked over at Gary and offered her beer.

"Cheers," Gary said as he leaned over to click Lili's glass.

We all took a sip and placed our drinks on the bar.

"Are you ladies visiting Savannah?"

"Yes," Lili said. "How about you?"

"I live here."

"Here?"

I said with a grin that Gary returned.

"Pretty much, I've been sitting right here at this bar for years. I'm not able to work anymore. I'm on disability."

"Oh. Sorry to hear that," Lili said.

"What work did you do?" I asked without thinking. Lili looked at me and smiled. Sort of her way of saying, no worries, ask away. We were on a mission.

"Bricklayer, mason work. It was a good trade. Young folks today are not interested in a trade. Want to make quick money. I fell off a ladder and broke my back. Got hooked on pain pills for a while. Now I just drink."

Lili and I let Gary talk. It sounded like he needed company. It turned out Gary was from New York, so we quickly bonded with stories from our youth. Funny how people you just met having a drink in a bar become life-long friends, even though you probably won't ever see them again. Maybe that was it.

"My husband, Carl, was a firefighter," Lili shared. "That's when we lived in New York."

"Was he there for 9/11?"

"Yes. He died eight years ago."

"Sorry to hear that," Gary said. "So was his death tied to 9/11?"

"I think so, but the government doesn't agree."

I watched Lili pick up her beer and take a full drink. I knew she had been fighting this battle for a long time and would continue until Carl got his due. It was only right.

"I know what you mean, I served in Vietnam. I fight to this day with the VA every time I go for my appointments. Luckily, I've got what I've got. But it's just enough to get by."

After a while, the bartender brought Gary another drink, and he looked my way for my story. I finished my Cosmo, and the bartender brought a refill. I told Gary all about my divorce and my prior life. The doctor's wife dumped for a younger woman.

"It still hurts, but I'm moving on with my life."

"Well, I'm with you there, Mabel. I've been divorced more than once. I let a good woman go. I suspect your ex-husband did too."

We all three toasted to our life stories.

"So, Gary, what's the story with this bar? Has it been here awhile?" I said. "Is it haunted?"

Gary laughed. "Not as far as I know, but just about every other building in Savannah is."

Lili and I waited for Gary to tell us a little more about the bar. We bought him another drink. We would have to make sure he didn't drive home.

"Earl has been the owner of this place for years. He lost his wife to cancer. For a while, he thought he was going to lose the bar. Toward the end, he tried to get his wife into some experimental treatments. He got her in, and it bought her a little more time, but it wasn't a cure. I've seen that happen to a lot of my buddies. Gives them a few more years, but then the cancer comes roaring back."

"That's what happened to my Carl. He had lung cancer. It's an awful cancer. I pray every day they will find a cure."

"I wouldn't hold your breath. Oh, sorry, ma'am."

"Oh, I'm not. They don't call it big Pharma for no reason."

"So, anyway, Earl fell on some hard times," I prompted Gary.

"Yeah, he tapped out everything he could, mortgaged the building—everything. But finally, when he ran out of options, he had to borrow from some loan sharks."

"Mob?"

Gary gave me a knowing look. After all, he was from our neighborhood. The mob was like the corner grocery store. They had their hands in everything.

"Not directly. But my speculation is exactly that, Mabel. They were involved. The loan shark was a good friend. Someone Earl trusted with his life because a long time ago, this man saved his life. They served together. He talked him into putting the bar up as collateral. To get the money, he had to sign over part ownership."

"Goodness," Lili said. "Did he get the bar back?"

"No, he did not. His widow got the bar. She owns half now with Earl."

"His widow?"

Lili looked at me and then back to Gary, who seemed to know quite a bit about the goings with Earl.

"So, what happened to the guy, this loan shark friend?" I asked Gary.

"He was murdered. It's all over the news. Found him at your campground."

"Busted," I said to Lili.

"I wanted to be polite, but I have seen you both in here. Joe told me all about you."

"Well, while we're here in Savannah, we have been coming to Earl's. The murdered man, Oscar, and his wife were traveling with us on our trip out west," Lili said.

"If you have been in here, you met Selma, our long-time bartender. Everyone knows her and loves her."

I nodded my head. "Yes, we know Selma and that she was arrested for the murder. Police and FBI have been talking to everyone at the campground."

"Both Mabel and I have been to the jailhouse to visit her. Although I just met Selma, I felt like I've known her all my life."

"Selma is like that. A good woman. She won the lottery, and that guy took advantage of her lack of financial smarts. Just like he did with Earl."

"Oscar?" I said.

"So, Oscar was the shark?" Lili asked Gary.

"He was the one who got Earl to sign over the bar?"

"Yep, the man had a silver tongue. He was a real wheeler-stealer. Smooth talked people into investing in his get-rich-quick schemes. Earl knew better, but he was desperate. His wife was dying. Selma was lonely and fell for the guy when he separated from his wife. She never had that kind of money in her life. He was a bona fide con man."

"What's going on with the bar?" Lili asked.

"The guy's widow claims she owns half the bar, although Earl hasn't seen it in writing. She's been trying to talk Earl into selling to some investors. She wants to cash out and move on. The bar is all Earl has, and he doesn't want to give it up. It's his life and his last remaining link to his wife. They were very happy here."

"Were the investors from Las Vegas by any chance?" I asked.

"Earl thinks so," he said in a whisper. "He doesn't want to sell, but now these guys are putting the pressure on him."

Gary looked into his drink like it held some answers, and then he finished it.

"Gary, how do you know all this?" Lili was wrapping up our interview and making sure the source was credible.

"Because I'm Earl's brother, that's how. If he loses this bar, then he has lost everything that ever meant anything to him. Maybe we can put our heads together and make sure that it doesn't happen."

"Maybe," Lili said and looked at me.

"I hope you believe in ghosts." I said.

"Oh, I do, I do," Gary said.

CHAPTER 41

Lili was fine to drive home, didn't even finish her beer. We asked the bartender to order Gary a ride home.

"Don't have to. He lives upstairs in one of Earl's apartments."

When we got back to the campground, Lili told me she'd talk to Bob about our conversation with Gary.

"What are you going to say?"

"That we went into town and ended up at Earl's."

It was true, even though she left out some finer details. I said goodbye and went into Betsy.

After a little nap, I went over to Lili's place for happy hour. Bob was working on the fire pit and Joe was already there. I took the chair next to him.

"I saw you and Lili at Earl's talking to Gary. I went in to pick up a check for some work I did for Earl. You were deep in conversation. I waved, but I don't think you saw me."

"We were there for lunch. It was the first time we met Earl's brother," I said. "He's interesting, and the conversation got deep."

"He spends most of his time sitting at the bar. I give him a ride to the VA for appointments. He's a good guy.

Very close to Earl. He gave him the money for the down payment on the bar."

Although Joe didn't flat out gossip, he did like to share information. I guess that's the southern way of looking at it. Bob joined us and was sitting back quietly, drinking his beer.

"Has Oscar's wife dropped in anymore at the bar?" Bob interjected.

"Yes, she has."

"Was she alone?"

"No. Two men in business suits were with her. They sat with Earl. Whatever they said put Earl in a bad mood for the rest of the night."

Joe finished his drink and went into his camper to get ready for the evening. I started to say something but decided it was best to stay quiet. I knew Lili had talked to Bob; pillow talk is what she likes to call it.

"Mabel," Bob said and took a deep breath and closed his eyes momentarily. "I'll make some calls."

"Meg and Louie?"

He nodded.

"Good. It will save me a call."

I had already texted Meg about Gary, and she had left me a short, and to the point, voice mail.

"Mother, stay out of this."

We finished our cocktails as Bob grilled up some hamburgers for dinner. Lili went inside and came back with a bowl of potato salad. We were going to make it an early night. While we dug into our food, Joe came out and headed to my pickup.

"Have a good show and keep your eyes open," I said as he got into Thor.

"Yes, ma'am I'll do that and thank you for the use of Thor."

I went back to Betsy to wait for Irma. She was bound to show up.

"Irma. Here, Irma."

It sounded like I was calling a kitty cat. Not the madam of a cat house. I fixed a nightcap and decided to wait up a little longer. She was in a different time zone, after all. I fell asleep in my lazy girl chair, as I liked to call it, and had one of those dreams that leaves you with a feeling it was real and not a dream.

Chief Little Bear was standing in my camper. He was as big as life. Next to him was Irma, but she was uncharacteristically quiet.

"Talk to Oscar's widow before it's too late." He said in a very deep voice. As he lifted his tomahawk like a nun pointing a ruler, I woke up and sat straight up in my chair. I knew the dream was more than a dream. It was a message. Chief Little Bear had come to me in a dream to deliver a message.

"Irma, where are you?"

I sat there for a little while longer and then got up and stretched my back. It took me a minute to set up my bed. I fell into a restless sleep as soon as my head hit the pillow, the vision of Irma and Chief Little Bear still on my mind.

"Copy that," I said to the ghosts. "Copy that."

CHAPTER 42

I didn't feel the best the next morning. Lili and I were out for our walk, and the fresh air did help. I told her about my dream and my restless night.

"So now you have two ghosts? One wasn't enough?" Lili just shook her head. "Mabel, sooner or later, we will be leaving and heading out. Tom and Jerry told Bob we are free to go. More and more, Bob thinks Oscar was involved with those Vegas guys and that they killed Oscar."

"If they did, then Selma, pardon my French, is screwed. Even Meg can't fight the mob."

"That is unless Selma gets help from those two FBI agents."

"You mean, Lt. Dan and Agent Bill? I doubt they are going to go out of their way to help Selma unless there's something is in it for them."

"Either way, Mabel, it's going to be a long time before a trial. Nothing we can do just sitting here. We did our part. You got Meg to represent Selma, and she stopped that transfer to the state penitentiary. You even got Meg back to practicing law. It is time to move on."

"So, are we heading out? Is that what you are trying to tell me?"

"I'm afraid so. I would say the day after next. That should give you time to break the news to your roommate."

"Lili, believe me, I am more than ready to head to Nashville. Joe is too, but he won't go until this is settled for Selma. I was hoping for a few more days."

"Did you forget your daughter? She has plans to move you back to Long Island and stick you in a retirement home. The longer you stay here and the more you get caught up in this murder, the more pressure she will put on you to pack up and move back to Long Island."

"You're right. She really is pushing that senior living thing. She's been emailing me brochures."

"You will have to cross that bridge when you come to it."

"She thinks I'm considering it since it was a condition she negotiated when she agreed to represent Selma."

"Whatever we do Mabel from here on out we need to be careful. Somebody murdered Oscar. If it was the Vegas mob, then they killed him because he didn't pay his gambling debts. They might have found out he had offshore accounts and was going to leave the country."

"Well, if that's the case, they are going to go after the Barracuda next. It's what Willie Nelson does. He's their bill collector," I said.

"Bob had some thoughts since the Barracuda has been spotted rubbing shoulders with those guys. The Barracuda hooked up with Willie Nelson and negotiated a deal to pay off Oscar's debt by turning over her half of the bar and put pressure on Earl to sell them the bar at what I guess is a low-ball offer. Then she can walk away with the offshore accounts and life insurance and start a new life."

"Meg mentioned the mob using a cash business like a bar to launder money. I highly doubt Earl is the type to go into partnership with those guys and let them use the bar to launder money," I said.

"We probably need to visit the grieving widow one more time. Maybe I'll bring the Barracuda a peach cobbler since she didn't care for my tuna salad."

"I agree and visit Selma to say goodbye."

We were not looking forward to that visit, and that included the ghost in my camper.

CHAPTER 43

A little later, Lili and I headed into town. I drove Thor. My baby Groot bobblehead on the dashboard brought a smile to my face. Sid sent me a text to show me a baby Yoda bobblehead. I might need a truck with a bigger dashboard.

"Have you heard from Irma today?"

"No, it's a little strange. I'd say I'm worried about her, but what's to worry she's already dead. Plus, I'm not looking forward to telling her we're heading out. No telling what she will do or even worse what outfit she might show up in."

I parked Thor, and we made our way to talk to Selma. She didn't look good. In fact, she looked worse. I may have to text Meg.

"Are you eating?" Lili asked.

"I am, but I have lost my appetite."

A look of sadness etched her face.

"I just heard from my son. His leave was denied. He can't get here anytime soon. I can't thank you enough for talking to your daughter, Mabel. She saved my life. I would have died if they transferred me."

Lili looked at me and raised her eyebrows. On the ride over, she said we should try to find out more about the Barracuda and Earl.

"They don't give us a lot of time with Selma, so we need to find out what she knows about those two. Did they have a relationship or just friends? Mention Gary. You ask. You're good at that."

She meant I was good at sticking my foot in my mouth. I spoke before I gave it any thought. It got me in trouble, but sometimes, it got me out of trouble.

"Selma, the other day Lili and I were having lunch at Earl's, and we had a chance to talk to his brother Gary. Do you know him?"

"Sure. Gary loaned Earl the money to buy the property and start the bar years ago. But Earl's repaid him and then some."

"He seems like a nice guy. He was very friendly." I wanted to keep the conversation going.

"Gary is there pretty much every day, warming the same bar stool. He lives in one of the apartments above the bar. His drinks are supposed to be on the house, but he always pays and tips well. That's just who he is."

"He talked to us about the Barracuda and Earl. Are they close?" I asked facetiously. Lili closed her eyes for a moment but kept quiet.

"Hell, no! Earl can't stand her. But the Barracuda and Earl's wife were close, and she was very attentive to her at the end. It brought his wife a lot of comfort. So, maybe he goes along for his wife's sake. He and Oscar go way back. They served together."

"Yes, Gary said Oscar saved his life."

"He did, Mabel, but not in combat. They were both in a bar and some guy pulled a knife on them as they were leaving. He was going to rob them, when Oscar tackled him and that was that. I guess you could say he saved both their lives."

"Gary told us that Earl signed over part ownership of the bar to Oscar. It was the only way to get the money to help cover his wife's medical expenses."

"There were all kinds of rumors going around. When his wife got really sick, we were all worried. It was so heartbreaking. She was a sweetheart. Earl is a private man. Keeps it all in. But now and then he would break down and talk to me. I know he didn't have the money to keep up with her treatments. Our paychecks were late sometimes, but he always paid us. His insurance didn't cover much. He was pretty desperate. I know that much. Maybe you can check that out at the courthouse?"

"If they recorded it," Lili said. "We got the feeling that Oscar wasn't much on paperwork."

"Well, maybe that would be a good thing. I've learned a little about paperwork and finances since I met Oscar. I was stupid. I didn't know to insist on paperwork from Oscar for my investments. My son finally insisted. He was in town on leave, and he confronted Oscar. I have my name on the oil rig, for what it's worth, in writing."

"I'll ask Meg to check it out. My guess would be they did not record it. Oscar was a wheeler-dealer, and he did business on the fly."

"I know he took out a mortgage on the building to pay for his wife's medical costs. He tried to get the bank to loan him more but had no luck. Like I said, he was desperate. He blames himself for not being able to do more for her."

"Selma, have they told you if the autopsy report is in?" Lili asked as she glanced at a watch she wore today.

"Yes, this morning, Meg called me. Guess what. The bullet that killed Oscar came from my gun. I'm cooked."

Our time to visit with Selma was up. We said our goodbyes.

"I didn't have the heart to tell her we were leaving," Lili said as we left the jailhouse. "We'll come back right before we leave for Nashville."

"Maybe it's best if we do an Irish exit. Not sure she can take much more."

"What's that?"

"It's when you duck out the back door without saying goodbye. Irma does that all the time."

"It doesn't look good for Selma," Lili said.

"Lili, someone stole her gun from the bar and killed Oscar with it. Don't forget that picture Daryl showed us of the two suits lugging something in a tarp. Oscar was killed and then Selma was set up to take the fall."

"It could be the Barracuda. She certainly has motive. He was asking her for a divorce. As his widow, she stands to walk away with plenty, life insurance, offshore accounts, and part ownership of Earl's bar," Lili said.

"Meg told me that they probably will offer Selma a deal. She'd have to weigh going to jail for a certain number of years as opposed to the rest of her life or worse."

"I don't know, Mabel. I just don't know. I wish we could leave for Nashville on a better note."

"One thing I do know is that Irma won't rest until this murder is solved. She's invested in it. Maybe I should just turn around and go home. Sell the camper and move back to Long Island."

"I think you need a drink," Lili said. "It will clear your head. Come on, let's go over to the hotel and visit with the Barracuda. Maybe Irma will show up and have better luck this time, and she'll confess."

I parked Thor, and we made our way to the lobby. I went up to the desk where a smartly dressed young woman greeted us. She reminded me of Natalie from the Triple A office.

"Can I help you, ladies?"

I decided to play the old card.

"Yes, dear, we have a friend who is staying at this hotel, Eleanor Johnson. We're in town and wanted to come by and say hello. Can you tell me what room she is in?"

"Oh. I'm sorry, but I'm not permitted to give out room numbers. But I can call her for you."

I just smiled, and Lili did the same. I could see her eyes darting to the long line that was forming behind us.

"We wanted to surprise her. It's her birthday, and she doesn't have anyone. She's a widow, all alone." Then I added. "Kids don't call her. Can you believe that? Now you don't strike me as that kind of girl."

Lili and I smiled more. I turned around and smiled at the line of unhappy people growing behind us.

"People are always in a rush nowadays." Lili said.

"They're here on a tour and have a bus waiting outside. Not nice people," she said in a conspiratorial tone.

"You have beautiful eyes," Lili said. "Just like my granddaughter, who's about your age."

That seemed to do the trick. She probably had a soft spot for her granny. Plus, someone behind us helped by shouting, "Lady, the bus is waiting."

"Room 503. Wish her a happy birthday."

"We will, sweetheart," Lili said and patted her hand.

"Thank you," I said as we walked toward the elevators. The line had doubled in size. "Poor dear, she needs some help."

"I hope she doesn't get into trouble," Lili said. "We'll tell the hotel manager what a great job she's doing before we leave."

We got off on the 5th floor and found room 503. I was about to knock on the door, but I stopped. I looked at Lili, and we both could see the door was slightly ajar.

"Housekeeper?"

"The housekeeper would not leave the door slightly open." Lili looked down the hallway. "I don't see any housekeeping carts. What should we do?"

It was at that moment that Irma showed up.

"Let me ask the ghost. She's here."

"Follow me," Irma said.

We both watched the door open wider. Lili made the sign of the cross.

"Lili, wait out here. I don't want anything happening to you."

"What about you?"

"Well, I've got Irma. She'll protect me." I made a sign of the cross.

"How is she dressed?"

"Like a cop."

"Nope, I'm with you."

Lili got right behind me.

We made one more sign of the cross as we walked into the room. We could see it was a suite. I opened my purse and took out a small berretta.

"Eleanor? It's Mabel and Lili. Are you here? Your door was open," I said, holding my berretta in front of me. Lili was still behind me.

"Lili, stay here and if you hear a shot, run and get help."

Lili started to argue, but I quickly walked to a hallway that led to the bedroom. When I walked in, Irma was standing at the foot of the bed.

"You can put the gun away, Mabel. Tell Lili to call the cops."

I looked at the Barracuda lying on a king-size bed. A pillow covered her face.

"Is she dead?"

"Yep and my money is she got a ticket straight to the hot zone. I bet her reunion with Oscar wasn't much fun."

CHAPTER 44

Lili called 911 and reported finding a body in room 503 and gave them the name of the hotel. They kept her on the phone, and we waited in the suite. The FBI arrived and escorted us into the hallway. It was Lt. Dan and Agent Bill. Somehow, they got there first. Next, we saw Tom and Jerry getting off the elevator.

"Ladies, why am I not surprised to see you?" Tom said. Then he turned to the FBI agents. "But we are surprised to see you two."

Agent Bill gave him a thin-lipped smile. "We were in the neighborhood." He then turned to us. "You both should wait for me in the hotel lobby."

"This is our crime scene," interjected Jerry.

"We'll be in touch," Tom said, as he shook his head and they followed Lt. Dan into the scene of the crime.

When we got to the lobby, a member of the hotel staff was telling numerous unhappy guests they couldn't go to the fifth floor.

"But what about our stuff?"

"The hotel will bring it to your new rooms."

"What's going on?"

"It's a crime scene," I said, as Lili and I made our way to a couch facing the front desk.

We saw the front desk clerk who had given us the Barracuda's room number. She looked distraught, and we hoped she wasn't worried that we would tell about her giving us the Barracuda's room number. We walked over to her and Lili did her best to calm her down and reassure her that she was not in trouble.

"Don't bother. I'm quitting. I'm done living in a city filled with ghosts."

"Where are you going?" Lili said.

"Back home to Indiana."

"Good luck, dear."

She reached over and gave Lili a hug.

Since it looked like we were probably in for a wait we had lunch in the coffee shop and then returned to have a seat in the lobby. The FBI was everywhere. They were all wearing their FBI jackets, so you knew they were with the FBI. We saw Tom and Jerry. They waved and stopped to talk to some of their men and then went back up the elevator. I saw Irma buzzing around the hotel like an angry hornet. She kept popping in and out, and then Lt. Dan and Agent Bill got off the elevator. I got up and cornered her and begged her not to do anything rash.

"Please take a break."

"I'll be back."

I watched her slither up to Agent Bill. He swatted his ear like he felt a mosquito. He was looking at me. I smiled, but he didn't return the smile. I turned around and sat down with Lili. They spent a few minutes talking to a group of agents and went back up the elevator.

"Well, here goes."

Lili got out her cell. I suspected she was texting Bob because she made a sign of the cross. I did the same to show support. In less than a minute, her cell buzzed.

"It's Bob."

I could only hear her side of the conversation, but she wasn't saying much. Bob was doing all the talking. She looked at me and rolled her eyes and then hung up.

"What did he say?"

"Just that he and Joe are on their way over and we will talk later."

We picked up some magazines to pass the time while we waited in the lobby. After a bit, Lili's cell buzzed.

"It's Bob again."

I watched Lili close her eyes and shake her head as she took the call.

"Well," I said when she placed her cell back in her purse and started to look at another magazine. Lili could be calm under any circumstance. I had seen her in action over the years.

"They're here but can't get into the hotel. So, they are going to Earl's. You heard me tell him we have orders to stay until the FBI talks to us."

Someone had snuck up the stairs to the fifth floor and got caught taking a video. So now, all the hotel guests were quarantined in the lobby. It was getting crowded. Free snacks and drinks were being offered to keep everyone calm. One of the guests sat down next to us. He was upset.

"I need to get into my room. I've got a plane to catch," he said. "I need to grab my briefcase and my carry-on luggage." He got back up to go argue with the hotel staff.

We were getting tired of waiting.

"Lili, maybe we should take the hotel up on a drink?"

"I've a better idea. Why don't we leave and head over to Earl's? I'm sure the FBI can track down two little old ladies. We'll ask Lt. Dan and Agent Bill for forgiveness—later."

"Instead of permission. Let's go."

We were about to stand and sneak out when the elevator opened and out came Agent Bill. He was heading right over to us. We sat back down.

"He doesn't look happy," Lili said.

"Yes, and he has his bad cop look on his face. Where's Irma when we need her? Maybe we could ask her to pull the fire alarm."

At that moment, Irma showed up, and she was dressed like a fireman. Good grief, I thought. I need to be careful what I wish for.

"Mrs. Gold, Mrs. Young, do you want to tell me what you were doing here?" Agent Bill demanded to know as he sat down across from us. The guy who had to catch a plane saw him and came right over.

"Officer, I need to get in my room. I need to catch a plane."

"Sir, you'll have to reschedule your flight." Agent Bill flashed his FBI credentials. He went back up to the front desk like they could reschedule his flight.

"Well, Mrs. Gold. Care to explain?"

"We came to see how the Barracuda was doing." I could see Irma standing close by with a fire hose.

"No!" I said adamantly to Irma.

"No?" Agent Bill replied with a tone.

"She means Mrs. Johnson," Lili said quickly while I mustered a smile. "Barracuda was her nickname. Everyone called her by her nickname."

Irma, the fire chief, had vanished and reappeared. She was wearing an FBI jacket. Agent Bill was glaring at me. He really needed to go to diversity training. This was not any way to talk to senior citizens.

"Well, when we got to her room, we noticed the door was slightly ajar. We went in, and I called out for the Barra—I mean Eleanor."

Agent Bill got out his notepad to take notes.

"So, you walked in the room and called for the Barracuda, sorry, Eleanor, Mrs. Johnson, and then what?"

"Well, I got out my registered firearm, for which I have a concealed weapons permit. I went into the bedroom."

Agent Bill took some more notes and now was waiting for the rest of the story.

"Can I see your license?"

"My driver's license?" I asked the G-man.

"NO. Your concealed weapons license, permit whatever they call them in Florida."

"Oh, of course, officer."

"Agent…"

He corrected me again with the tone. I got my purse and spent some time taking a lot of stuff out of my bag, lipsticks, comb, brush, cough drops, Kleenex, and phone, all the usual stuff that lands at the bottom of your purse. I got my wallet and fumbled some more.

"Oh, here it is. It was right behind the picture of my two granddaughters."

I showed him the picture, but he wasn't interested so I flashed my concealed weapons permit. Agent Bill was now fuming. I was waiting for the smoke to come out of his ears. I knew exactly where it was, but I thought I'd give him a little of his own medicine. He took it from me, looked at it like it was a national secret, and then handed it back.

"It's going to expire in a month. You might want to get it renewed. Okay so, you and Mrs. Young walked into the room, you got out your registered firearm, and then what?"

"What do you mean, then what?"

Agent Bill was losing his patience, but he managed to keep his cool. I took a minute to return all the stuff to my purse while he waited.

"I found her, and well, the rest is history. You know. You were up there."

"No, it's not. What's next?"

He was holding his notepad in a ready position and started tapping it with his pen.

"Well, what was next was that the Barracuda was lying on the bed with a big pillow stuck to her face. That's when I told Lili to call 911."

"Did you touch the body?"

"Oh, my heavens! NO! I mean, I thought about it. My son teaches yoga, and he told me we can now do chest compressions instead of mouth to mouth. I walked really close to the bed, and well, it didn't look like she was breathing."

"How do you know that?"

"I looked at her chest, and it was not going up and down. You saw the woman. She has to be a double D."

"The 911 lady told us to wait, and that help was on the way."

Lili came to the rescue, and I took a much-needed breath. "Like Mabel said, she wasn't breathing. It was obvious."

"Probably had something to do with that big old pillow on her face," I added.

"You think?" Agent Bill said.

"Just saying. No disrespect."

Lili and I waited while Agent Bill finished his notes and put his notepad away.

"So, what happened to her," I asked.

"Well, ladies, since you walked in on the body and just happen to show up at every crime scene—to the point where I am beginning to feel you're part of the team, I will tell you that I am sorry, but your friend Eleanor is dead."

"Well, we sort of gathered that," Lili said with a motherly smile.

"So, somebody snuffed her out," I said in my best Dirty Harry impression.

"Yeah, somebody snuffed her out with that big old pillow you saw on her face. The technical term is asphyxiation."

"Right, but what about cameras," I asked Agent Bill. Well, he did say we were part of the team. Maybe we'll get one of those FBI jackets like Irma was wearing. I could see her near the elevator, standing guard.

"Yes, Mrs. Gold, we're checking the cameras. Thank you for that reminder, though."

"What is the FBI doing here?" Lili asked as he got up to leave.

"Well, we heard that the hotel had free drinks, and we're almost off duty, so we thought we might take the hotel up on the offer."

I gave him the evil eye with a smile, of course.

"Aren't Tom and Jerry in charge?" Lili asked, following up with her own line of questioning.

"Official business, which means it's none of yours," Agent Bill said as his cell rang.

"Crap," he said, looking at his cell.

Irma had positioned herself right over his shoulder and was looking at the number. A smile appeared on her face. She walked back to her duty station.

"Is it Agents Mulder and Scully?" I asked. He didn't see the humor.

"Lili, we might have to introduce Agent Bill here to some of our book club members."

Lili nodded in agreement.

It must have been someone important because Agent Bill looked nervous as he took the call and walked out of earshot. We had never seen Agent Bill nervous before, so Lili and I got comfortable in order to watch him sweat.

"Yes, sir." We heard Agent Bill say as he took a deep breath. "Sir, as best as we can tell, she's been dead for about 12 hours. Yes, sir." Agent Bill followed up with another deep breath. If he kept that up I was sure he was going to hyperventilate.

"Yes, sir, that's correct. It has the markings of a hit." Agent Bill said, now looking our way. "She was last seen in the bar here at the hotel with two men that we have had our eyes on. We're running the video feed through facial recognition."

Agent Bill hung up and directed all his FBI attention to Lili and me. We sat up straighter.

"You heard all you need to hear. Mrs. Johnson was murdered. Now head on back to your campground, and please, ladies, stay out of our investigation. Got it?"

We watched a local news crew make their way into the lobby.

"Crap. I will definitely need a drink now."

"Yes, sir," we both said.

We got up to head out the hotel where a large media presence was forming. No sooner had we made it outside the hotel than Irma showed up.

"Get over to the Earl's." She was still wearing her FBI jacket.

"We are heading there now," I said.

"Talk to Bob and tell him what happened."

"Oh, we will. Don't worry about that."

"Irma?" Lili asked.

I nodded my head. "We should have stopped for that free drink."

"I've got a meeting with Little Stella—finally. She's hard to track down. I'm going back to pin her down and see what she knows. Later."

"I think I can almost see her if I squint my eyes a little more," Lili said squinting her eyes for me. "What did Irma say?"

"She said we should talk to Bob and tell him what happened. She's found Little Stella and plans to talk to her. See if she knows anything about Oscar and the Barracuda. You remember her? She was best friends with my mother-in-law, Big Stella."

"You mean the Little Stella, the one who was married to a head of one of the families."

"Yeah, that's the one."

When we walked into Earl's I stopped so fast Lili bumped into me.

Bob and Joe and someone I recognized were waiting for us.

"Shoot."

"Hello, Mom. We need to talk."

It was my oldest son, who was the spitting image of his father.

"Hello, son. Can I buy you a drink first?"

CHAPTER 45

We were heading back to the campground. I drove Thor, and my son rode shotgun. Bob, Lili, and Joe decided it was a good idea to give us some space. They would meet us back at the campground for drinks. Bob said he would grill steaks for dinner.

"You've been talking to your sister."

"I have, Mom, and I understand you asked her to represent the woman who was arrested for shooting a member of your traveling group?"

"Yes, her name is Selma. She didn't do it, but they arrested her anyway for his murder."

"Well, Mom, usually when they arrest you for murder, they have a pretty good reason."

"They make mistakes. So, you have been talking to your sister? Is that why you are here?"

"I am. And lo-and-behold when I got to the campground I ran into Bob. He and that nice fella Joe were on their way out and he told me you and Lili were with the FBI...about another murder."

"Yeah, well, only because we were at the wrong place at the wrong time. We just dropped in to visit someone, and well, she was dead. That's all. The FBI is talking to everyone. Not just Lili and me."

"So, what happened?"

"Well, like I explained to Agent Bill, he's from the FBI. Not much of a people person."

"Yeah, usually they're not."

"Anyhoo, Lili and I dropped by the hotel to visit Oscar's wife, the Barracuda. Oscar's the guy who was murdered and the Barracuda's his wife or was his wife.

"The Barracuda?"

"Yeah, it's what Oscar called her. A term of endearment. We wanted to check on her and make sure she was doing okay, and when we got to her room, well, like I said, she was dead."

"How did you know she was dead?"

"It might have been the big pillow over her face."

He just shook his head.

"Look son, Lili and I are just trying to help Selma. She didn't shoot Oscar. She's being set up. We just want to help her."

"That sounds like you and Lili. Mom, do you have any booze back at your campground or should we pick some up?"

"Is the pope Catholic? Bob has bourbon. Good stuff. You want to drive my truck?"

My son looked at me like it was Christmas morning. I parked, and he took over.

"I like Groot up there on the dashboard. What do you call your truck? I know you gave it a name."

"Thor."

"Love it."

"By the way, your sister thought an F-150 was a gun."

"That sounds like Meg. You know, while you and Lili were being detained and questioned by the FBI, I had a chance to get to know Bob. He told me he was Special Forces before becoming a homicide detective."

My son regretted that he had never had the opportunity to serve in the military. He fancied being a Navy Seal. Instead, he's been navigating the unpredictable waters of stocks and bonds and pensions and Wall Street.

"Yes, he's the leader of our caravan. He helped me pick out Betsy. I am glad you're here. I want you to see my Betsy."

"Betsy? Did you get a dog?"

"No, but I might. Betsy is my camper."

"Before we get to your campground, there is something I need to tell you."

I looked at my son. Now what, I was waiting for the other shoe to drop.

"Tiffanie asked Dad for a divorce."

"What? Is that so? Well, I'm not surprised. She's going to take him for all he's got left."

"Not if he gets custody of the twins. She never took to motherhood. She doesn't want primary custody."

"Are you kidding me? Your father changing diapers? He wouldn't know where to start."

"Bianca said she would help take care of them."

"Mother of God and all the saints above," I said, repeating Big Stella's favorite expression. "I can't see her taking to motherhood either. We will see about that when those babies keep Bianca up all night."

"It was his handler, Cliff's suggestion. Seems like he went through a divorce, and he got custody of his kids."

"Great. Now we have the CIA giving your father marital and parenthood advice. Where was he when we split up?"

"Well, to be honest Mom, I was glad for an excuse to come and see you. I was in Atlanta on business, and I decided I'd drive over for a short visit. I have to drive back tonight. I have an early morning meeting."

"Oh," I said, disappointed.

"So, what is this murder business all about?"

I was about to say something when I looked up, and there was Irma in the back seat. She had a piece of duct tape covering her lips. She raised her hands and made a cross with her two pointer fingers. I got the message. Don't say anything. Then she was gone.

"Oscar and his wife were part of our group. We had just met. Really didn't know them that well. It all happened so fast. First Oscar and now the Barracuda. Sorry, Eleanor, don't want to talk bad about the dead."

He seemed to be satisfied with that explanation because he had something else on his mind.

"Meg wants you to come back home and look at some retirement communities."

"Over my dead body."

"Yeah, that's pretty much what I thought you'd say. I'll report back to Meg that the leader of your group has a solid military background, and you will be well protected."

"Thank you."

No need to mention that Meg already knew Bob, and that background of his made little difference to her. She was bent on my moving back and into a retirement community. I had to keep one step ahead of her. When we pulled into my spot, I could see the group was set up for happy hour and a cookout. We sat for a minute before we joined them.

"Jack, please don't worry about me. Lili and I promised Agent Bill today we would stay out of his hair."

"That was very nice of you, Mom." He smiled. He had my smile. "I'm sure the FBI is happy that you are allowing them to investigate their case."

"We just wanted to help Selma, and that's why I got your sister involved. Meg wanted to go back to being a lawyer. Did she tell you that?"

"Just found all that out when I talked to her the other day, and she suggested I visit and check on you. But not surprised. She needs to do something with her days."

"Buy her a glass of wine. She'll spill the beans." I said with a wicked grin as we got out. "Let me show you Betsy, and then we'll join the group."

After a tour of Betsy, he gave me a big hug. "I love her, Mom. She looks like a Betsy. But I do think a little puppy would be good for you. Keep you company."

Little did he know I already had company.

He skipped drinks, "Driving back tonight and a meeting in the morning." We had a great meal of steaks and corn on the cob and a peach cobbler for dessert. I was glad to see that he and Joe hit it off.

"Joe, I'll be happy to take care of all that money you're going to rake in when you make it big in country music."

I noticed before he left, Jack Jr. took Bob aside. I figured for a "watch out for my mom" chat.

"Don't worry, Jack. I'm fine," I said as he gave me a hug and a kiss and got in his rental for the drive back.

"Love you, Mom. But look, if not a retirement community, at least think about moving back to Long Island. You would be nearer to us. We could take care of you."

"Jack, I'm going to be sixty something—not eighty. I told your sister I'm giving it some thought. The operative word is SOME."

"Plus, you can babysit those twins," he said with a wink.

"Get out of here, buster." He was laughing as he drove off.

"Right." I thought as I watched until he was gone. It'll do Jack good to see what I went through raising our five kids. Karma is alive and well.

CHAPTER 46

Lili and I were heading out for our morning walk when I saw Joe waiting for us.

"Hey Joe, what's up?"

"This morning, when I was getting ready to head into town, I saw a man snooping around Eleanor's camper."

"You did?"

"I asked him who he was, and I told him the camper is off-limits because it was part of a criminal investigation."

"What did he say?"

"He wanted to know if it was the police or the FBI."

"I told him both, and he left."

"Well, that's strange."

"I recognized him. I've seen him at Earl's a couple of times. He was the driver of that Bluebird that was here in the campground not too long ago. Just thought I'd let you know. I'd be careful if I were you. He had a gun in a side holster."

Joe left, and we continued our walk.

"Lili let's head back toward that section of the campground where Gordy is parked. Remember, he told us about a Bluebird. See if it's back."

"It's getting complicated, Mabel. I stayed up last night talking to Bob about what happened yesterday and about our little chat with Agent Bill. Your son also spoke to Bob, and he's worried. If we keep our noses out of this, we won't be tripping over any more dead bodies."

"This is our last day, Lili. I promise we'll keep our noses clean. Oh dear, do you see what I see?"

"Yes, the Bluebird. Mabel, let's turn around before that driver sitting out front sees us."

"Roger that."

When we got back, I told Lili we'd meet up a little later and I headed into my camper where Irma was waiting for me.

"I like your son. Not as controlling as Meg."

"He is a good son. We had a nice visit."

"Mabel, we need to step it up. Keep working on this case. I'm sure now that we have two murders it's going to be enough to get me to the Promised Land."

"Irma, Bob wants us to stay out of the murder solving business. Lili is leaning in that direction. Joe told us that he saw some guy snooping around the Barracuda's camper. Thought it was the driver of that Bluebird that took off as soon as the feds and cops showed up. When Lili and I were out on our walk, we saw the driver and the Bluebird. Maybe we have done all we can, Irma. Why don't you talk to Saint Peter and see if he'd give you credit for the work you've done so far? Bob wants to leave. Like tomorrow."

"Nope, I get no credit unless we solve the murder. I already asked him. I think you and Lili need to go back down to Earl's. Find his brother and talk to him."

"Irma, you heard what I said. We may have to do this without Lili."

"That's too bad because she is a lot smarter than you when it comes to people."

"I'm sorry, but tomorrow we are heading to Nashville. It'll be fun. It's known as Music City. You like music. You used to be a showgirl."

"Mabel, I'm counting on you. Help me and then I'll be out of your hair. Then you can go to Nashville and dance the two-step at one of those Nashville saloons and celebrate.

"Finish this and I'll be gone. You can head west in peace. Boring without me, but you will be in peace."

CHAPTER 47

Meg texted she was now working on getting Selma out on bail.

"I have asked the judge to allow her to stay at the campground with an electronic monitor. I should know soon."

Our job here was done. Well, except for Irma, but I'll blow up that bridge when I get to it. She is more or less along for the ride. I just hope she doesn't go into full poltergeist mode.

I was going for a morning walk. Lili had texted that her back was acting up and was using a heating pad.

"Getting old is not for sissies," Lili texted.

We were due to leave today but turned out we had a reprieve. Seems there was a mix-up with our Nashville campground reservations. Nashville was busy with the CMA festival. As soon as he got confirmed reservations, we were leaving.

It was a beautiful day in the woods. A little foggy, but I was deep in thought thinking about what Jack Jr. told me the other night. If this were a few years ago, I'd have been happier than a clam and be telling everyone karma rules the day. But with my new life on the road, I

288 · RITA MOREAU

was starting to move forward and leaving that dark part of my life behind me.

I stopped on the trail, got out my cell, and called Henry. He was texting me daily since he found out about the campground murder. But it was time for an old school phone call. He answered on the first ring.

"Mom, you okay?"

"Yes, Henry. Thought I'd give you a call instead of a text. It's nice to hear my children's voices. Where are you, Henry?" I could hear noise in the background.

"Elbow deep in cupcake batter. Bianca just got an order for a big wedding. She's working with a caterer she knows. It's a last minute cancelation gig. How about you?"

"I'm out walking. Look, I'll cut to the chase so you can get back to the cupcakes. Your older brother paid me a surprise visit. He was in Atlanta on business. Both he and your sister Meg are driving me crazy wanting me to move to a retirement home near you guys."

"Mom, you're not exactly the retirement home type."

"You got that right. I'm just getting my feet wet with camping. I like it a lot."

"Then do that. Stay true to yourself, Mom." Henry was an old soul.

"Jack Jr. said your dad and the barfly are splitting."

"We heard. Dad called and talked to Bianca. He might end up with the twins."

"That's what Jack Jr. said. Anything else?"

"No. That's it. I got to go now, Mom. Love you," Henry said, and then he was gone.

"Yeah," I said to no one around. "Karma is alive and well."

Usually, there were more walkers out, but between the fog and the threat of rain, I found myself alone on a stretch of the trail. I decided it was time to turn around. As I did so, I saw a man standing in the middle of the trail. I stopped dead in my tracks. It was Willie Nelson or his clone. He started to walk toward me.

"Good morning, Mrs. Gold. I didn't mean to frighten you, but we need to chat."

He was in front of me, blocking my path.

"Has anyone ever told you that you look like Willie Nelson?"

"All the time, but not thanks to Dr. Gold, if that's what you are thinking. I do have a friend who was his patient. I think you know who I mean."

"What do you want?" I said braver than I felt as I took a step back. He took two forward.

"I want the best for you. You and your friends should continue your camping trip. You might want to head out soon. Real soon."

He then came close and leaned over to whisper in my ear, "It would be better for your health." He stepped aside to let me pass.

"Watch out for bluebirds," he called out to me as I took off. "They can be nasty birds."

And with that warning he disappeared into the woods. My hands were shaking. Where was Irma when I needed her?

I made my way, as quickly as possible, back to my camper. Irma was nowhere to be seen, so I just sat there for the longest time and contemplated my health.

CHAPTER 48

"Where were you? I could have used some help from the beyond," I said to Irma, who was sitting at the dinette. I had closed my eyes for a moment and when I opened them there she was dressed in tan fatigues and looking at a cover of a book I was reading. The latest Carol J. Perry Witch City Mystery.

"I was nearby, but in stealth mode. I've had your back, Mabel."

"Well, what were you going to do if he pulled out a gun?"

"Same as before, I would have stepped in front of the bullet."

"That's nice to know, Irma. Thank you for that. But would it have helped?"

"Probably not, but he was only there to give you a message, not to kill you. Remember, I worked with men like him while running my house. If he wanted to kill you, you'd be dead, and we'd be having this conversation in purgatory."

I poured myself a shot of cream sherry, my Aunt Sadie's favorite libation, and sat down at the dinette. She was still staring at Carol J. Perry's latest cozy mystery.

"Irma, you're in luck. Lili texted me and told me we have another day or two before we leave."

"That's good news because I had that talk with Little Stella."

"You did. What did she say?"

"She sends her best."

"Please give her mine. Anything else?"

"I asked her about Oscar and if she knew him from before."

"Before?" I drank my shot of cream sherry.

"Before she was dead. She knew a lot of people from your old stomping ground but turns out she didn't know him. She agreed to ask around and get back to me if she hears anything."

"That's it?"

"She's like me, Mabel. She's waiting to get out of purgatory. She's not the big shot she was back in your neighborhood. A lot of her peeps have moved on."

I got up and poured another shot of cream sherry. My nerves were still shaky from my close encounter with Willie Nelson.

"So, with that little meeting today I'd say it seems like you're making somebody a little nervous."

"Well, we did overhear Agent Bill saying that the Barracuda's murder had the marks of a mob hit."

"He's a fed. Everything they see has the marks of a mob hit. It's called job security. I'd check out that bird problem he mentioned."

"The Bluebird? I'll ask at the campground office and see what they say."

"Copy that." Then the spook spooked out.

CHAPTER 49

We were at the fire pit, and Bob was laying out Nashville, our next stop. Joe was considering joining us, but later. The elephant in the campground was Selma. He was a lifeline. I understood. Irma was right there with him.

"Nashville is the capital of Tennessee, and it's situated on the Cumberland River. It's best known as the capital of country music. We will be visiting all the hot spots, including the city's famous Music Row and honky-tonks."

Bob was excited because he was able to secure reservations at a campground that was close to the action. He was ready to leave. I was about to rain on his parade.

"I met someone on my walk today."

"Who?"

His detective radar turned on quickly.

"Well, let's just call him Willie Nelson."

"The same guy from Earl's Bar?" Joe said. "Met Oscar the night he was killed."

"Yes, and yes. There aren't too many guys who look like Willie Nelson. I'd say Willie Nelson and this guy."

"Did he threaten you," Bob asked.

"In a manner of speaking, let's just say he delivered a message. He said it was time we headed out."

"I'll make some calls. In the meantime, I want you and Lili to stay close to the campground. By his reaction, I could tell he was worried.

"Joe, let me know if this guy shows up at Earl's. There's a connection here, but it's not our job to figure it out."

"Yes, sir," Joe said as he got up to leave. "Talk to you all later."

We called it a night. I looked at my cell. I saw the usual suspects. Meg's text to check on me. I texted I was fine, and we were leaving for Nashville. Sid sent me an emoji message. A heart and thumbs up. I saw one from Louie.

"Mabel, just checking in to see how you are doing."

I texted Louie back, the same as Meg. I figured Bob would be calling them both right now about Willie. I started to put my cell away, and I saw a new text come in from Ernie, *"Call me at this number when you get this text."*

I called the number, and he answered on the first ring.

"Mabel, I understand you had a visitor today."

"Yes. How did you know? Are there cameras on the hiking trail?"

"Let's just say word gets around. I promised Louie I would look out for you. Tell me what happened."

"Well, this Willie Nelson character suggested we'd enjoy the music much more in Nashville. Who would have thought a trip out west would be so much fun?"

"He's dangerous."

"I sort of got that."

I was quiet since I didn't think Ernie was calling just to check on my health.

"Did he say anything else?"

"He did give me some Bluebird tips."

"What did he say?"

"He said to be careful because they are not friendly birds."

"What does that mean?"

"There has been a Bluebird in the campground with a driver for two men in suits. They have been spotted at Earl's Bar.

"I'll check them out."

"How are you going to do that? Drones?"

"Mabel, you are a character."

"I have detailed files," I said with my best Terminator impression.

"Good night, Mabel."

"Good night, Ernie, and thank you," I said as the cell went dead.

CHAPTER 50

The next morning when Lili and I were having coffee, my cell rang. We'd decided to skip the walk since the forecast said heavy rain and possible tornados. Lili told me that Bob felt it wasn't the best day to leave for Nashville. I answered my cell. It was Gary.

"Mabel, this is Gary, Earl's brother. Selma gave me your number when I was visiting. I hope you don't mind me calling."

"Hey, Gary, no problem, is everything okay?" Lili was watching me intently.

"I've got something I'd like to run by you, and then maybe you could run it by your daughter."

"Sure. If you think it will help Selma."

"I've got an appointment today at the VA. I'll call you later, and we'll set up a time to meet."

"Gary?" Lili said after I hung up.

"Yeah, he said he has something that might help Selma. Wants to run it by me and get it over to Meg."

We finished our coffee and Lili went back to her camper. I headed in the other direction to the campground office to settle my bill. While I was there, I was also going to ask about the Bluebird. Couldn't hurt, I hope.

"Good morning, Mabel. I heard you folks were heading out," the campground manager said with a little too much glee.

"Yeah, Tony, it's time as soon as the weather clears."

"It sure was strange that day, all those boxes falling all over the place. Those FBI agents were jumping around like they heard gunshots."

"Yeah, that was weird."

If he only knew how weird I thought as I paid my rent for the campsite. Tony gave me a receipt and said we could pay by the day if the weather didn't clear.

"So, Tony when Lili and I were out walking we saw a Bluebird. You don't see too many of those campers. When I was looking to buy my camper, I looked at one, but it was too big for me and I'd have to tow a car."

I didn't want to flat out ask about the Bluebird and its driver, so I waited for his response.

"Well, for years they were built right here in Georgia. Bluebird built motorhomes and school buses. It went out of business after the recession hit in 2008. Before that, if you had a Bluebird, you could stay at their campground next to the factory. It was called the Bird's Nest. But that's all gone too."

"So, someone said that Bluebird we saw had a driver."

"Yeah, that's a little unusual. The two men he's driving for are not your typical campers. They're businessmen. They said they were in real estate."

"Oh. Well, I might take a walk back that way. That Bluebird was a beauty. Is it still there?

"They left."

"Oh, they did?"

"Yes. No offense Mabel, but I'm looking forward to peace and quiet."

"I am too, Tony. No offense taken."

CHAPTER 51

We were back at Earl's. "The scene of the crime," I joked. Bob didn't quite see the humor.

A couple of tornados had touched down along our route to Nashville, and more was forecasted. Bob decided we'd give it one more day and leave the day after tomorrow when the weather was supposed to be better. He checked on our reservations and they were willing to hold our spots until then. He was ready. Lili looked my way. I shook my head. No Irma. "How about we go by tomorrow and see Selma," Lili said. "Let her know our plans."

"I agree, although I'm not looking forward to saying goodbye."

I looked around for Gary. I had not heard from him since his call. But then he was more of a day drinker. Maybe he changed his mind.

"Howdy folks." Joe came in the door and stopped by our table on his way to set up for his gig.

"Howdy, Joe," we all said like a choir.

"We'll be leaving day after tomorrow. June's a busy month in Nashville. Will we see you before long?" Bob waited as we did to hear Joe's plans.

"I've got a few more weeks here at Earl's. I haven't talked to him about Nashville. Then there's Selma. I'm keeping her son in the loop."

"We look forward to seeing you, son, when the time is right." Joe got up and shook Bob's hand. Lili and I gave him a hug.

"Remember, I want you to meet my daughter Cecilia. It looks like she's going to join me in Nashville."

"I am looking forward to that, ma'am."

He made his way toward the stage to set up.

We were sitting in a booth tonight. More out of the way, but we still could see who came in the bar. As we were sitting there, I looked up. It was the driver of the Bluebird. I recognized him from our walk, and so did Lili.

"Know that guy, Mabel?"

Bob caught the look of recognition in my eyes.

"He's the driver of that Bluebird that's been in and out of the campground."

"The one Willie Nelson's double warned you about?"

"Yes. Lili and I saw him one day on our walk. Tony in the office said they had left the campground."

We watched as he went up to the bar and said something to the bartender who nodded her head and disappeared behind a swinging door that led to the kitchen. When she returned, she was followed by Earl and Gary. The driver got up, walked behind the bar, and followed both men through that door.

"Wonder what that's all about?" I said.

"Don't know," Bob said. "But I intend to find out."

Bob got up, picked up his beer and took a seat at the bar. As soon as he left Irma appeared standing by our booth. Chief Little Bear was with her.

"She's back," I said.

"Hey, Irma," Lili said.

"She's got company, Chief Little Bear."

Lili tried squinting her eyes looking for the two apparitions.

"I think I can see an outline."

"They aren't saying anything." I didn't really know how to greet a Native American chief. A dead one at that.

"Here comes Bob."

Irma and Chief Little Bear disappeared.

"Gone."

"Well?" Lili asked Bob. I could see Joe heading over. Joe sat down next to me.

"You saw the driver?" Bob asked Joe.

"Yeah, saw Earl and Gary come out. Earl's office is in the back. Probably went back there."

"Bartender said the guy came in and asked for Earl."

We sat for a while, and Joe got up and went back on stage. After about 10 minutes we saw Earl. He came out and started chatting with his customers. No Gary or Bluebird driver.

"Maybe he slipped out the back. Hold on, I'm going to check."

We watched Bob go out the front door and, in a few minutes, he was back.

"There's a back door. No sign of the driver. That's how he left."

"Bob, Gary called me and said he wanted to meet and run something by me and if it was helpful, I could get it to Meg. I was waiting for him to call back. I never heard back from him, so I assumed it wasn't all that important."

"I see. If he still wants to meet, I'd do it here. No dark alleys."

"That was my plan."

"Let me know when you're meeting. I'll be close by just in case you need me."

"Roger that."

CHAPTER 52

The next morning Lili and I went to say goodbye to Selma. Neither one of us was looking forward to that. We got in Thor for the drive.

"I told Bob we were going to see Selma, and that we'd be back a little later. He said to text him if Gary reaches out to meet with you."

"I will, Lili. First, let's take a little drive in the campground. I want to see if that Bluebird is back."

"You're reading my mind."

I made a turn into the section of the campground where we had seen the Bluebird. But there was a different motorhome parked in the spot where we had seen the Bluebird.

"Gone," said Lili.

We made our way into town. When we got to the jail, we saw Tom and Jerry outside the building. Tom stepped forward.

"Mrs. Gold. Mrs. Young. We're glad to see you. I was about to call your daughter Mrs. Gold. Selma is not doing well. She's stopped eating. If I let you visit her in her cell see if you can talk her into eating."

Tom led us to her cell. She had lost a lot more weight. She looked up and smiled. That seemed to take effort.

"Selma, you need to eat," Lili said as she sat down on the cot and took Selma by her hands.

"You are skin and bone. You must eat. You have to keep up your energy."

"I know, Lili. I know. This is all so horrible. I just don't have an appetite."

"Listen to me, honey, don't give up. If you don't do it for yourself, do it for your son. Don't leave him like this."

Selma looked at Lili. She got the message. A light-bulb went off. It would be something that would haunt her son for the rest of his days.

"Plus, Meg is working on getting you out on bail. They won't let you out if you're sick. They'll send you to the hospital."

I stretched the truth a little, but anything to put hope back in her eyes.

"She did? Wow, out on bail? She had not mentioned that to me."

"Don't say anything to her. It's something she shared with me but didn't want to tell you until she got it worked out with the judge."

"I won't say anything. Okay, Tom and Jerry have tried to get me to drink some protein shakes. I'll start with those and be a little more open to the bland jail food."

That was when we saw Selma smile. She looked like the Selma we first met. A feisty broad who was a fighter.

"I'll go ask Tom and Jerry for one of those protein drinks," Lili said. "Be right back."

I took Lili's place and sat next to Selma and held her hand.

"Tom and Jerry are bending the rules a little for their favorite bartender," I said.

"I've known those two since they were kids."

We waited until Lili returned with the shake.

"Now drink this, but slowly."

We watched Selma take a sip of the protein shake.

"Hmm, not bad," she said. When she finished it, we could see some color in her face. Lili looked at me and smiled.

"So, when are you heading out?" Selma asked. "I knew this day was coming."

"Tomorrow," I said. "Next stop is Nashville."

"I love Nashville."

"Anytime you need us, we can drive back," Lili said.

"Well, let's hope the next time you see me, all of this will be behind me. At least they can't pin the Barracuda's murder on me. I have a rather good alibi," Selma said with a chuckle.

I decided to ask Selma about Gary.

"Selma, Lili, and I met Gary. He said he was by here to see you."

"Yes, he comes by to visit. He keeps my spirits up."

"How about Earl?" Lili asked.

"Not as much, but then he's got the bar to run. Gary visits for both of them."

"Selma, Gary said he talked to you about something. He called me and said he wanted to run it by me and if I thought it could help you would I discuss it with Meg?"

"He did?" Selma said, somewhat confused. "I don't remember anything, but then I've been out of it lately."

As we sat there, Selma closed her eyes. It looked like she was falling asleep.

"Time to go," Lili said in a whisper.

But not before Irma popped in. She was dressed like a nurse, like they used to, starched white nurse's uniform and hat.

Lili must have seen me look up.

"Our friend?"

I nodded yes.

"Ask Selma about the driver of the Bluebird," Irma said.

Selma opened her eyes. So, I went ahead and made the plunge.

"Selma, do you know a guy who drives for the owners of a Bluebird?"

"Yeah, he came in and got friendly with Gary, who gets to know anyone who spends any time at the bar."

"Ask her if she ever saw him do anything weird?" Irma said.

"Selma, did he ever act weird?"

"He *was* weird. But, no, there was just this one day when the bar was empty, and he was nursing his beer. Gary had a doctor's appointment at the VA. I had to run to the back of the bar. When I came back, he was behind the bar."

"He was? Lili asked.

"He was holding my gun. I stopped and stood back for a moment. I saw him put it back. I waited a few seconds and then walked out. Before he left, he asked if I owned a gun. I told him I did. I got the gun from underneath the bar and showed it to him. I told him it was there just in case I needed it. He finished his beer and left."

Selma thought about this and then said, "Do you think he stole my gun?"

"I think you should mention this to this to Tom and Jerry." I said.

"I will."

Selma stood up and walked around her cell. Irma was holding her elbow. She sat down, and Lili and I said our goodbyes. We left Nurse Irma sitting next to Selma, holding her hand.

CHAPTER 53

Lili and I were silent for most of the drive back to the campground. Seeing Selma looking so frail had been a shock. Having to say goodbye didn't help. As we pulled into the campground, we saw Bob. He was getting their camper ready to leave. The chairs were still under the awning by their camper, but he had cleared up everything else.

"Let's talk to Bob. He can sort it out. That's what he used to do," Lili said as Bob walked over to us.

"How'd it go? You look like you need a drink."

I guess by the look on our faces, he knew something was up.

"Have a seat, ladies." He grabbed a cold bottle of beer and handed it to us. We sat under the awning. I don't usually care for beer, but it sure tasted good.

"Well?"

Lili began, "We went to say goodbye to Selma and when we got there Tom told us she had stopped eating. Was about to call Meg. She looked terrible. She was skin and bones. Tom let us sit with her in her cell and he asked us to coax her to eat. We got her to drink a protein shake, and she promised to eat. Mabel asked her about the Bluebird driver."

"What did she say?"

"She said she knew him. He had been in the bar, and he and Gary got to be friends. One day he dropped by the bar. It was empty and Gary was at the VA. Selma had to run to the back of the bar and when she came back, she caught him behind the bar. He was holding her gun. She watched him as he placed it back. He didn't see her."

"Interesting," Bob said.

"Yes," Lili added. "Mabel told her to mention it to Tom and Jerry."

"I'll give them a call just to make sure that Selma told them. Might not be anything but you never know, and you can't discount anything, especially actions that are out of character."

We met back at happy hour. Joe joined us. I took a minute to tell Joe about our visit with Selma and what she told us about the Bluebird driver.

"I talked to Tom and Jerry. They said they would follow up on this driver and the Bluebird. It's a long shot, but at least they agreed to investigate further," Bob said.

"I talked to the bartender about the guy," Joe said. "It pretty much matched what she told you. The driver came in and asked for Earl. She went back and got Earl, who was in his office with Gary. They came up and took the guy back to Earl's office. She said Earl shut the door. Which is odd, Earl never shuts that door. It's always open."

"Sounds like Earl wanted privacy to talk to the driver," I said.

"Yes, ma'am. I agree."

"Then he left by the back door which leads out to the parking lot," Bob said.

We sat there figuratively scratching our heads. Where was the ghost when you needed her?

"Let me call Meg and Louie. Might be we'll stay one more day," Bob said.

That's when I saw Irma. She leaned over and gave Bob a kiss on the head. I noticed Bob scratching his head.

"Reminds me of my son," she said.

CHAPTER 54

The next morning, I was up bright and early. I wanted to make sure Bob had not changed his mind about staying one more day. I was looking forward to Nashville and secretly hoping I'd be able to toast Irma in heaven. As I sat there drinking my coffee, I saw Lili heading over. She was carrying what I hoped was breakfast. She managed to bake up miracles in that little oven of hers.

"Bob took the Harley out for a spin. Nice day for a ride."

We sat drinking our coffee and enjoying delightful, tasty blueberry muffins, while contemplating a long walk around the campground, when I looked down and saw my cell vibrating.

"It's Gary." I went ahead and put him on speakerphone.

"Mabel, can you meet me at the bar? We need to talk. It's important."

"Does this have to do with what you called about the other day?"

"I don't want to say over the phone. Can you come on down now?"

"Okay."

"See you shortly. I'll be waiting." Click.

"What do you think of that?"

"I think you need to get a hold of Bob. Let him go with you when you talk to Gary."

"He might not talk if he sees Bob."

"Then I'm coming with you."

"Lili, I don't think that's a good idea."

"I don't either, but I think the ghost probably does," she said squinting.

I looked and there was Irma. Standing next to her was Chief Little Bear.

"I think she's dressed like a Cherokee warrior. Chief Little Bear is next to her," I said. "She's wearing a dress and its red calico cotton with yellow stripes with seven-pointed stars."

"Mabel, I'm wearing an official Cherokee tear dress. It's a practical dress. Not too long to get dirty in the dust or wet in the morning dew."

I explained to Lili about the dress, waiting to see what was going on with those two ghosts. That's when Chief Little Bear spoke. "I am here to warn you. A storm is near."

Then they were gone as quick as they came.

"A warning that a storm is coming, and that's all he said. Could be a rain shower or could be a hurricane."

CHAPTER 55

When Lili and I got to the bar, it was closed.

"This is odd," I said. "It's almost noon."

Just then, we saw Gary. He walked toward my pickup, where we were standing.

"What's up with the bar?"

"I don't know. I had an early appointment at the VA. I called you from the VA, and when I got here, I found the bar closed. Follow me; I have a key to the back door."

We followed Gary, where we found the back door open.

"Stay behind me."

We went through the kitchen, and we could hear voices inside the bar. It sounded like Earl and someone else. When we got to the swinging half door that led to the bar, I peeked over Gary's shoulder. Earl, the Blue-bird driver and the two men in suits were standing up front, near the stage. Unfortunately, Gary coughed, and they heard us. The driver pulled out his gun and walked over and pointed it at us.

"Boss, it's the brother and the two old broads."

One of the suits got up and walked over to the driver.

"Put your gun away, Roy. Where are your manners? Pull up chairs for the ladies."

Roy walked over to a table and pulled out chairs and pointed at us to sit.

"I'm sorry," Earl said as Lili and I sat down. Gary stood behind us.

"My name is Iman, and this is my brother Cyrus. We are, or I should say, we *were* associates of Oscar."

"Are you guys from Vegas?" I said.

"No, a little further away. Dubai. We work for some men who own a bank in Dubai."

Roy stood next to the two men from Dubai. He still had the gun out. The conversation we interrupted continued as if we weren't there.

"There was no reason to kill Oscar's wife," Earl said. "I did what you said. I went along with the cops arresting poor Selma for Oscar's murder."

"Well, the *Barracuda,* as you call her, had ideas of her own and was going to sell this bar out from under us. We didn't intend for anything to happen to her. Roy just got a little carried away," the man who introduced himself as Iman said with a scowl. Cyrus was quiet. Maybe he didn't speak English. Just whatever you speak if you live in Dubai.

"Oscar took the last of everything dear to me." Earl was talking to Gary.

"I should have known better. All my savings were gone. I was desperate to help my wife. It didn't help. She died, anyway. I called Oscar that night and told him I had the money to repay the loan. I just wanted my bar back. He showed up and told me he had a better deal. Let some investors use the bar for laundering their money." Earl pointed to the two men from Dubai.

"We argued. I wanted my bar back, and I had the money from what I received in the life insurance policy after she died. That's when Oscar said he was signing the bar over to your associate in Dubai." Once again Earl pointed at the two men.

"I was supposed to stay on at the bar and run it like normal. He said I wouldn't even know anything was different. I would never have to worry about money. He said they would even take care of you, Gary. All I had to do was just go along."

"You shot Oscar," Gary said.

"I snapped. I grabbed Selma's gun from under the bar and threatened him. He reached for it and we started struggling and I shot him. If I had known it would get Selma arrested for the murder…"

Earl hung his head and started sobbing. Gary went over to him and put his arms around his brother.

Imam spoke. "It was lucky for you that Roy was outside in the parking lot. He was under orders to keep an eye on Oscar."

"Yeah, I cleaned up your mess," Roy said.

We continued to listen. It was as if they didn't care that Lili and I were sitting there and hearing everything. It wasn't a good sign. They were going to kill us.

Iman continued, "Roy and Cyrus took the body and dumped it in the campground. Not too far from where we were in the Bluebird and left the gun right next to it. It was fortunate that Roy knew it was Selma's gun. You did good Earl, telling the police the story we told you to tell them. That everyone witnessed their argument earlier in the evening. Didn't take much for them to figure out the gun belonged to Selma. Oh, one slight thing, we did wipe the trigger so that your fingerprint would not be on it."

"Now what?" Earl said.

"Now? Well, you might say you are no longer needed. They will find you here with a suicide note admitting that you killed the *Barracuda*—you all come up such colorful nicknames, and so descriptive too—and you will admit to killing Oscar as well, and complaining that they took everything from you, including this bar. You should be happy about that since Selma will be set free. See? We're doing you one last favor," Iman said and nodded at Roy.

Then we watched Roy step forward with an evil grin on his face and point the gun at Earl's head.

"Wait," Gary said.

"We'll go along with your money-laundering scheme. Just don't kill my brother. Please don't kill us. These ladies are heading out of town. They won't say anything."

"Well, Gary, there was a time we might have been able to discuss that and work out those details, but that time has passed," Iman said. "I'm so sorry, ladies."

"You can't just shoot all of us?" I said. "What are you going to do with our bodies?"

"You Americans," Iman laughed at my question and his brother joined him. I didn't think it was that funny.

"Oh, we can shoot all of you and they will never find your bodies. Roy here is not only a good driver, but he's a good cleaner. We will be long gone back to Dubai. Our job here will be done. We have papers to show our associate owns this bar." He gave Roy the signal.

Just as Roy was raising the gun to Earl's head, Irma the warrior and Chief Little Bear appeared, and all hell broke loose. Lili had her eyes closed and was saying her prayers. Gary was still standing next to his brother. He was holding his hand. Irma stepped in front of Earl and the bullet passed right through her and missed Earl, who stood there, patting his chest for a bullet hole. He turned and saw Gary pull out a gold cross and kiss it.

"What the hell," Gary said.

The next thing I saw was Irma tackling Roy. A bottle flew out from behind the bar and she caught it and smacked Roy on the head. He fell to the floor. Out cold. His gun flew across the room right to Gary, who picked it up.

"How did that happen," Gary asked.

"Ghosts," I said.

The two men from Dubai started to run, but not before Chief Little Bear stopped them. It was as if there was a solid plate of glass in front of them. They were stuck and couldn't move. Irma smacked them on the head with the bottle and boom they were out cold on the floor. Gary turned to the stage and picked up a box filled with spare guitar strings. He quickly used them to tie their hands behind their backs.

While he was doing that, I pulled out my cell and called 911. Irma was now in front of me. "I'm out of here. I'm going to go talk to Saint Peter. Wish me luck."

Chief Little Bear had vanished.

"This place is haunted," Gary said. "Are you ladies okay?"

"Yes," we said in unison as we heard sirens not too far out. "We have to work on that," I said to Lili who grinned and shook her head.

Gary was standing next to Earl. He knew what was coming. "Earl, the cops will be here any minute. You know what you have to do."

"I do, and I'm ready to get this over with. Please take care of Selma and tell her I am sorry."

We heard the siren's now in the parking lot. Doors opening and slamming shut.

"I'm ready to talk to the cops," Earl said. "I'm ready, Gary. I'll be waiting in my office." We watched Earl go into his office for the last time. Gary started to say something, but then Tom and Jerry bolted in.

"Why am I not surprised to see you two ladies," Tom said. Gary came over.

"What's going on, Gary? Who are those men you have hog-tied over there?"

"Come with me. It's a long story. Earl has something to tell you."

Tom followed Gary into Earl's office, while Jerry waited outside the door. It didn't take long. Tom led Earl out of the office and out the front door. Out of respect, he did not handcuff him.

Next, Lt. Dan and Agent Bill showed up with their entourage of FBI agents. We watched as they took Roy and the two brothers from Dubai with them.

Iman came close to me, "I saw the warriors."

"Yeah, well, they'll be back if you have any ideas of sending your people from Dubai to pay us another visit."

"Never meant you two ladies any harm. It was nothing personal, just business," Iman said as he and his brother and Roy were escorted out the bar.

Agent Bill walked over, "Wrong place, wrong time again ladies."

Lili and I just smiled.

CHAPTER 56

Bob and Joe arrived next. "We got here as quickly as we could," Bob said, giving Lili and me a big hug. "Thank God, you're both okay, but we'll talk later."

"Yes sir," I said.

As he held Lili in his arms Gary came up to me. "Did you say your daughter was a lawyer? The kind you need if you murdered someone. I might need her number for Earl."

"Sure," I said and gave him Meg's number.

As Gary started to leave, I asked him, "Gary, what was it you were going to tell me?"

"I did some digging down at the courthouse. When Earl signed over half the bar to Oscar, he never recorded it. Not big on paperwork, I guess."

"Well, that's a good thing. So, the guys from Dubai were going to muscle their way into the bar even though they didn't have a legal leg to stand on." I walked out front with Gary.

Tom had Earl in the back of their police cruiser. Jerry came over to me. "We will need a statement from you and Mrs. Young later, but you can go. You know the drill. We know where to find you."

"Yes, sir," I said. "How about Lt. Dan and Agent Bill? Will we need to talk to them?"

"They're good. I spoke to them. Now, why don't you all go back to the campground and have a stiff one."

"I'll drive back with Mabel," Lili said to Bob and Joe, who rode over together. "She shouldn't drive alone."

"We'll be waiting for you back at the campground," Bob said. "Don't take any detours, you two."

CHAPTER 57

"Is she here?"

"No, probably up talking to Saint Peter."

No sooner had I said that when Irma popped into the back seat of my truck. She was wearing the same dress she'd worn when I first met her. It reminded me of my Aunt Sadie.

"Speak of the devil," I said to Lili and nodded my head to the rear.

"Hello, Irma. Nice work back there."

"Thank you, Lili." Irma was quiet.

"I take it the meeting did not go as planned, Irma. You're back. So, what happened with Saint Peter?"

"He sent me packing. He said good job, but I got a way to go before he lets me through those gates. He did let me see my sister Betsy. She said she would be waiting for me. Ciao. I'm Going to look for my cowgirl boots."

"What did she say?"

"Saint Peter told her that her job here is not done. She's coming with us to Nashville."

"Damn," Lili said. "I mean, I'm sorry for her but glad she's coming along."

"You might want to speak to Lili a little later about the cussing," Irma popped back in. "She's picking up your bad habits."

"Yes, ma'am," I said and smiled.

I looked in the rear-view mirror.

Irma gave me a big wink.

CHAPTER 58

In the end, Earl confessed to murdering Oscar.

Roy, the Bluebird driver confessed to killing the Barracuda when she told them she had a better plan for the bar and wouldn't go along with their money laundering plans. He was in FBI custody and probably had a lot to tell them about the two suits from Dubai. It might get Agent Bill a promotion. Bob heard from Ernie. It seems alphabets wanted to talk to the two brothers from Dubai about alphabet stuff.

Once again, our trip to Nashville was delayed for good reason, to celebrate Selma's release. She never looked happier. Gary took over running the bar and put Selma right back to work. Gary got in touch with Meg and she had a new client.

When Meg called, I could tell that she was happy and excited. "You're keeping Louie and me busy, Mom. The FBI called and wants to talk to Earl. Looks like I can swing a plea deal for him. I think it will work out to be a good and fair deal."

Like I said, my daughter is a good lawyer. Hope I never need her services.

Louie texted he planned to offer Meg a partnership. He was expanding his office and setting up a space for Meg.

"Partnership?" I said to Louie when we talked.

"That's what I plan to talk to her about. She's a damn fine lawyer."

Finally, one fine day, we set out for Nashville, but not before karma spread her wings one more time.

"That oil well hit pay dirt," Selma told us the night before we left. "It's like winning the lottery all over again. Who knows? I might even buy this bar," she said looking at Gary. They seemed to have a particular look in their eyes.

"Love dust," Lili called it.

Joe said he would join us in Nashville. Just about the time my daughter Cecilia was due to arrive. It was good to be back on the road with Thor. I had my eyes on the road, and Irma had the TripTik for the next part of our trip.

Trixie, our GPS, spoke up with directions.

"Howdy, Trixie," Irma said.

I felt good. I loved the camping life, and for the first time in a long time, I loved my life.

"We're not in Kansas anymore, Irma."

"Roger that, Mabel. Roger that."

A Note to the Reader

Dear Reader,

Thank you for reading and I hope you would check out my other books. I would be most grateful if you would spread the word. In addition, I hope you would take a minute or two to post an honest review on Amazon.

If you would like to chat, I would love to hear from you.

Please email me at author@ritamoreau.com.

Drop in and say hello at

www.ritamoreau.com
www.facebook.com/RitaMoreauAuthor
www.amazon.com/RRMoreau

Until next time,
Rita

Acknowledgments

Rita Moreau lives in Florida with her husband, George, who brags to everyone that he is the author's husband. Without his motivation there would be no author.

To PatZi Gil for her support and friendship I am forever grateful.

Thank you to my Beta readers, Georgia Tawil and Barbara Ellis, who possess very sharp eyes.

To my niece, Indya Gordon, for sharing her good eats and recipes.

To the Town of Indian Shores Library volunteers who have supported me all during my writing journey.

Last but not least, I am very grateful to you my readers. If my novels bring you a good laugh and a little time for you, then my job is done.

LILI'S GOOD EATS
Kahlua Cake

Ingredients

Devil's Food Cake Mix
1 cup sour cream
1 cup Kahlua
¾ cup vegetable oil
1 cup chocolate chips
4 eggs

Instructions

Combine ingredients and pour into a Bundt Cake Pan. Lili usually sprays the pan with Bakers Joy. Bake for 55 minutes at 325°F.

Mabel shared this one with Lili. It is a hit with the book club gals back in Boca Vista.

Linguine with Tomatoes, Feta, Olives, and Lemon

Ingredients

2 tablespoons olive oil
2 to 3 cloves garlic, peeled and minced
3 large tomatoes, peeled, seeded, and chopped
1 tablespoon chopped fresh oregano or 1 teaspoon
    dried, crumbled
12 to 16 ounces linguine, cooked and drained
8 to 12 Greek or Italian black olives, pitted and
    quartered lengthwise
4 ounces feta cheese, coarsely crumbled
Juice of 1-2 lemons
Salt and pepper

Instructions

Heat large skillet over high heat until very hot. Reduce heat to medium and add olive oil. Add garlic and sauté about 10 seconds.

Stir in tomatoes and oregano and simmer 7 to 8 minutes.

Add hot drained linguine and toss to coat pasta thoroughly with sauce. Add olives, feta cheese, lemon juice and salt and pepper to taste. Toss just to combine.

Lili says to serve immediately.

Indya's Maw Maw Peach Cobbler

Ingredients

1 stick of butter at room temperature
1 cup of self-rise flour
2 cups of sugar
1 cup of milk
4 cups of peaches

Instructions

Heat 1 cup of sugar and peaches to a low boil

Combine 1 cup of sugar and 1 cup of flour and 1 cup of milk in a casserole dish. Spread the butter. Pour the peaches and syrup on top. Bake for 45 minutes at 350°F until brown and bubbly.

Indya's Maw Maw Squash Casserole

Lili says the key is not to stir. Maw Maw is a southern term of endearment for grandmother.

Ingredients

2 cups of squash
1 cup of chopped onion
1 can of cream of chicken soup
1 Jiffy cornbread mix (cook by directions)

Instructions

Cook squash and onion until tender and mash. Once the cornbread is done let it cool and then crumble into a bowl. Add cream of chicken soup and squash and onion mix. Mix and add to a casserole bow. Spread butter on top. Bake for 45 minutes at 350°F until brown and bubbly.

Cinnamon Coffee Cake

Ingredients

1 cup oil
2 eggs beaten
1 tsp vanilla
1 cup milk
1 cup sugar
3 cups flour
3 tsp baking powder
1/2 tsp salt
1 1/2 cup brown sugar
2 tsp cinnamon
1/2 cup butter melted

Instructions

In a large mixing bowl. combine oil, eggs, vanilla and milk together. In a medium bowl, blend together sugar, flour, baking powder and salt. Combine egg mixture with flour mixture. Pour half the batter into a lightly greased 9 x13 pan.

In a medium bowl, prepare streusel by combining brown sugar and cinnamon.

Sprinkle half of streusel on top of the batter. Top with remaining batter and then sprinkle the remaining streusel on top. Drizzle with melted butter.

Bake, uncovered at 350°F. for 25-30 minutes.

CPSIA information can be obtained
at www.ICGtesting.com
Printed in the USA
LVHW021650130521
687357LV00010B/568

9 798676 266394